Twice as Tempting

Susan Coventry

Susan Coventry

ISBN: 978-1542872881

Cover Design: Woodchuck Arts
Edited by: FirstEditing.com

DEDICATION

To my faithful readers. Thank you.

ALSO BY SUSAN COVENTRY

A New Chapter
See You Then
Starring You and Me

Chapter 1

Kelly Cruise rushed toward the bank of elevators, her heels clicking loudly down the hospital corridor, but Damian caught up with her in a few short strides.

“What’s your rush? he asked once they reached the elevators.

“I told you. I have to get back to work. We have a new employee who just started a few weeks ago, and I don’t want to leave her alone for long.” Kelly glanced impatiently at the numbers above the elevator door, willing the elevator to hurry up and reach the maternity floor.

“What are you doing tonight?” His tone was casual, but his eyes were intense.

“I have a date,” she snapped, and she waited for his reaction.

Damian just stared at her for a few beats until she filled in the blanks. “What?” she asked. “Did you think I would just sit around and wait for you to come back to Michigan?" The sarcasm dripped off her tongue, and she cursed herself for losing her cool.

Mr. Strong and Silent continued to stare at her, but his mouth remained shut.

"You did, didn't you? You expected me to wait around for eight months until you came waltzing back into my life. Well, it doesn't work that way, Damian. My life didn't end just because you weren't in it."

"I…" he began.

The elevator bell rang, and the doors opened. Kelly and Damian had to step aside to let a stream of passengers out, and then Kelly stepped in, expecting that would be the end of their conversation.

She was wrong. The big lug stepped into the car with her, and the door closed with an ominous groan.

"Look, Kell. I'm sorry that I didn't call you after I left. My life was kind of in upheaval, and I had some stuff to work out. But now I'm back, and I'd like to go out with you again."

Why is this elevator so damn slow? Kelly glared at him with one hand on her hip. "Why? So we can have sex for a while and then you can take off to California again?"

"I'm not going back," he said just as the elevator reached the ground floor.

The doors slid open, and they both stepped out. Kelly was rendered speechless, and the ground felt shaky beneath her feet. Her footsteps slowed while they walked toward the hospital lobby. "You're not going back to California?" she asked, just to make sure that she had heard him right.

"No."

"Never?"

"Well, it's hard to say never, but no, I don't plan on it."

They had reached the lobby, and Kelly leaned against an overstuffed chair for support while Damian stood before her with an inkling of a smile at the edge of his full lips.

"How long have you known this?"

"For a few months, but I've actually been thinking about it for a lot longer than that."

"Yet you didn't see any reason to tell me before now?" Her voice rose, and Damian's smile instantly disappeared.

"Kell…"

"Don't Kell me." She stood up straight and tried to contain the fury that threatened to burst out of her. "It doesn't matter anymore. You're not allowed to walk in and out of my life at will and expect me to lay down and spread my…"

Damian placed his hand firmly on her elbow and half-dragged, half-pushed her out the lobby door into the bright sunshine. He manhandled her down a path that snaked around the hospital grounds until they were alone.

"It wasn't like that, Kelly."

"The hell it wasn't!"

Damian paced in front of her with anger emanating off him in waves. "Yes, we had sex, but it was more than that to me."

Kelly's fists were curled so tightly that her red nails dug into her skin. "How do you expect me to believe you when you *never* called me. Not once in eight months. Eight months, Damian!"

Damian's shoulders slumped, and he shook his head from side to side. "I made a mistake."

"No, Damian. I did." Kelly turned on her very expensive heels and stalked off, unwilling and unable to look back lest Damian see the tears that streamed down her face.

Kelly was so rattled from her run-in with Damian that she almost cancelled her date with Ken, but then she decided not to let Damian ruin her evening.

For a few months after Damian had left, she lost her mojo. She hadn't even been able to look at another man without thinking about him, and she'd fallen off her game. Well, now she was back, and Damian could just take his place at the end of the line!

Kelly changed from her work clothes into her date night clothes, which, on that particular night, consisted of her most form-fitting jeans, a white off-the-shoulder peasant top, and strappy heels. She layered on a few silver bangle bracelets, added some dangly earrings, and fluffed up her hair. Kelly had been blessed, or cursed as she thought of it sometimes, with a curvy body, and she liked to show it off. Her chestnut brown hair was long and wavy, and she often wore it up in a high ponytail, but tonight, she kept it long and loose. Thanks to her Latin American heritage, she had caramel-colored skin and golden brown eyes that were large and expressive. Kelly had learned how to use her assets to her advantage back in high school, and she wasn't above using them still, at age thirty.

She waited for Ken in the living room of her small apartment on the third floor of the building. This would be their third date, but he hadn't been up to her loft yet. She had met him at the bookstore where she worked and where she had met most of the men she'd dated in the past few years. Ken was a graphic designer who had come into the store several weeks ago and bought several books on health and fitness. He had recently embraced a new, healthier lifestyle, and he'd bought books about eating "clean" and becoming your "best self." Ken was of medium height and build, with sandy blonde hair and light blue eyes—not her usual type, but handsome in a wholesome sort of way.

He wasn't anything like Damian, who had a rough-and-tumble appearance, with his jet black hair, stubbled jaw, and piercing dark brown eyes. Damian was tall and muscled, with strong, calloused hands from working on cars and a gruff voice to match. And then there was the tattoo of a lightning bolt on his right upper arm…

The sound of Ken's car horn broke through her thoughts, and she took a deep breath to steady herself. "Damn you, Damian Kostas. I will not let you ruin my date!" Kelly slung her purse over her shoulder and raced out the door.

They walked into the crowded new bar/restaurant that was currently all the rage in the small community of Clarkston, Michigan. It was Friday night, and the place was loud and full of people looking to have a good time. Kelly was no exception. After the day she'd had, she was ready to cut loose. *Who knows—maybe I'll invite Ken up to my apartment tonight.*

The hostess sat them at a high-top table for two, across from the square-shaped bar in the center of the room. Ken immediately buried his head in the menu, and Kelly had just opened hers when she heard something that made her freeze. *No way. It can't be.*

She lifted her head up, and her fear was confirmed. Damian sat at the bar facing in her direction, alongside an older gentleman with gray hair and a full gray beard. The sound that she had heard was Damian's laughter, which had carried across the room and wormed its way under her skin. She watched him smile and laugh with the older man until…

He looked up and locked eyes with her, and his face lit up with a slow, easy smile.

"What sounds good to you, Kelly?" Ken asked, his head still bent over the menu.

A buff Greek God to go, please! "Um…I'm not sure. What are you having?"

"I'll probably have a salad with grilled chicken and vinaigrette dressing."

Yawn. How boring! If Kelly were eating with Damian, she would have probably ordered a fully loaded cheeseburger and fries. But that wouldn't go over well with Mr. Health and Fitness. "I guess I'll have the same," she said and closed her menu. She purposely kept her eyes down and slowly unrolled her silverware from the white cloth napkin.

The waitress came over and took their orders, and while Ken was placing his, Kelly snuck a peek in Damian's direction. The cad was still staring right at her, and this time, he raised his beer glass in a mock salute.

Kelly resisted the urge to stick her tongue out at him and turned her attention back to Ken, who was asking her a question.

"Kelly? Are you ok? You seem a little…distracted."

"Sorry, Ken. I was just thinking about a run-in I had with a disgruntled customer earlier today, and it kind of got to me, but I'm sure I'll feel better after we eat." She gave him her best smile and hoped that he would buy the lie. *Disgruntled customer? Really? That's the best you could come up with?*

Ken reached his hand across the table and placed it on top of hers. "I hope it won't only be the food that makes you feel better. I'd like to make you feel better too."

There was no mistaking the intention in his eyes or his words, and Kelly slipped her hand out from under his. She gave him a weak smile and then excused herself to go to the ladies' room. She went the long way around to avoid direct contact with Damian, but she felt his eyes upon her as she sashayed across the floor. She might have purposely swung her hips and flipped her hair back for good measure.

Kelly didn't really need to use the facilities, so she primped instead. She teased her hair at the top to give it added volume and applied a fresh coat of lip gloss. Silly, since she would be eating soon, but it gave her something to do. When she opened the door of the restroom, she bumped right into a solid wall of muscle!

"Damian! What are you doing here?" she hissed, and she pushed on his chest to back him further down the hallway.

"It's a free country, Kell. I can eat wherever I want to."

She wanted to wipe that smug look right off of his exotic Greek face! "Did you know that I would be here tonight?"

"Nope."

"Are you sure that Emma didn't happen to mention it?"

"Positive. I came here to meet a buddy of mine about a business deal, not to spy on you."

"Huh. Well, then why don't you concentrate on your *business deal* and stop staring at me while I'm on a date!"

"Doesn't look like a date to me. And how would you know that I was staring unless you were looking at me too?"

Arrogant, egotistical, infuriating man!

Before she could form a response, he continued. "Instead of standing here talking to me, you should get back to your *date*." With that, he turned and walked away, leaving her tongue-tied in the middle of the empty hallway.

Thankfully, Damian left the restaurant shortly after their confrontation, so Kelly was able to eat her salad in peace. Well, relative peace. Her stomach was churning, and her head hurt, and it was difficult to concentrate on Ken when all she could see was the anger on Damian's face when he told her to get back to her date.

The date that she had been looking forward to had quickly turned into a disaster thanks to Damian. Kelly had no choice but to cut her losses, and after they finished eating, she asked Ken to take her home. He obliged and didn't even bother asking her if he could come up to her apartment. The poor guy! He was probably wondering what had gone wrong, but there was no way that Kelly could tell him the truth.

Instead, she gave Ken a chaste kiss on the cheek and thanked him for dinner. "Call me?" she said as she stepped out of his car, but she wouldn't be surprised at all if he didn't. *Thanks a lot, Damian*, she hissed on her way up the stairs.

Once inside her apartment, Kelly plunked down on her cushiony sofa, kicked off her heels, and laid back with her hand on her forehead. She would have liked to lament to her best friend, but Emma was still in the hospital, having just given birth to a beautiful baby girl. She could have called one of her other girlfriends, but none of them knew about Damian. He had only been in town for six weeks, several months ago, so she'd never had the chance to introduce him to anyone else.

A few short, glorious weeks. Just long enough for the gorgeous Greek to get under her skin and ruin her for any other man.

Chapter 2

As Kelly sat in the rocking chair with baby Ava cradled in her arms fast asleep, she relayed her latest man drama to Emma. It was a Monday afternoon, and Kelly had left the new employee, Jill, alone at the bookstore, so she could pop in on her best friend.

Emma had listened intently and nodded along, and now Kelly waited for her to speak.

"You know I love you, right?" Emma began.

"Yes."

"And you know I'm usually on your side when it comes to men."

"Yes." *This isn't sounding good*, Kelly thought.

"But this time, I have to side with Damian, and it's *not* because he's about to become my brother-in-law."

Kelly scowled. "So, you don't think he's to blame at all?"

"I think it would have been nice if he would have called you, but it's not like you two were in a committed relationship, Kell. You said yourself you were just in it for fun, remember?"

Ava squirmed in Kelly's arms, and she glanced down at the sweet baby girl, who fell instantly back asleep. "I might have said that, but after what we shared, I thought he would at least call."

Emma sighed. "Why don't you try talking to him again? Calmly this time. My wedding is only a few months away, and I don't want my maid of honor and the best man at each other's throats!"

"So, you think that Damian and I should try to be *friends*?" Kelly gave Emma a look of disbelief. "We didn't start out like you and Zack, Em. We went from zero to one hundred in thirty seconds!"

Emma smiled and rolled her eyes. "I know, and I tried to warn you. But you could at least try to be pleasant toward him, for me and for Zack."

Ava let out a little cry, and Kelly quickly stood up and transferred her into Emma's waiting arms.

"Is it time for her to eat or something?" Kelly asked nervously. She loved holding her "honorary niece," but she wasn't too keen on the crying.

"She might have gas," Emma said.

"Geez, look at the time! I should probably get back to work. Don't want to leave Jill alone for too long."

"How's she working out?" Emma asked as she positioned Ava on her shoulder and patted her back.

Emma was the owner of A New Chapter, the bookstore where Kelly worked as the marketing guru and second in command. A few weeks before Emma was due to have her baby, she had hired Jill, one of their best customers, to pitch in while she was on maternity leave. They had another employee, Brett, who worked part time around his college schedule.

"She's doing great. Don't worry. Everything's under control."

Emma visibly relaxed. "Thanks, Kell. I really appreciate your help, and you know I'll be back as soon as I feel up to it."

If Kelly knew her friend, it probably wouldn't be long. The bookstore was Emma's pride and joy, although now she had an actual baby with that distinction.

Emma walked her to the door. "Promise me that the next time you see Damian, you'll try to be pleasant. Please," Emma added.

"I promise," Kelly replied, but inwardly she thought, *I hope it won't be anytime soon.*

Later that afternoon, Kelly was teaching Jill how to close out the register when the door chimed and in fluttered Alex, Damian and Zack's mom.

Whenever she thought of Alex, two words came to mind: flamboyant and gregarious. *Quite the opposite of Damian*, Kelly thought while she gave Alex a warm, welcoming smile. Kelly had met Damian's family through Emma, and she would probably have continued contact with them now that Zack and Emma were getting married. Kelly was happy to see Alex, and she stepped out from behind the counter to give her a hug.

Kelly was instantly enveloped in Alex's enthusiastic embrace, and the sweet familiar smell of her perfume tickled Kelly's nose.

"What brings you here?" Kelly asked. It couldn't have been the books, because Alex often proclaimed herself to be "too busy to sit down and read." *That left…oh no…a party?*

"Well, dear, I'm just so excited to have Damian back that I'm planning a little get-together for him, and of course, I wanted to invite you."

Several replies crossed Kelly's mind, but before she could respond, Alex continued. "We, Joe and I, really enjoyed your company over the holidays last year, and we've missed you."

Seriously? Why couldn't her son be this sweet?

"Now that Damian's back, I hope we'll be seeing a lot more of you."

"Uh…Mrs. Kostas?"

"Call me Alex."

"Ok, Alex. Does Damian know that you're inviting me to this get-together?"

"I don't know if I specifically mentioned it, but I'm sure he'll be thrilled!"

Kelly shook her head. "I wouldn't bet on it," she said.

Alex eyed her with curiosity, but the smile never left her face. "Why? Did you two have a lover's quarrel?"

Oh God. How can I look this woman in the eye when she thinks that Damian and I are lovers?

"Because, you know, Joe and I argue all the time, but it's lots of fun to make up!"

Kelly wanted to melt into the floor, or at least don Harry Potter's invisible cloak and disappear.

"Mrs. Kostas…um…Alex. I appreciate the invitation. I really do, but Damian and I aren't together anymore." She couldn't bring herself to say the word "lovers" no matter how open Alex seemed to be to the idea.

Alex looked confused. "But the other day at the hospital…I saw the way you two looked at each other. Maybe you just need some time to get reacquainted, and what better way than at my party!"

She's not giving up. Now I see where her son gets his stubbornness! I'll tell you what, Alex. I will come to your party *if*, and only *if*, Damian wants me there. Which means he has to ask me himself."

Alex looked like she was about to protest, but then she thought better of it. Kelly was proud of herself for standing her ground, because, as wonderful as Damian's family was, she didn't want to show up to their party unless the guest of honor wanted her to be there.

"Ok, dear. I'll tell him, but if that boy doesn't get his act together, I'll box his ears."

Kelly giggled at the image of Alex scolding her imposing adult son.

Alex had one hand on the door when she turned and said, "Dinner is at my house on Friday at six o'clock. I hope we'll see you there."

Kelly just nodded. The ball was in Damian's court. *Let's see how he plays it.*

Chapter 3

Two nights later, Kelly was kicked back, binge-watching old episodes of *Friends*, when Ken called. She was surprised to see his name on the display after their last date, and if she were being honest, she had hoped it would be Damian calling instead.

"Hi, Ken," she said and muted the television.

"Hi. I'm glad you picked up. I wasn't sure after our dinner last week."

Poor guy. If it weren't for Damian waltzing back into town, she might have actually enjoyed Ken's company.

"About that, I'm sorry, Ken. I had an off day." *That was putting it mildly!*

"Maybe we could try again. There's an outdoor concert at Depot Park on Friday, and I wondered if you would like to go with me."

Damn! Of course, it had to be on the same day as Alex's dinner—which Damian hadn't officially asked her to yet.

"Kelly? You still there?"

"Yeah, I'm here." *What to do, what to do…* "I have plans on Friday, but I'm available on Saturday night."

Ken sighed. "I'm playing racquetball with some friends that night."

Racquetball? Really? People still play that? "Oh. Well, I would like to see you again, but I guess it'll have to be another time."

"Yeah. Ok. I'll call you next week."

When Kelly hung up, she let out a stream of curse words. A few weeks ago, she had been optimistic about dating Ken. He seemed like the kind of guy who had his act together. He had a well-paying, interesting job (according to him), he was sweet, and he was into healthy living. He wasn't drop-dead gorgeous, but he was good-looking, and she was mildly attracted to him. Emma had laughed when Kelly had told her that. "Mildly attracted? That doesn't sound very promising, Kell," Emma had said. But after Damian, Ken was the first guy that she could even say that about, so she had been willing to give him a shot. She hadn't felt that spark (or fireworks), like she had with Damian, but hey, a good relationship was built on a lot more than sex. At least, that's what people said.

Besides, now it was Wednesday evening, and Damian hadn't made any effort to contact her. Kelly felt certain that Alex would have relayed her message, as anxious as Alex was to include her, but her son obviously didn't feel the same. Maybe their "relationship" had just been about sex after all, and Damian was ready to move on to the next conquest, which was why Kelly wasn't ready to kick Ken to the curb just yet. She felt a twinge of guilt at having turned him down for Friday, but there was still a chance that Damian might call. Plus, she had promised Emma to be nice to Damian, at least until the wedding, which was three months away. She could play nice for three months. The question was—could he?

The next day, Kelly decided that she might not be able to hold up her end of the bargain after all. She had worked until five, rushed to her Zumba class, and was now driving home, hot, sweaty, and disgruntled. Damian still hadn't called, and at this point, she seriously doubted that he was going to. She was half-tempted to call Ken and ask if his offer for Friday night still stood, but when she pulled into the parking lot of her apartment complex, she became distracted.

There was a large, black Chevy truck parked in her designated space, and she could see the outline of a man sitting inside it. Kelly was just pissed off enough to consider laying on the horn, but then the driver's side door of the truck opened and the man stepped out.

Holy shit. It's Damian!

Kelly struggled to get her bearings as she parked her Volkswagen Jetta two spaces down from Damian's truck. *Breathe, Kelly*, she reminded herself before she stepped out of her car.

Damian waited for her on the sidewalk, his hands shoved in the front pockets of his ripped Levi's. He wore a black t-shirt with The Rolling Stones emblem on the front, and his usual scuffed brown work boots. The wind ruffled his wavy black hair, and she noticed the stubble that graced his chiseled face. *The man is too sexy for his own good!*

Kelly was still wearing her workout clothes: a bright pink tank top with a built-in sports bra, tight black yoga pants, and neon cross-trainers. Her long hair was caught up in a ponytail except for the tendrils that had escaped at the sides, and she was makeup free, having wiped it off before her workout. Even though she wasn't "dolled up," she felt sexy under Damian's approving gaze.

"Hey," he said when she joined him on the sidewalk.

"Hey," she volleyed. *Not a bad start.*

"Got a minute?"

"Well, as you can see, I'm hot and sweaty, but as long as you don't mind…" Her words trailed off because the look on his face practically singed her hair. She must have reminded him of all the times they had been "hot and sweaty" together, and now she was reminded too!

"I don't mind," he said gruffly.

Kelly motioned for him to follow her, and he stayed a comfortable distance behind while they tromped up the stairs to her third-floor apartment.

Damian had been there several times before, but he looked around as if he were seeing it for the first time.

"Have a seat," Kelly said. "I'm going to grab some water. Do you want anything?"

Damian cleared his throat. "Got a beer?"

Kelly rummaged around in her fridge and came up with a lone Guinness that might have been left over from the last time Damian had been over.

"It's been in there a while," she said and watched his lips curl up when she handed him the beer.

"It'll do."

Kelly sat in the chair across from Damian and took a long sip from her bottled water. She felt overheated from her workout, or maybe it was from the company, who stared at her intently with a masked expression.

Not a fan of small talk, Damian plunged right in. "My mom is having this dinner thing tomorrow night, and she wondered…I wondered…if you'd like to come."

Part of her wanted to give him a hard time for waiting so long to ask, but the sensitive side of her decided to let him off the hook.

"Sure," she answered and watched him visibly relax.

"You sure your *date* won't mind?"

Is he asking just to needle me, or does he really care? "I've only gone out with Ken a couple of times. It's not like we're…a couple."

Damian's eyes flickered with satisfaction at her response. "Ok, then. Six o'clock on Friday." He set the empty beer bottle on the glass table in front of him and stood up as if to leave.

Kelly fought a wave of disappointment but stood up too. "That's it? That's all you have to say?"

"Well, yeah," Damian replied and shoved his hands in his pockets again.

She could interpret his silence in a number of ways, but the last thing Kelly wanted was to argue with him again. She decided to leave well enough alone, although she was dying to ask him a slew of questions. Best to go with a simple one for now.

"Did you get a new truck?" The last time Damian was in town, he had flown in and had used a rental car to get around. Now that he was supposedly back for good…

"It's used, but the guy I bought it from kept it in good condition."

"It suits you," she said. "Big and manly." As soon as the words were out, she wished she could retract them, especially when Damian shot her that smug grin.

"I'll take that as a compliment," he said and sauntered to the door.

Kelly admired the way he filled out his worn-in jeans, but she quickly averted her eyes when he turned back around.

"Friday night," he said, and she nodded, afraid to open her mouth again.

Chapter 4

When Kelly arrived at Mr. and Mrs. Kostas's house, she noticed that Zack's Range Rover was already there, and she breathed a sigh of relief. At least if things didn't go well with Damian, she could count on the support of her best friend.

Kelly had taken great care with her appearance, as she usually did when there was a man involved. Tonight she wore a belted tunic top over a pair of leggings, and a pair of low-heeled ankle boots. Emma had warned her ahead of time not to show too much skin, so Kelly had chosen one of her more conservative outfits.

Alex was the one who opened the front door, and she immediately pulled Kelly in for a hearty hug. "I'm so glad you're here," she said with a wink.

Emma was the next one to greet her, and she hugged Kelly too. *This is one expressive family!*

Gracie careened around the corner and wrapped her arms around Kelly's legs. "Aunt Kelly's here," she announced to the whole room.

Damian had been standing at the picture window with his back to her, and he slowly turned around.

Kelly melted right on the spot. Big, bad Damian cradled his infant niece carefully in his muscular arms and rocked her gently back and forth. Something about the scene made Kelly want to snap a picture, but Emma beat her to it.

"Smile for the camera, Uncle Damian," Emma teased, and she snapped a couple of pictures with her cell phone.

Kelly followed Emma all the way into the living room and exchanged greetings with Zack and Joe Kostas. Three Kostas men in one room was quite a sight to behold. Kelly had labelled Zack and his brother Greek God numbers one and two, and their father Joe was still handsome in his sixties. *What a gene pool!*

"What can I get you to drink, Kelly?" Alex asked, relishing her role as hostess as usual.

Kelly noticed that Emma held a glass of wine, so she said, "I'll have what Emma's having."

Zack let out a loud laugh. "Just as long as it's not rum and Coke."

Emma scowled at him while he relayed the story of the time Emma got drunk on rum and Cokes at his co-worker's wedding. By the end of the story, everyone in the room was laughing, including Emma.

Kelly sat back and sipped her wine, and tried not to look at Damian overmuch. Every time she did sneak a peek, he caught her, which meant that he was looking too! He hadn't said much, but that was to be expected. He was usually content to sit back and let everyone else do the talking. However, when asked a direct question…

"So, Damian, what are your plans now that you're back?" Kelly ventured.

The room stilled, and all eyes focused in on Damian. *Oops…he hates to be the center of attention, but inquiring minds…*

Damian handed the baby off to Emma, plopped into the nearest chair, and casually crossed his leg over the opposite knee.

"First off, I need to find a place to live," he said.

"Son, we already told you. Take as long as you need. You're not bothering us by staying here," Joe said.

"Ha! Dad, you should know that it cramps Damian's style to live with his parents," Zack teased.

"I'm not *living* here. This is a temporary solution until I find my own digs."

Then Emma piped in. "Hey, Kell, aren't there some apartments available in your complex?"

Now the focus switched to Kelly, and she wanted to crawl into a hole. "Well…yeah…I think so…"

"I don't know about that," Damian said.

"Why not? I think it's an excellent idea," Zack said, ignoring Emma's signal to knock it off.

"I might look at some rental houses instead," Damian said.

"In Clarkston? That'll probably cost you a small fortune," Joe said.

Thankfully, Alex came fluttering into the living room and announced that it was time for dinner. Everyone filed out, but Damian stayed back and put a hand on Kelly's arm to stop her.

"Is that true about there being apartments for rent in your building?"

Kelly felt like his hand was burning a hole through her sleeve, or maybe it was the fact that standing this close, she could feel the heat rolling off of him. "Not in my building, but there are some units available in the complex."

He didn't let go of her arm. "How would you feel about that?"

"What? About you living there?" She tried to play it cool, but the catch in her voice betrayed her.

"Yeah. Would that be a problem for you?"

Kelly looked into his smoldering brown eyes with the flecks of gold and shook her head. "Would it be a problem for you?" she asked.

His eyes appraised her for a moment, lingering on her mouth. "No," he finally said.

They might have said more, but Alex called, "Kids, come on. Dinner's getting cold."

Damian let go of her arm. "See why I have to get out of here," he said and chuckled gruffly.

Kelly giggled and followed him into the dining room.

After dinner, Alex shooed Damian and Kelly out of the kitchen, inviting them to "relax and catch up."

Her attempt at matchmaking was so obvious that Kelly wanted to laugh, but she didn't want to make Damian any more uncomfortable than he already was.

"Walk outside with me," he said and headed toward the front door without waiting for Kelly's response.

As soon as they were outside in the bright August sunshine, Damian appeared to relax. They walked around to the back of the house that faced a small yet picturesque lake and took a seat on a swinging wooden bench overlooking the water.

With Damian's bulky frame taking up much of the seat, Kelly had to scoot far over to the opposite side to avoid contact. They sat in silence for a few minutes and stared out at the water rippling gently in the breeze.

"It must have been fun growing up here," Kelly commented as a pontoon boat carrying a large group of passengers floated by.

"It was," Damian replied. "Zack and I used to be out on the lake all summer long, until Mom came out waving her arms to call us in."

"I can totally picture that," Kelly said.

"Listen, Kell, about the other day at the hospital…"

Kelly held up her hand. "Let's not go there, Damian. I'm enjoying this right now. No need to dredge up the past."

Damian shoved his hands in his hair and shifted on the bench. "I just wanted to say that it was wrong of me to expect that you'd want to pick up where we left off."

Kelly sighed. "I'm not completely blameless here. I shouldn't have expected you to call me after you left. We never made any promises to each other."

They locked eyes for a long moment.

"What do you say we call a truce? At least for the next few months, until Zack and Emma's wedding."

Kelly wondered what his definition of a truce was—exchanging pleasantries at family gatherings or something more…intimate? *Don't go there, Kell!*

"I suppose we owe it to them, huh?"

"Yeah. Plus, Zack said he'll kick my ass if I'm not nice to you."

Kelly tipped her head back and laughed. "Emma told me to be nice to you too, but she didn't threaten bodily harm!"

Damian stuck out his hand. "So, truce?" he asked with a gleam in his eyes.

"Truce," she said and placed her hand in his. He clasped it firmly, and she felt instant heat from the contact. Suddenly, she remembered those hands on other parts of her anatomy, and she had to shake her head to return to the present. True, they had once been lovers, but Damian hadn't said anything to make her believe that he wanted to go down that path again.

The sound of Alex's voice calling them in for dessert broke Kelly's train of thought, and then she realized that she and Damian were still holding hands.

"Be right there, Ma," he called gruffly and reluctantly let go of Kelly's hand.

"I think I'm going to check into that apartment sooner rather than later," he said as they trudged up the sloped lawn to the house.

"Great," Kelly said. *Just great!*

Chapter 5

Kelly had just opened the bookstore on Monday morning, when Emma walked in balancing a bag from the Clarkston bakery and two steaming cups of coffee.

"You're an angel," Kelly said, relieving Emma's burden. "I knew you wouldn't be able to stay away for long!"

Emma had just given birth to Ava a few weeks ago, but as the owner of A New Chapter, she was having a difficult time staying away. "I promised Zack I would only stay for a few hours," she said. "Just long enough to get a few things done and to talk to you about Damian."

"What about Damian?" Kelly said while she reached into the bag and pulled out a cinnamon sugared donut.

"Well, how did it go on Friday night? We haven't had a chance to talk since then, and I'm dying to know."

"Not much to say," Kelly replied before she bit into the yummy goodness of the donut.

"Oh, come on. You two sat outside for quite a while alone, so there must be something to tell."

Kelly rolled her eyes. "And you thought *I* was the hopeless romantic!"

Emma fished a double chocolate donut out of the bag and waited for her friend to spill. She didn't have to wait long.

"Damian and I called a truce. We're going to play nice at least up through your wedding, but that was all we agreed to. Nothing else." Kelly knew that she sounded disappointed, but Emma was her best friend, and there was no reason to hide her feelings.

"I wouldn't call living in your apartment complex nothing!"

Kelly almost choked on her donut. "Wait, what? Did he already get a place?"

Emma smirked. "Yep, and he happened to mention that he's in the building directly across from yours. You two are going to be neighbors!"

Kelly's eyes grew as big as saucers. She had known it was a possibility, but now that it was a reality…

"So, what do you make of that? Out of all the possible residences in the Clarkston area, he chooses to live right next to you!"

Kelly was afraid to be optimistic. "I'm sure he chose the apartment because it was within his budget and he was anxious to have a place of his own. It has nothing to do with me."

"Hmm…we'll see," Emma said and wiggled her eyebrows.

"Em, I know you would like it if Damian and I got back together, but don't hold your breath. I'm afraid that ship has sailed. Besides, I'm dating Ken, remember?"

Emma cocked her head to one side. "I thought you weren't sure about him. How can you date a guy who's into healthy living when you're sitting there eating a donut?"

Kelly giggled. "There's nothing wrong with eating healthy, but if I indulge once in a while, Ken doesn't have to know."

"Says the queen of cheeseburgers and fries."

"You're one to talk!"

"I know, but at least Zack doesn't mind. Anyway, I think it's awesome that you and Damian are going to be neighbors."

Before Kelly could respond, the front door chimed, and in walked Mrs. Simmons, an eighty-year-old grandmother who happened to be one of their best customers.

"Good morning, Mrs. Simmons. How can we help you today?" Kelly asked and gave her a bright smile.

"You can help me by starting that romance book club we talked about," she replied gruffly.

"Romance book club?" Emma asked, directing her inquiry at Kelly.

"While you were busy having a baby, Mrs. Simmons asked me to host a romance book club meeting at the store. She and several of her friends are interested."

"I think that's a great idea! I wish we'd have thought of it sooner."

Kelly shot her a scolding look. "I don't know, Em. I'm not really into public speaking. I prefer to keep a low profile."

"Nonsense!" Mrs. Simmons proclaimed. "You're young and beautiful. Now is not the time to keep a low profile. Look at me, still going strong at eighty!"

How can I argue with that? "Ok, fine. But if it's a disaster, don't say I didn't warn you!"

Emma smiled and turned to Mrs. Simmons. "We'll work out a date, and you'll be the first to know."

"Thank you, dear," she replied and then disappeared into the romance section.

"Thanks a lot, Em," Kelly hissed.

"Hey, you're the expert on romance novels, not me," Emma said and walked away.

If only I could be as good at romance in real life…

The next few days passed quickly, and Kelly drove home from the bookstore on Friday evening with the entire weekend stretched out before her. Emma had insisted that Brett and Jill could handle the store for the weekend and that Kelly deserved some time off. Kelly should have felt grateful, but she actually felt let down. She had half-hoped that Ken would call her for a date, but her phone had remained silent. Now the weekend loomed ahead of her with no plans in sight.

Kelly had just started to prepare a mental list of chores that she could do when she pulled into the apartment complex and spotted Damian's black truck parked in front of the building across from hers. The tailgate was down, and there were several packing boxes stacked inside.

Kelly parked her Jetta in her assigned space, checked her reflection in the rearview mirror, and caught sight of Damian sauntering toward her. Kelly took a deep breath, smoothed down her skirt, and stepped out of the car.

"Hey, neighbor," he said with a dazzling smile.

"Hey," she replied. *Now what?*

"Just get home from work?" he asked, eyeing her up and down.

"Yeah. Congratulations on your new apartment. That was fast."

"Yep. I don't mess around," Damian said and leaned against the tailgate of his truck.

Kelly took in his usual attire of faded jeans and a graphic t-shirt, which today sported the Chevy logo in large black letters across the front. He wore the same worn-in work boots that she had seen on him numerous times before but never tired of. Damian was not a man who dressed to impress, and the truth was, Kelly admired that about him. He simply was who he was, with no apologies. She'd never seen him put on airs or adjust his behavior to fit in. He was a man who was definitely comfortable in his own skin, and oh, what glorious skin it was…

"Is that all of your stuff?"

"Yeah, why?"

"It doesn't look like much. There's no furniture."

Damian chuckled. "I need to buy some. I only had the essentials shipped here from California."

Kelly guessed that the number of boxes in his truck would barely contain all the clothes in her closet! "Well, then that explains why you didn't need help moving in!"

"Actually, this is my third load. I could have used some help earlier, but Zack was at work, and my dad was on the golf course."

"Ah, well, don't let me interrupt. Go back to your unpacking and…welcome to the neighborhood," she added flippantly. Kelly had just turned around to head to her own apartment when Damian called out…

"Wait."

She stopped mid-stride and faced him again. "What?"

"You busy tonight?"

Uh-oh. "Um…"

"Because I was thinking about ordering Chinese take-out, and if you're not busy…"

Kelly eyed him suspiciously. Was this part of the whole calling-a-truce plan, or did he have an ulterior motive? Because if he did, she would *not* make it easy on him this time. There was no possible way!

"Never mind. Forget I asked." With that, Damian turned around, hopped into the back of his truck, and bent over to pick up some boxes, which provided Kelly with a perfect view of his…

"Chinese sounds good," she blurted.

Damian set the boxes back down and slowly stood up.

Damn the man for having such a hold on me! But she had to eat, and her refrigerator was currently void of food. It was a practical solution, but she would definitely draw the line at dinner.

"Cool," he said. "If you want to change, I'll order the food, and you can come over in a few minutes."

She put her hands on her hips and quirked an eyebrow at him. "I thought you said you didn't have any furniture?"

Damian nodded. "Good point."

"Have them deliver the food to my place, and you can come over here."

If Damian's smile could have spread any further, it would have fallen right off of his ruggedly handsome face.

"What? Did I say something funny?"

"No. It was nothing. I'll be over in a few."

Kelly was still confused as she walked up the stairs to her apartment. It wasn't until she had stripped down to her bra and panties that understanding struck. "Oh, I get it now. I said that he could *come* over here." She giggled and then shook her head. "Damian, you are one naughty boy, but I've got news for you. Nobody's *coming* under my roof tonight!"

Just to prove her point, Kelly pulled on an old pair of gray sweatpants with the letters MSU printed down one pant leg, and a matching green and white MSU t-shirt. Not her best look, but nothing said "hands off" like an old pair of sweats! She even resisted the urge to touch-up her hair and padded out to the living room barefoot to await Damian's arrival. She idly flipped through a fashion magazine until her doorbell rang.

"Come on in," she called. She set the magazine aside but remained seated. She didn't want to jump up and answer the door lest she appear too eager.

Damian strolled in looking the same as he had a few minutes earlier, yet there was something different. The smell of his spicy cologne wafted in with him, along with the scent of mint from either his mouthwash or toothpaste.

That rat! He had obviously "spruced up" before he had come over!

Damian raked his eyes over her and smirked. "You changed into something more comfortable, I see."

Kelly rolled her eyes at him. "What time will the food be here?"

"They said about fifteen minutes," he replied, taking a seat on the opposite end of the couch.

Observing him leaned back against the puffy couch cushions reminded Kelly of the times they had made love there, and she swallowed hard. Searching for a neutral topic, she asked, "So, what are you doing for work?"

"Remember that guy you saw me with at Hilltop the other night?"

"The older gentleman?"

"Yeah. His name's Jim Farrell. He owns a custom car shop up the road in Ortonville. I worked for him before I moved to San Diego. Anyway, he's getting ready to retire, and I plan on taking over his shop."

"Wow, really?"

"Why is everybody surprised when I tell them? I've got brains, you know!"

Kelly giggled at the sly reference to his buff body. Whenever she used to compliment his physique, he'd counter with, "I've got a mind too."

"I know you do. This is just the first I've heard of your plans. I think it sounds great."

"Yeah, well, I still have a lot to learn about the business end of things, but Jim's going to work with me until I get it figured out."

"What's the name of his shop?"

"Jim's Custom Cars. Not very original, I know. I'll have to change the name."

Kelly's brain started whirring—she was a marketing guru after all. "Maybe I could help you with that," she suggested, her eyes lighting up.

"You'd want to do that?"

"Sure, why not? It's what I do. I'm the one who came up with the name for the bookstore, and I'm the one who does most of the marketing for the store."

"Yeah, but car stuff…"

Kelly put her hands on her hips indignantly. "It doesn't matter what the product is, marketing is marketing."

Damian crossed his arms over his chest and gazed at her intently. "Ok, smarty. So, what's a chassis?"

"It's…um…it's that thing…um…"

"That's what I thought. You don't know a damn thing about cars!"

The sound of the doorbell saved Kelly from having to retort. Damian jumped up to get the door while Kelly went into the kitchen to procure the plates and utensils. The whole scene felt surreal; it was like she and Damian hadn't missed a beat.

They'd eaten Chinese in her apartment before and followed it up with heart-pounding, against-the-kitchen-counter…

"Here we are," Damian said and set down the containers on the kitchen table.

When Kelly turned around with the utensils, he studied her inquisitively. "You ok? You look a little flushed."

"I'm fine. I think I just stood up too fast." *Liar, liar, pants on fire! Literally!*

Damian accepted her explanation and began to dish out the food. "I don't suppose there's any more beer in your fridge?"

"Actually, I picked some up on the way home from work the other day. Just because…you know…I felt like having a beer." Her second lie of the evening! She had picked it up on the off-chance that Damian might visit her apartment again.

Kelly pulled two beers out of the fridge and plunked them down on the table.

"Thanks," Damian said, and he shot her another one of those spectacular Kostas's smiles.

They dug into the food with gusto, as they had every time they'd eaten together, and Kelly enjoyed their companionable silence. Maybe having Damian for a neighbor wouldn't be so bad after all, as long as everybody kept their clothes on!

After they had finished eating and Kelly had put away their dishes, the silence turned awkward. If they had been dating, Kelly might have suggested watching a movie, or going out for ice cream, or… Who was she kidding? They would have most likely ended up in bed, but since that wasn't happening, she wasn't sure what to do.

Damian stood up abruptly and shoved his hands in his front pockets, a sure sign that he felt uncomfortable too. "I should probably get going," he said and moved toward the door.

Kelly followed a few steps behind him. "Yeah, ok. Thanks for dinner," she said.

"No problem." Damian had one hand on the doorknob, but he suddenly turned around. "You know, I might ask for your help with some marketing stuff, even though you don't know shit about cars."

Kelly's lips curled up in a satisfied grin. "You could teach me," she said flirtatiously.

The air crackled between them. "Are you a good student?"

"I got all A's and B's in school."

"You might get dirty."

"I'm ok with that."

Damian smirked, but Kelly stood her ground. "I'm good at what I do, Damian."

"Don't I know it!" He eyed her up and down and then opened the door.

"Goodnight, Kell," he said and headed down the stairs.

Kelly watched him leave, and just before he was out of sight, she yelled, "Hey, you forgot your leftovers."

"That's ok. I know where you live."

The last thing she heard was his deep chuckle before he disappeared into the night.

Chapter 6

His hands trailed up and down her bare arms, leaving prickles of heat in their wake, and her nipples tightened beneath her t-shirt.

"You want this just as much as I do," he said, his voice deep and gravelly.

"Yes," she whispered.

He tugged up the hem of her shirt and pulled it off in a quick swoop, baring her breasts to his hungry gaze. Then his fingers went to the drawstring on her sweatpants, and he slowly untied them, his fingertips barely grazing the skin above her waistband. He began to ease the pants down her legs when…

A loud rumble sounded. And then another, and then…Kelly woke with a start. She sat straight up in bed and looked around frantically. *Where is he? He was just here a minute ago, undressing me.* She glanced down at her MSU t-shirt and sweatpants, which were still perfectly in place, and sighed. It was just a dream. A hot, sexy dream starring her and Damian that she didn't get to finish thanks to someone's extremely loud vehicle.

Kelly heard the rumble again and hauled herself out of bed. She grabbed her robe off the bedpost and glanced at her bedside clock. Seven-thirty. Who was making all that racket at seven-thirty on a Saturday morning. Didn't they realize that some people might still be sleeping, or trying to finish a really juicy dream? Kelly shuffled over to the living room window and peered out through the blinds.

There was the culprit, backing out of his parking space in his oversized, obnoxiously loud black truck! She watched Damian leave through the tiny slat, but not before he glanced up at her apartment. She let go of the blinds like they were on fire and backed away from the window hurriedly. She didn't want him to think that she was spying on him after all. And why was his truck so loud anyway? She would have to teach him the proper etiquette for apartment living!

Since she was up, she put a pot of coffee on and thought about her plans for the day, which right now consisted of absolutely nothing. She could vacuum and dust, which would take all of twenty minutes in her tiny apartment, or she could get a head start on reading her new romance novel. It was a no-brainer.

After breakfast, Kelly showered and dressed, and she had just sat down with her new book when her cell rang.

"Hey, Em," she answered, sitting cross-legged on the couch.

"Hey. How's your weekend going?"

"Well, it's been interesting so far," Kelly replied, twisting a long strand of hair around her finger.

"How so?"

"Damian and I had dinner together last night," she blurted.

Emma's smile came right through the phone. "Really? How'd that go?"

"It was nice."

"Nice? That's all you've got? Nice?"

Kelly giggled. "We shared Chinese food and talked. That was all, Em. End of story."

"Hmm…"

"I'm serious. He left right after dinner, but then this morning…"

"What about this morning?"

"The bugger woke me up out of a sound sleep with his obnoxiously loud truck."

Emma laughed. "Sounds like you two are back in business!"

"Not like you think, but we might work together on the marketing for his car shop."

"But you don't know anything about cars," Emma said.

Kelly sighed. "That's what he said, but I can still help him with a marketing plan."

"Sorry, Kell. You're right; I don't doubt you."

"That's more like it. So, what about you? What are you and Zack up to today?"

"Funny you should ask, because that's why I called. Do you have plans tonight?"

"No, but thanks for reminding me."

Emma ignored her sarcasm and forged ahead. "How would you like to babysit your new niece?"

Kelly must have hesitated for a bit too long, because Emma hurriedly continued. "It would only be for a couple of hours. Just long enough for Zack and I to go out to dinner. We haven't had a date in what feels like forever, and…"

"I'd love to, Em."

"Really?"

"Yes. You don't need to convince me. I would love to watch Ava for you."

Emma breathed an audible sigh of relief. "Great! Can you be here at six?"

"Sure. Will Gracie be there too?"

"No, she's with her mom this weekend. It'll just be you and Ava."

Kelly felt a flicker of nervousness, but she quickly squashed it. She didn't have much experience with kids, not having any nieces or nephews by blood, but she had already formed an attachment to Gracie and Ava. Besides, it was only for two hours. How hard could it be?

"Ok. I'll be there at six."

"Thanks, Kell. I really appreciate it."

Now that Kelly had something scheduled for the evening, she was able to relax and enjoy the rest of the afternoon. She escaped into her new romance novel, which was an angst-filled story of forbidden love between a boss and his secretary. Cheesy, yes, but engaging nonetheless!

She drove into the Village of Clarkston for lunch at her favorite deli and returned home to accomplish a few housekeeping chores. All in all, it wasn't a bad day, and she only looked out the window for Damian three or four times. Not too bad!

When she knocked on Emma's door at six o'clock, Zack and Emma were standing in the foyer, anxiously waiting for her.

"Geez. You two act like you've never been out of the house," Kelly teased. "Where's the baby?"

"She's sleeping in her bouncy seat in the living room, but she'll probably wake up soon. Bottles are in the fridge, and instructions on how to heat them up are on the counter. I just changed her diaper a little bit ago, so you should be all set for a while," Emma said in a rush.

Kelly thought they were both acting a little strange, but she could understand their need to be alone. She hugged Emma goodbye and pushed them out the door, calling, "Don't worry. Go out and have fun!"

Kelly shut the door behind them and tiptoed into the living room to have a look at her beautiful niece. Ava was sleeping peacefully in her pink and purple bouncy seat, with a fuzzy pink blanket tucked right up under her chin. Her skin looked like porcelain compared to the shock of thick black hair that stuck straight up from her tiny head. The hair had obviously come from the Kostas's side, but the baby's face reminded her of Emma. Amazed that a sleeping baby held her so rapt, she was startled when the doorbell rang, and Ava's eyes jerked open.

Kelly scowled as she rushed to the door. Whoever was there obviously didn't know that a baby lived here; otherwise, they never would have rung the doorbell! Ava started to whimper while Kelly quickly swung open the door. She shook her head at Damian, who was the culprit for the second time that day.

"What are you doing here? You just woke up the baby," she scolded.

Ava's cries became louder, and Kelly walked away, leaving Damian to trail after her.

"I came over to babysit. What are *you* doing here?" he asked.

Kelly bent over and carefully lifted Ava out of her seat. The minute she was in Kelly's arms, Ava's cries died down to a soft whimper. "I'm babysitting. What does it look like?"

Damian shoved his hands in his pockets and gave her that irritating smirk, the one that made him look like he had a secret. "Oh, I get it. I'm going to kill Zack!"

Damian plopped down on the leather couch while Kelly paced back and forth in an effort to soothe the baby. "What do you mean? What did Zack do?"

"He called me about an hour ago and asked if I could babysit, but he didn't say anything about you being here."

"That's odd, because Emma called me this morning. Unless…"

"Bingo! They're trying to play matchmaker," Damian said without a hint of anger in his voice. If anything, he almost sounded pleased.

"Well, that's ridiculous," Kelly muttered. "Ava doesn't need two babysitters, so you're welcome to leave if you want to."

Damian quirked an eyebrow at her. "Why should I leave? She's *my* niece," he reminded her.

"Just because you're related by blood doesn't mean that I love her any less," Kelly huffed. With that, Ava emitted a burp that instantly eased the tension and caused them both to laugh.

"See, even her burps are adorable," Kelly said.

Damian chuckled. "We're mature adults, Kell. Why don't we both stay?"

Kelly stared at him for a few seconds before caving in. "Ok, fine." She stopped pacing and took a seat on the opposite end of the couch from Damian.

He promptly closed the gap between them.

"What…what are you doing?"

"I can't see her face from over there," he explained. "Relax, Kell. I don't bite. Well, maybe in some situations…"

Kelly swatted him on the arm—the right one with the lightning bolt tattoo up by his shoulder. She loved that tattoo for some inexplicable reason, and she used to trace her finger over it whenever they were…

"It's my turn to hold her," Damian said, and Kelly tried not to flinch when she transferred the baby into his arms. He was sitting so close to her that their thighs touched, and she suddenly felt very warm.

"I'll go heat up her bottle," Kelly said, jumping up. Any excuse to get away from him for a few minutes.

"I'll come with you."

"Why? It'll only take a minute. I'll be right back." Damian stayed seated, but she swore she felt his eyes on her while she walked away.

She took her time in the kitchen and tried to ignore the cooing sounds that Damian made in the next room. He was a man of many contrasts: tough on the outside, yet soft and gentle around kids and in the bedroom. Although he could be rough sometimes too. *STOP IT*, she scolded herself.

"You ok in there?" Damian called.

"Yep, I'm good," she yelled. She took a couple of deep breaths, extracted the bottle from the microwave, and returned to the living room.

Ava was cradled in Damian's beefy arms, sound asleep. "You must have the magic touch," Kelly said and then instantly regretted her choice of words.

"You would know," Damian said gruffly.

"Are you flirting with me?"

"Maybe."

"Why?"

"Why not?"

Kelly glared at him. "I thought we weren't going down this path again."

Damian sighed. "Just because we called a truce doesn't mean that I don't want you."

Kelly felt a surge of heat in her loins, but she ignored it. "I'm still mad at you."

"I know."

"And I don't want to be the woman that you just mess around with. Not this time."

"I get that."

"Do you, Damian? Do you really?"

He stood up and gently placed Ava back in her bouncy seat. Kelly was still standing in the middle of the room, clutching Ava's bottle tightly in her hands.

He walked toward her, and she inhaled sharply as he reached out and took the bottle out of her hands. He set it down on the coffee table and then took one step closer until she could feel the heat between their bodies.

"What do you want from me, Kell?"

You. I want you. She swallowed nervously, but she looked him straight in his golden-brown eyes and said, "I want the whole package, the courtship, the romantic gestures, the…"

"Hearts and flowers?"

"Yeah, maybe." It was hard for her to think straight with him standing this close.

"I didn't know you cared about that stuff."

He reached out and tugged on a strand of her hair, and continued to stare at her with at least one recognizable emotion in his eyes—lust. But she was determined not to give in—not this time.

"Well, I do…sometimes." Right now, she would settle for a kiss, but a kiss would lead to another, and then another…

"I made it too easy for you the first time around," she added.

Damian took a step back. "Too easy? Ha!"

"You disagree?"

"Yes. Nothing about you is easy."

Kelly felt her dander rising to a dangerously high level. "Are you saying that I'm *difficult*?"

Damian took another step back. "Well, you're not easy, that's for sure!"

Kelly gaped at him and racked her brain for a retort, but she appeared to be fresh out of them. Instead, she turned on her heel and stomped out of the room. Damian followed two steps behind.

"Where are you going?"

"Home," she replied, swinging her purse over her shoulder.

"Come on, Kell…"

"Don't Kell me," she hissed and threw the door open. "Oh, and by the way, when you leave your apartment at seven thirty on a Saturday morning, you don't need to rev your engine. You may not believe this, but some people were still trying to sleep!"

She shoved out the door without waiting for a response, but he yelled one out anyway.

"How did you know I revved my engine if you were sleeping?"

Kelly threw her hands in the air and got into her car before she dared spew anything else at him. *That cocky, arrogant, son-of-a…* Kelly stopped herself before she finished that thought. Along with promising Emma that she would be nice to Damian, she had promised to curb her swearing! Great—that made two promises that would be impossible to keep!

Chapter 7

Kelly braced herself for Emma's phone call, which came as expected a short time later.

"What in the hell happened between you and Damian?" Emma began.

"Oh, so it's ok for you to swear, but not me?"

"Answer the question, Kell."

Kelly gave her the short version and ended the story with, "I don't think I can do this, Em."

"Do what?"

"Stand up in your wedding with…him!"

"I'm not hearing this. I am *not* hearing this," Emma repeated emphatically.

"I'm sorry. You know I love you, but if Damian and I can't be in a room together for more than fifteen minutes without blowing up, how are we going to make it through your wedding day?"

"I'll tell you how. You two are going to suck it up and behave like rational adults, that's how! I will not have either one of you ruining my wedding."

And then the phone went silent. Emma had hung up on her. Perfect. Now Kelly was the bad guy, and Damian had probably gotten off scot-free.

Kelly did the only thing she could think of to relieve stress (that didn't involve alcohol or men). She retrieved her iPod from the bedroom, stripped naked, and poured herself a steaming hot bath. She sank into the water up to her neck and let herself get lost in the tunes of yesteryear. She could always count on the boy bands to make her feel better, and when she finally stepped out of the tub, she felt like her old self again.

Kelly wrapped the towel snugly over her breasts and padded out of the bathroom at the exact moment that her doorbell rang. *Now what?*

She glanced at the kitchen clock on her way past—nine o'clock—flicked on her outside light, and peered through the peephole. Damian stood there, looking skittish as he transferred his weight from one foot to the other. He reached his arm out like he was about to ring the bell again, but he stopped when she said, "What?"

He looked straight into the peephole and muttered, "Can I come in?"

Kelly glanced down at her towel and then back through the hole. "I'm kind of busy right now."

"Please. I'll only stay a minute."

Well, when he put it like that and when he gave her that sheepish look… She yanked open the door, making sure to keep her body shielded behind it, and once he was inside, she quickly slammed it shut.

Oh boy. This is a big mistake. Damian looked her over like he might have with a new car, inspecting all the nooks and crannies. By the time their eyes met, his were fogged over; a look that she was intimately familiar with.

Now who's in the driver's seat? "What do you want?" she asked, fully aware of the double entendre.

Damian swallowed hard and shook his head as if to clear it. Kelly was still warm from the bath, and she felt a trickle of perspiration roll down her back. She waited somewhat impatiently for him to speak.

"I…um…came over to…apologize."

Progress. "Go on," she said, aware that her towel was starting to slip. She quickly placed one hand above her breasts to keep the towel in place, which drew Damian's attention right there.

He swallowed again and said, "I didn't mean to imply that you're…difficult."

She started to soften—damn it! For Damian to set aside his pride and apologize to her when she hadn't made it easy on him… ok, so maybe she was a *little* difficult.

"Ok," she replied and gave him a slight smile.

"Ok?"

She nodded. "Ok."

"So, we're good?"

"For now. Just don't wake me up at seven-thirty tomorrow morning, and we're good."

Damian smirked. "I'll try not to."

An awkward silence fell over them, and Damian put his hand on the doorknob. "I should go."

"You probably should," she replied, although part of her wanted to yell, "No, don't!"

He searched her eyes and must have sensed her uncertainty, because he pulled the door open and slid out before any more words could be said.

After he left, Kelly leaned back against the door and exhaled loudly. "That was a close one!"

A few minutes later, she was tucked in bed, her current romance novel by her side. She reached over to the bedside table to silence her phone, and it buzzed with an incoming text.

You can answer the door in a towel anytime.

Kelly's smile stretched across her face, and she read the text three more times while deciding how to reply.

But not for everyone. Just for me.

Kelly giggled at that and then wondered if he really meant it. Had he been jealous when he had seen her out with Ken? Or was this just a strategy for getting her back in his bed?

You're lucky I answered the door. (She didn't want him getting too cocky!)

I agree.

He agrees? Hmm…what is his angle? Before she could respond, her phone pinged again.

Sweet dreams, Kell.

Kelly dropped the phone like a hot potato. If he only knew about the dream she had had the other night! She picked up the phone and typed:

You too!

And then she hurriedly shut it off. There would be no more flirting tonight—except between the sexy boss and his hot secretary in her romance novel. Just what she needed to read about before bed—not!

"Try this," he said and reached across the table with a sample of Szechuan chicken between his chopsticks.

She opened her mouth wide, and he slid the chopsticks inside. He watched her carefully as she chewed the piece of meat and then licked the sauce off her lips.

"Pretty good," she said. "But how do you do that?"

"Do what?"

"Hold those things. I've never learned how."

"It's pretty simple. Give me your hand."

She reached her hand across the table and watched it get swallowed up in his strong grip. He placed the chopsticks between her fingers just so and clamped down on them.

"There. Just like that."

But he didn't let go of her hand, and she felt her pulse quicken.

"Kell," he whispered and leaned close enough that she could see the gold flecks dancing in his eyes.

She didn't have to reply, because their lips crashed together of their own volition. She tasted the remnants of their meal on his lips and opened her mouth wider to accept his tongue. She was no longer aware of anything else but this—the warmth of his lips, her hand still locked in his, the heat of their bodies, and then…

Her brain registered the rumble of his damn truck! Kelly blinked her eyelids rapidly until they opened all the way, and she noticed the light shining in through the slats in her blinds. "It better not be seven-thirty," she hissed as the engine revved again.

She leaned over and peered at her alarm clock. Eight o'clock! Ok, so he'd done as she had asked. How could she be mad at him? But still, this was the second time he'd interrupted her sleep, not to mention her sexy dream.

Kelly reluctantly crawled out of bed, grabbed her robe, and headed out to see what he was up to. She peeked out the living room blinds, but this time, he looked right up at her and waved.

Pulling her robe tighter around her, she opened her front door and stepped onto the landing. Nobody seemed to be stirring except for him, and a few squirrels who chased each other around a nearby tree.

Kelly cupped her hands around her mouth and called, "Where are you off to so early?"

"Church," he replied, like she should have known.

But she had no idea that he went to church, and she couldn't help but be a touch surprised.

"This early?"

Damian chuckled. "I'm having breakfast with my parents first, and then we're going to church together."

"Oh," Kelly said, slightly miffed at herself for being so nosy.

"Sorry for waking you up again."

"At least it wasn't seven-thirty," she said and smiled.

Damian smiled back. "See you later," he said and hopped into his truck.

She suddenly remembered that she was standing outside in her robe, with her hair sticking up in every direction, so she turned and hurried back inside. She couldn't resist one more peek out the window, and she saw that Damian was still smiling as he drove away.

Chapter 8

Kelly felt relieved when the workweek started up again. Instead of focusing on Damian's comings and goings from their apartment complex, she turned her attention back to the bookstore. In between waiting on customers, placing orders, and shelving books, she began to plan her first romance book club meeting.

Her first order of business—selecting the book, which was not an easy task given the wide variety of romance novels to choose from. She decided to steer away from erotica, because she didn't want to offend anyone's sensibilities, but she wanted a story with at least a little sass!

Kelly was examining the array of possibilities laid out before her on the bookstore counter when Ken came strolling in. She quickly reassembled the books into a neat pile and shoved them aside.

"Hey, Ken," she said and greeted him with a smile.

"How's it going?" he asked, giving her a genuine smile in return.

She did like the guy, and it wasn't his fault that Damian had swooped back into town just when she and Ken were getting to know each other.

"Not bad. What brings you in today?"

"Well, I could lie and say I'm here to buy a book, but I won't."

"Ok…"

"Look, Kelly. I really like you, but I can't tell if you feel the same. I thought so at the beginning…but then something changed."

"Yeah, I know, and I'm sorry about that. Something came up, and I got a little distracted, but I like you too."

A warm smile spread across his face. "So, should I ask you out again?"

Why not? My infatuation with Damian is just that—an infatuation. Maybe, with Ken, it will be different. Maybe I haven't given him a fair chance. "Sure. Ask me again."

Ken cleared his throat noisily. "Kelly, will you go out with me on Saturday night?"

"Yes," she said.

"Great. I'll call you later in the week, and we'll make a plan."

Just then, the door chimed, and in walked Mrs. Simmons. "Sounds good," Kelly replied and then nodded toward her customer.

Ken took the hint and turned to leave, passing Mrs. Simmons on the way out.

"Good-looking young man," Mrs. Simmons said when she approached the counter. "But not as good-looking as that other fellow."

Kelly was confused. "Which other fellow?"

"That dark-haired, broody man that has a body like Adonis."

Kelly's eyes widened, and she let out a loud laugh. "You mean Damian?"

"I don't know what his name is, but I've seen him in here before, and he's one fine specimen."

"Mrs. Simmons!"

"What? I'm not dead yet!"

Kelly giggled again but decided to change the subject. "So, I'm trying to select a book for our book club meeting. Got any suggestions?"

"You're the expert, dear. I'll leave it up to you, but choose something spicy. It'll keep people coming back!"

On Wednesday evening, Kelly pulled into her apartment complex at the same time that Damian was getting into his truck. He looked up and waved while she pulled into her parking spot, and then waited for her to get out.

"Good timing," he said when she stepped out of the car.

Depending on how you look at it… "Good timing for what?"

"I was just on my way to the furniture store. Want to tag along?"

Kelly raised her eyebrows. "You want me to go furniture shopping with you?"

He shrugged. "Why not? I could use a woman's opinion."

"You could always ask your mom."

"Are you kidding? She only shops for furniture that can seat a thousand people. She has no idea how to shop for an apartment."

Kelly giggled. It was common knowledge that Alex loved to entertain. Her motto was "the more the merrier," much to the chagrin of her boys.

"Do you have to leave right away? I just got home from work, and I usually like to change…"

Damian interrupted while giving her the once-over. "Nothing wrong with what you're wearing," he said with a glint in his eye.

Kelly had on a black knit dress that hugged her curves and fell to just above the knee. Her three-inch heels showed just a peek of her toes, which she had painted a bright pink. Some days, she liked to dress up, and this happened to be one of them.

"Ok…I guess."

"Don't worry. I'll feed you," Damian said while he gave her a hand into his truck.

"I didn't say anything about food," Kelly snipped.

"Didn't have to. I know you, remember?"

Kelly rolled her eyes as he went around and hopped in the driver's seat.

"This thing is mammoth," she said, glancing around the roomy interior of the truck. "What do you need all this space for?"

"It's good for hauling things, plus the backseat is like a couch. Big enough to make out on if you know what I mean."

He shot her a sideways glance, and Kelly glared at him. "You would think of that." And then, to change the subject, she asked, "So, what kind of furniture are you shopping for?"

"My first priority is a bed. I've been sleeping on an old pull-out couch that my parents loaned me, but that thing is killing me."

"You poor thing," Kelly teased.

"I'm serious. I'm walking around with a constant backache."

"Maybe you need a massage." *Oops, walked right into that one!*

"You offering?"

"No. It was just a suggestion. Anyway, what else are you looking for?"

"A kitchen table and chairs, and a leather recliner."

"Is that it?"

"Yep, for now. What else do I need?"

Just the basics. That was Damian in a nutshell. Simple man, simple needs. She liked that about him.

When they entered the furniture store, Damian headed straight for the clearance center. Frugal with himself, yet generous with others—another admirable trait.

There were several beds set up against one wall, complete with mattresses and pillows so customers could test them out. Damian plopped down on the first bed they came to and sprawled across the mattress in a giant star shape.

"Not bad," he said after a few minutes. "Try it out." He scooted over to one side and patted the space beside him.

Kelly's nerves were already sparking simply from being in his presence. There was no way she was going to lay down on the bed with him!

"C'mon, Kell. Give it a whirl." He patted the empty space again and smirked, obviously enjoying her discomfort.

"Why should I? You're the one who's going to sleep on it, not me!"

"Hmm…" Damian looked like he was considering saying something else but decided not to. Instead, he rolled off the bed and sat down on the next one. He sprang up and down on it a couple of times, and then lay flat on his back.

"Now, this one's even better," he said.

Damian shut his eyes for a second and sighed. He looked like he was in…heaven.

"What's so great about it?" Kelly asked, her curiosity piqued.

Damian kept his eyes shut but patted the edge of the mattress. "You've got to try it, Kell. At least just sit on it. It's like a big puffy cloud."

He looked harmless, lying there with his eyes closed, and she was curious, so she perched carefully on the edge and bounced up and down a couple times.

Damian's arm shot out so fast she barely saw it, and now he clamped her wrist in his tight grip. He moved over and tugged her backward at the same time so that she landed flat on her back next to him.

Kelly's mouth gaped open, and she was about to curse at him when a salesman approached.

"That's a nice one, isn't it?" he said, smiling down at them.

Damian still had a hold of her wrist, but he loosened his grip just enough to slide his hand down and intertwine their fingers together. To the salesman, they must have looked like a happy couple trying out beds together, but inside Kelly was seething.

"Yes, it's very comfortable. Isn't it, sweetie?" Damian looked at her pointedly.

"If you want to try out some more, we have a lot of choices in our main showroom," the salesman offered.

"NO! I mean, no thank you, that's not necessary," Kelly said through gritted teeth. "I think this one's fine, don't you, *sweetie*?"

Damian chuckled and redirected his attention to the salesman. "Why don't you check back with us in a little while?"

"Sure. Take your time. My name is Bob if you need anything else."

After Bob walked away, Kelly untangled their hands and scrambled off the bed.

"You…you…"

"Relax, Kell. I was just having fun. Remember all of the fun we used to have?"

Yes! I remember too well. She shot him a look and said, "I think we should move on to the kitchen table and chairs."

And they did, but Damian wasn't done having *fun* yet. When they perused the various tables, he kept leaning his weight on them to see how they would hold up under it. She knew why he was doing it and chose to ignore him. Leave it to him to make something sexual out of furniture shopping!

An hour later, they left the store with a promise from Bob that Damian's furniture would be delivered over the weekend. By the time they got back in the truck, Kelly was exhausted and hungry.

"What can I feed you?" Damian asked.

His question was innocent, but it brought to mind her dream from the other night, when he had been feeding her Chinese food. A public place. They needed to eat in a public place, she decided.

"What if we get a pizza and take it to Depot Park?"

"Really? That's what you want? Because I can spring for a nice dinner, Kell."

"No. I'm serious. It's a beautiful night, and I'd like to eat at the park."

"Ok, then."

They ordered a pizza from Rudy's Market in downtown Clarkston, bought some beer to go with it, and took it to the park. It was the end of August, still warm but with a hint of fall in the air. Summer was winding down, which was always a letdown to Kelly, who loved the warm weather.

They sat across from each other at a picnic table under a large oak tree and dug into the pizza and beer. Other than a few murmurs about how good the pizza was, they didn't talk much, but it was a comfortable quiet, and Kelly enjoyed it.

"So, how's the car shop coming along?" Kelly asked once they had finished eating.

"Not bad. Jim's been teaching me the business side of it, so I haven't been able to get my hands dirty yet. He's working on a custom Corvette job right now, and I'm dying to get under the hood."

Kelly smiled at his description and at the way his eyes lit up when he talked about cars. She might not know much about them, but she understood his enthusiasm. She felt the same way about her job.

"I should bring you there sometime—show you around."

"Get my hands dirty?" she teased.

"Or maybe you could just hand me the tools," he teased back.

"I could do that."

"Wouldn't want you to break a nail," he said and reached across the table for her hand.

Her traitorous hand slipped into his of its own volition. Kelly watched Damian rub his thumb back and forth over the top of her hand a few times and then looked up to find him staring at her.

Uh-oh. There was that look again, and she was fairly certain that the look on her own face matched it!

"We should probably go," Kelly said, but she didn't pull her hand away.

Damian nodded but made no move to get up. "Kell," he began.

"No, Damian. Don't say anything. This has been… nice. Let's just leave it at that."

He nodded again, but this time, he pulled his hand away, and Kelly instantly missed his warmth.

They were silent on the short drive back to their apartments. Before Kelly could open the passenger door to get out, Damian said, "Let me help you down."

He hurried around to her side and gave her a hand while she carefully stepped out of the truck. "I need a stepladder to get out of this thing," she said, smiling up at him.

"Not if you've got me," he replied and smiled back.

They stood close together, wedged between his Chevy and the SUV parked next to him.

"Thanks for hanging out with me," Damian said, and in a swift movement, he bent down and kissed her cheek.

It was a far cry from the kind of kiss he'd given her in her dreams, but it thrilled her in a different way, and she appreciated the gentlemanly gesture.

"It was…fun," she replied, borrowing his word from earlier.

Just then, the owner of the SUV approached and motioned to his vehicle. Kelly and Damian broke apart to let the man get in his car, and the moment was lost.

She gave Damian a brief wave, turned, and walked across the road to her building. She didn't look back until she was standing outside of her door with the key in the lock. When she glanced over her shoulder, he was still there, in the middle of the road, his hands tucked in his pockets, watching her.

Chapter 9

"Where are you taking me?" she asked. He had tied a bandanna around her eyes so she couldn't see, and now he was leading her down the hall.

"Patience," he replied.

The blindfold was something they hadn't used before, and she kind of liked the idea of relinquishing control to him.

The apartment was small, so she knew that he was leading her to his bedroom, but she decided to be a good sport and played along.

He backed her up to the edge of the bed and gently pushed on her shoulders to get her to sit.

"Can I take the blindfold off now?"

"Why don't you lay back first?"

She thought her heart might pound right out of her chest. His little game was starting to feel like something more, but she lay back and sank into the soft mattress. She didn't have to see it to know that it was the same mattress that they had tried out in the furniture store.

Suddenly the bed dipped on her left side, and she felt Damian's presence surround her.

"Do you like it?" he asked, his voice low and breathy.

She nodded, unable to trust her voice.

"Do you want me to take the blindfold off now?"

His voice came from above her, and he was so close that she felt his breath against her cheek.

"No," she whispered.

"What do you want, Kell?"

"I want you to kiss me," she said.

And the next thing she knew, his lips were on hers—warm, hard, demanding. His hands entangled in her hair, and he had lowered himself over her so their chests rubbed together enticingly. Her hips automatically arched up to meet his, and then…

The sound of her alarm clock broke through.

Kelly reached an arm out and swatted at the clock until she found the off button. "Ugh!" she yelled to the empty room. She pounded her fists against the mattress a few times to release her frustration. "This has got to STOP!"

She sat up in bed and took a few deep breaths. Thank goodness she had a full day ahead of her. First, she had to work, and then she was going out with Ken. Anything to take her mind off Damian, which was easier said than done.

The first thing she did when she left the apartment was glance at his parking spot, which was already empty. Damian had mentioned that he worked at the car shop on Saturdays, so she figured that was where he was. She tried not to think about the gentle kiss that he had given her last night, or the way he'd held her hand at Depot Park. He had been about to tell her something, but she had cut him off. Now Kelly wondered what he had wanted to say.

When she pulled into the parking lot of A New Chapter, there was Mrs. Simmons standing outside, waiting for the store to open.

"Did you run out of books already?" Kelly teased as she unlocked the door.

"No. I came to see if you picked out a book for our romance club yet."

Mrs. Simmons was a widow, and Kelly suspected that loneliness was often what brought her to the store. She came in at least three or four times a week, sometimes just to browse, but she bought a lot of books too. She also supported the store by telling all her senior friends about it, so Kelly and Emma did their best to please her.

"I haven't chosen one yet, but I'm getting closer. Do you want to see which ones I'm considering?"

"Love to," she replied.

Kelly pulled a stack of romance novels out from behind the counter and showed them to Mrs. Simmons. Since Kelly had already read them all, she gave Mrs. Simmons a synopsis of each, and then listened to her opinions. Kelly's back was to the door, so when it chimed, she didn't see who had entered, but Mrs. Simmons did, and her eyes grew wide.

"What?" Kelly whispered.

"I think someone's here to see you," she said and then turned and walked away.

Kelly turned around, and there he was in the flesh, the hunky star of her dreams!

"Hey, Kell," he said.

"Hey," she replied, trying not to act surprised. "I thought you'd be at work."

"I'm on my way. Just thought I'd stop by and say hi."

Kelly quirked her eyebrows at him. Damian wasn't the kind of guy who "just stopped by" unless he had a specific reason.

"And I wanted to ask you something," he added.

That was more like him. "Ask away," she said, her curiosity piqued.

Damian glanced around the store, but Mrs. Simmons was at the very back, flipping through books at the kid's table.

"I…um…" Damian cleared his throat and started over. "I wondered if you would go out with me tonight."

Kelly's heart skipped a beat, and then her stomach dropped and her brow furrowed.

"Maybe I shouldn't have asked," Damian said in response to her disgruntled expression.

"No, no, it's not that," she said, which brought a smile back to his chiseled face. "It's just that I already have plans."

The smile disappeared. "Oh. Ok, then."

Kelly wanted his smile back. She wanted to pull him behind the counter and wrap her arms around him. She wanted him to…

"Ask me again? Another time?"

"Yeah. Sure."

The store phone rang, interrupting their awkward exchange. Damian gave her a brief wave and left while Kelly picked up the phone.

"A New Chapter. How can I help you?"

"It's me," Emma said.

They hadn't spoken since the babysitting incident, and Kelly was happy to hear her friend's voice.

"Hi."

"I'm sorry," they said in unison and then broke out in giggles.

"I really am sorry," Kelly repeated. "And I promise not to ruin your wedding. It's just that Damian's got me so tangled up I can't think straight."

"What now?" Emma asked.

"Well, he just left the store after I turned him down for a date tonight."

"You turned him down? Why?"

"Because I already have plans with Ken."

"The vegan?"

"He's not a vegan. He eats chicken and fish."

"Can I give you my opinion?"

"By all means."

"Stop wasting your time on Ken when you know that you'd rather go out with Damian tonight."

"Well, it's too late for that. It would be rude of me to cancel on Ken. Besides, I can go out with Damian another time."

"Ok, but Damian's not going to chase after you forever. The man has his pride."

"I know."

They went on to talk about store-related things, but when Kelly hung up, her thoughts returned to Damian. Why did he have to ask her out tonight of all nights? It wouldn't be fair to cancel on Ken again, although she was considering it when Mrs. Simmons reappeared at the counter.

"He's the one," she said. "The Adonis I was talking about."

"Yes. He's the one," Kelly said.

Just before the end of her work day, Kelly made up her mind. She dialed Ken's number and tapped her foot impatiently as she waited for him to pick up. When he didn't answer, she was somewhat relieved, but then she had to explain to his voicemail why she couldn't go out with him. In the end, she left a rambling message apologizing for the last-minute cancellation and for leading him on. She mentioned that there was someone else but didn't go into details. When she hung up, she felt a twinge of guilt but decided that honesty was the best policy.

Her next call was to Damian, but he didn't answer either. Instead of leaving a message, she decided to try and catch him at home. When Kelly pulled into the parking lot and saw his empty parking space, she swore. She had just gone from having two potential dates to having none. *Maybe I'm being punished for cancelling on Ken.*

And then it struck her that Zack and Emma might know where Damian was.

"It's your lucky day," Emma said a few minutes later. "Damian and Zack are having a beer at Clarkston Tap. They just left a little bit ago."

Kelly breathed a sigh of relief. At least Damian wasn't out with another woman.

She hurriedly changed from her work clothes into something a bit more provocative. Her loose dress pants were exchanged for a snug-fitting pair of skinny jeans, and the conservative blouse got traded in for a silky tank top. She removed the elastic ponytail holder and let her hair fall in soft waves down her back. Shiny gold hoop earrings took the place of her demure diamond studs, and out came the strappy black sandals with the four-inch heels. A fresh coat of mascara and a swipe of lip gloss, and she was ready to go.

Kelly hadn't given much thought to what she would say to Damian—she just knew that she wanted to see him. She squelched the flutter of nerves in her belly while she parked her Jetta, and then she walked into Clarkston Tap. The place was a small bar/restaurant that catered primarily to the locals. Kelly had only been there one other time, and that was with Damian months ago. The low-key, simplistic vibe suited his personality perfectly…and there he was, a standout (along with his brother) among the crowd of men who were seated around the bar.

Several pairs of eyes turned her way as Kelly made her way over to him, but she barely noticed. Damian and Zack were watching sports on one of the overhead television screens, but it was almost as if Damian sensed her presence. He swiveled around on the bar stool and locked eyes with her, the corners of his lips turning up in a wide, sexy grin.

Her nerves instantly vanished when she saw his reaction, and she returned his welcoming smile.

Zack finally noticed the shift of his brother's attention, and he turned to greet Kelly as she approached.

"Hey. Look who's here! Did you come to relieve me?" Zack teased.

Damian gave him a playful shove. "Hey, I was doing you a favor, not the other way around!"

Zack hopped off his stool and offered it to Kelly. "I warmed it up for you," he said.

Just then, a waitress came over and asked for Kelly's drink order. She ordered a Coors Light and then turned her attention to Damian.

"Hi," she said playfully.

"Hi, yourself," he said.

Zack cleared his throat noisily. "You know what? I'm going to let you two do…whatever it is that you two do, and I'm going home to my soon-to-be wife."

"Don't let me chase you away," Kelly said, but she didn't sound very convincing.

"No worries. Damian and I had just about used up our allotment of words to each other anyway."

Damian smirked and took a long slug of beer.

"Tell Emma I said thank you," Kelly said.

"Will do. See you two kids later."

"Thank you for what?" Damian asked after Zack had left.

Kelly flipped her hair over her shoulder. "For letting me know where to find you."

"I thought you had plans tonight," he said, searching her eyes for clues.

"I cancelled them."

"I'm glad."

And then they were at a standstill. There were so many things that Kelly wanted to say to him, but she wasn't sure where to begin, and the bar probably wasn't the best place for a serious discussion.

Damian must have felt the same way, because he suggested, "Want to get out of here?"

"Sure," she said and then slugged down the rest of her beer.

"Wow! That was hot," Damian said as they were leaving.

She gave him a flirtatious glance over her shoulder. "I have many talents."

"Oh, I know you do," he said and followed her out the door.

Chapter 10

"Where do you want to go?" Damian asked as they walked across the parking lot.

Why does everything that comes out of his mouth sound seductive?

"We could go to my place so you can check out the new furniture," he suggested before she had time to respond.

He winked at her, and the memory of the two of them on the mattress at the furniture store came rushing back to her. "I don't know if that's such a good idea," she replied.

"Come on, Kell. Stop thinking I have an ulterior motive every time we get together."

"Ok, fine. But I'm coming over to see your furniture and to have a discussion. Nothing else."

"I got it," he said and opened her car door for her.

She slid in and rolled the window down.

"Beat ya home," he called and raced across the parking lot to his truck.

Kelly giggled at Damian's playfulness. She had certainly seen signs of it before, but she realized that there was so much more to learn about him. The weeks they had spent together eight months ago had been filled with fun: dinners out, the holidays, and lots and lots of sex. But then it had ended so abruptly when he had returned to California, and not seeing him or talking to him had left a deep void inside of her. She hadn't even realized how deep until he had returned looking hotter than ever and seemingly still interested in her. But this time, she was going to take the driver's seat. She refused to lay herself out for him on a silver platter like she had the first time, only to have him walk away.

No, this time, he was going to have work for her, and on the drive back to their apartment complex, she figured out how.

"It looks… nice in here," she said after he had shown her around his apartment.

"I know it's not as homey as your place, but I'm still working on it," he said. "Do you want another beer?"

"No, I'm good," she said as he extracted one from the refrigerator for himself.

There was only a sofa and the new black leather recliner in his living room, so Kelly took the chair. Less chance for any contact that way.

Damian looked at her when he came back into the living room, shrugged his shoulders, and sprawled out on the couch. "So, what do you want to talk about?" he said.

Kelly glanced at him while he leaned back against the couch cushions in his torn jeans, faded t-shirt, and work boots, and then swallowed nervously. *You can do this, you can do this*, she chanted to herself.

Damian took a long pull on his beer and waited.

"I have a proposition for you," she began.

Damian raised his eyebrows but remained quiet.

"I think it's pretty clear that we're attracted to each other."

"Um-hmm."

"And we already know that we're good together in… certain ways."

"Go on."

"But I think we should use the next few months, from now until Emma's wedding, to really get to know each other. To start over in effect."

Damian cleared his throat and sat up straighter. "But we do know each other, Kell."

"You think so? Then what's my favorite color?"

Damian looked her up and down and replied, "Blue."

"Lucky guess. What are my parents' names?"

"I have no idea."

"Exactly! That's what I'm talking about. We don't truly *know* each other, Damian. We were only together for a matter of weeks before, and we spent most of that time… "

"In bed," he finished proudly.

Kelly scowled at him. "Yes, and we've already established that that part of our relationship works, but what about the rest of it?"

"What rest of it?" Damian looked confused.

Kelly sighed. "We need to determine if we really like each other as people, not just as lovers."

Damian gazed at her intently for what felt like several minutes, as if weighing his options. He must have sensed that she was serious and that he was being tested. Finally, he said, "So, sex is off the table. So to speak."

Kelly nodded. "For the next three months."

"No kissing?"

Kelly stared at his lips and decided that maybe she could make an exception. "Some kissing would be ok, as long as it doesn't lead to… "

"How about touching?"

She glanced at his hands, one of which was wrapped tightly around his beer bottle, and the other that rested casually along the back of the couch. *Oh, what those hands have done to me!* "Maybe a little bit of touching."

Damian looked skeptical. "Why are you doing this, Kell? Tell me the real reason, because I know it's not just about your favorite color or your parents' names. Where is this coming from?"

Kelly squirmed under his intense scrutiny. She had bared her body to Damian before, but not her heart, not her soul. If this was going to work, she owed him an honest answer, so she plunged ahead. "All my adult life, I've given myself freely to men, and what do I have to show for it? A string of failed relationships, that's what. And I think it's because I've been going at it backwards. Instead of taking the time to develop something real, I've jumped right in and gotten ahead of myself. I've decided that I want something more than just a fling. I want someone to want *all* of me, and I want to feel like I'm worth the wait."

Damian took a long slug of his beer and wiped his mouth with the back of his hand. "So, for the next three months, we date and get to know each other without the sex."

At least he didn't laugh at me or tell me to leave. "Yes," she said softly.

"But some kissing and touching is allowed."

His attempt to understand the rules made her giggle. "Yes, but we can't get carried away."

"You know that this is going to be torture for me, right?"

"It won't be easy for me either," she admitted.

"And after the wedding is over…"

"The ban is lifted, assuming you still want me."

"Oh, I'll still want you."

Kelly swallowed hard. "So, do we have a deal?"

Damian leaned across the couch and held out his hand. "Shake on it," he said with a sparkle in his eye.

When she slid her hand into his rough warm grip, she almost called the whole thing off. Just the feel of his skin against hers and the memories of the pleasure he'd brought her in the past made her tingly from head to toe.

Damian smiled seductively, and she knew that it was going to be game on! If she was willing to "torture" him, he would do the same to her. The next three months were sure to be a bumpy ride!

"Ready to go?" Damian asked.

It was the following afternoon, and Kelly had the day off, so Damian had asked her to come with him to check out the auto shop. Kelly had left his apartment shortly after their discussion the night before, even though Damian had suggested they watch a movie together. She hadn't wanted to tempt fate by sitting in his darkened apartment on a Saturday night, so she had begged off early with the promise that she would accompany him to the shop the next day. She figured that this was the perfect outing for their first official "date," because a dirty auto shop didn't sound overly romantic, yet she was curious about where he worked.

"So, should I be asking some questions to learn more about you?" Damian teased.

"Sure. Fire away."

"What's your favorite movie?"

"*Gone with the Wind*," she answered immediately.

"Rhett or Ashley?"

"Rhett!"

"How come?"

"Because he's so much hotter than Ashley. The dark hair, those eyes, that smile…"

Damian chuckled. "Frankly, Scarlet…"

"I wouldn't have thought you'd like it too."

"I didn't say I liked it, but I've seen it a few times. My mom's a huge fan."

"So, what about you? What's your favorite movie?"

"*Die Hard*."

"Now that sounds more like you."

Damian smiled. "Bruce Willis is a badass in that film."

While she was enjoying their exchange, Kelly wanted to go deeper than learning about his favorites. "Why'd you leave Michigan the first time?"

Damian's smile instantly disappeared, and he tightened his grip on the steering wheel. "I wanted to get away."

"Yes, but why?"

He sighed, recognizing that she wasn't going to drop the subject. "Broken engagement," he replied cryptically.

Kelly's eyes widened. She'd had no idea that Damian had been engaged, and why would she? They hadn't taken the time to share their stories before. "I didn't know…"

"Well, now you do."

Maybe she should have let it go, but she couldn't. He had piqued her curiosity, and once that happened, there was no stopping her. "What happened?"

Damian shot her a weary glance and then trained his eyes back on the road. "We met in high school, junior year. After graduation, she went off to MSU, and I stayed home. I wasn't sure what I wanted to do with my life, but I knew that college wasn't for me. During her second year, we got engaged, but we decided to wait until she graduated to get married. A few months later, she decided that we were too different. We didn't have the same goals, or some shit like that. Anyway, I left for California shortly after."

Kelly was flabbergasted. The idea of Damian having been engaged was hard enough to wrap her head around, but the pain in his voice when he told the story was equally mind-boggling. That woman must have really hurt him to cause him to leave the state. Was *she* the reason that Damian was still a bachelor? Who was this woman, and why did Kelly have the inexplicable urge to punch her? *Or maybe I should be thanking her.* If Damian had gotten married, Kelly wouldn't be sitting next to him right then. She would never have known what it was like to kiss him, touch him, be with him.

Damian glanced over at her as if he were waiting for further questions. "So, that was it? You never saw her again?" Kelly asked.

"I heard that she got married a couple years later, but that's all I know. It was a long time ago, Kell. I'm over it."

But was he really? Kelly had her doubts, but she decided to keep them to herself for now.

"Here we are," Damian said, sounding relieved as they pulled into the gravel parking lot in front of Jim's Custom Cars.

The shop was a white brick building with two large roll-up doors and an attached office space on the right. The building was neat but unremarkable, and the marketing side of Kelly's brain was already plotting ways to make the building stand out. Damian used a key to let them in the customer entrance, and there was enough light streaming in through the large glass windows for Kelly to get a good look at the office space. It was sparse but clean, and featured a high wood-paneled front counter, a small waiting area with a few hard plastic chairs, and a water cooler. A glass-topped table held an assortment of car magazines, many of which Kelly was familiar with from working at the bookstore. A functional gray metal desk and matching file cabinets were positioned behind the counter, and framed photos of various cars and trucks covered the back wall.

Kelly scanned the pictures with interest and then asked, "Are these vehicles that Jim has worked on?"

"Yeah," Damian said.

"Wow. He does a good job."

"Come into the garage, and I'll show you our current project." Damian led her through another door into the open garage space. There were a few windows placed high along the back wall, but Damian flicked a switch, and the entire area filled with bright light. Again, Kelly noticed how clean the space was. Tool chests and work tables lined the outer walls, but it appeared that everything had its place. Kelly had been to auto repair shops before, but her impression of them wasn't very favorable. This was entirely different though, and she formed a new appreciation for Damian's job.

"Check out this beauty," he said, walking over to a baby blue Corvette with a white convertible top.

"What year is this?" Kelly asked, circling the vehicle to admire it from every angle.

"It's a vintage 1966," Damian said with considerable enthusiasm.

"Is there something wrong with it?"

"Just a few minor things, but the owner treats it like a baby. He won't accept anything but the best."

"And Jim's the best?"

"He's the best in this area. I learned a lot from him when I worked here after high school."

"And then you moved to California," she said, hoping to keep him talking.

"Yep, where I worked for my buddy Pete at his shop in San Diego."

There was one question that she had been dying to ask, and now seemed like the appropriate time. "What made you come back, Damian?"

He leaned against the side of the Corvette, his hands clasped in front of him, his legs crossed at the ankles, watching her intently while she circled the car and then stopped directly in front of him. He seemed to be contemplating his answer, so she tried prompting him.

"Did you know that Jim was retiring?"

"No. Not until I was here over the holidays."

"Was it for your family?"

"Partly."

"Was there some other reason?" She knew she was leading him, but she couldn't stop herself. Kelly had to know if she played any part in his decision to return to Michigan.

He opened his mouth to answer, but just then, the front door chimed, announcing a visitor. Damian pushed himself off the car and started moving toward the office, with Kelly two steps behind him, when Jim came into view.

Apparently, I'm not going to get my answer after all.

Chapter 11

"I moved back for you," he said, his eyes piercing into hers.

Her breath caught, and she took a step closer to him where he leaned against the Corvette.

"Couldn't get you out of my head. I thought time and distance would do the trick, but I never stopped wanting you, Kelly."

And with that, she flung her arms around his neck and pressed her lips to his. His hands automatically encircled her waist, and he spread his legs apart so that she could step between them. Her breasts smashed against his hard chest, and her hips aligned with his so perfectly that she felt the ridge of his erection.

She melted into his kiss, his scent, his touch. His warm hands travelled up and down her back, setting each and every nerve ending on fire. Kelly thrust her fingers into his thick dark hair, and he moaned against her.

Damian pulled apart just long enough to say, "Got to have you now…"

And then…her alarm rang!

Kelly blinked her eyes rapidly until she was fully awake. *This is becoming quite the habit*, she thought with a smile on her face. If she couldn't have Damian in the flesh, dreaming about him was the next best thing. Dreams would have to do, at least for next few months. She had made the rules after all, and she was determined to follow them!

When Kelly left for the bookstore a couple hours later, Damian's truck was already gone. He had told her yesterday that he liked to "get up with the birds" and go to work early. He had also mentioned that he usually grabbed a hot chocolate and a donut from the Clarkston bakery on his way to the shop. Such simple things, but she liked that she was learning his habits, and it only made her want to know more.

On the short drive to A New Chapter, Kelly recalled their conversation about Damian's engagement, and she realized that he had never mentioned his ex-fiancée's name. Since Kelly had also gone to MSU and she and Damian were the same age… Wouldn't it be strange if she knew the woman? Kelly had lived on campus and had been friends with many of the girls in her dorm, but that was eight years ago. Besides, it was a big school, and the woman could have lived anywhere. Surely, Kelly would have remembered if she had seen Damian in her building. With his dark, smoldering good looks and that hunky body, and…

"Oh my God, I'm doing it again!"

When Kelly pulled into the parking lot, she noticed that Emma's car was already there. Even though Emma had just had her baby a short time ago, she was having a hard time staying away. Selfishly, Kelly was glad to have her there. She missed their daily chats, and with Emma getting married soon, Kelly expected that they wouldn't be able to spend as much time together.

"Hey, bestie," Emma called when Kelly walked in.

"Hey, yourself. Couldn't bear to stay away, could you?"

"Well, I wasn't planning on coming in, but Alex insisted that I needed to get out for a while, so here I am."

"I take it Alex is babysitting?"

"You know it. Any chance to get her hands on her grandchild…"

Marriage and children—two topics that hadn't been on Kelly's radar, up until…

"So, how are things going with you and Damian?"

Just the sound of his name made her lips curl up. "Good. We're getting along good," she repeated.

Emma set down the stack of invoices she had been reviewing and looked her friend right in the eyes. "Are you back to…how things used to be?"

Kelly giggled. Emma was shy when it came to talking about sex, so she often used other terminology to describe it. "You mean sex?" Kelly said, just to rile her.

Emma turned a nice shade of pink and said, "Yeah, that."

"Actually, no," Kelly said with a hint of pride in her voice.

"NO?"

Kelly put her hands on her hips and glared. "I know what you think of me, but this time, it's different."

"Oh God. I'm sorry, Kell. It's just that when Damian was here before…"

"I know, but I've decided to take it slow this time. We're taking some time to get to know each other first."

"And Damian agreed to this?" Emma was obviously still flabbergasted.

"Well, yeah."

"Wow, Kell. That's…admirable, I guess. As long as you're happy, that's all that matters."

They worked companionably for the next few hours, until Emma left to pick up Ava. While Kelly neatened up the bookshelves, she reflected on how Emma had gone from being divorced to becoming a part of a family of four almost overnight. Up until recently, Kelly had touted her single lifestyle over that of her married friends. So, why was she suddenly yearning for something more? Just because Emma had joined the ranks of the (almost) married with children, it didn't mean that Kelly had to. Besides, Damian seemed to be content with his single status too.

"Ugh! Why does it always come back to Damian?" Kelly yelled to the empty bookstore. Her phone buzzed in her pocket and startled her. She fished it out and stared down at the simple text message.

Dinner tonight?

She hesitated for a moment but then typed: *Ok.*

Your place or mine?

She hesitated even longer this time, but before she could respond, her phone pinged again.

On second thought, maybe we should go to a restaurant!

Kelly giggled. Damian must have thought the same thing she had when she had read his invitation. It would definitely be safer for them to meet in a public place, rather than hole up in one of their apartments together.

I agree.

I'll need to go home and clean up after work, so, pick you up at six?

Kelly shook her head at the phone. He would hardly have to pick her up when she lived across the parking lot! She typed: *Sounds good* and then slipped the phone back into her pocket.

She floated through the rest of the workday with a permanent smile on her face, and when Brett came in to relieve her at five, he studied her inquisitively.

"I recognize that look," he said when he joined her behind the counter.

"What look?"

"You have a date."

"I have a certain look when I have a date?"

"Um-hmm. Your cheeks are a little flushed, and you have that dreamy, faraway look in your eyes."

"Wow, Brett. I had no idea that guys could be so observant!"

He smiled at her and adjusted his stylish glasses. The young girls were nuts over this guy, and Kelly could certainly understand why.

"Oh, we're observant all right. Is that what you're wearing on your date?"

Kelly glanced down at her black dress pants and floral print blouse. She had always dressed conservatively at the store, and Brett had never really seen her when she went out. "Hell no," she replied and then corrected herself, "I mean, heck no."

Brett chuckled. "I'm twenty-one, Kelly. I can handle a swear word or two."

"You're twenty-one?" she teased. "Anyway, as a guy, what would you suggest I wear tonight?"

"A dress," he answered immediately. "A simple sundress if you've got one. Men go crazy over a woman in a dress."

Kelly raised her eyebrows at him. "Really?"

"Oh yeah."

"Ok, then. I'll take your word for it. A simple sundress it is."

Kelly mentally went through her closet on the way home. She had an assortment of summer dresses to choose from, but based on Brett's description, she settled on one in particular. When she arrived at the apartment complex, she noticed that Damian's parking spot was empty. *Good! That gives me plenty of time to get ready.*

She plucked the dress out of her closet and held it up to herself in the bedroom mirror. The coral hue popped against her bronzed skin. Kelly had been blessed with a caramel-colored complexion thanks to the Latin American blood on her mom's side of the family. While her dad was as pale as could be, Kelly had inherited her mom's skin tone, along with her rich brown hair and golden brown eyes. She also attributed her curves to her Latino heritage, and while she used to curse them in her junior high school days, she came to embrace them during high school. While many of her friends had been "late bloomers," Kelly was fully developed by the time she was thirteen. It didn't take long for her to learn how to use her looks to her advantage, which sometimes got her into trouble. She recalled her mother's constant reminder that beauty would fade and that it was what was inside that counted. Kelly agreed, but tonight, while she was still fairly young, she would embrace her beauty and milk it for all it was worth!

She had just slipped her sandals on when the doorbell rang. When she opened the door wide, her mouth opened to match it. A more polished version of Damian stood before her, and she perused him from head to toe just to make sure that it was really him! Kelly realized that she had never seen Damian dressed in anything other than worn jeans, t-shirts, and his favorite scuffed work boots. Even though he was still dressed casually, tonight he had on olive green cargo shorts with a collared black polo shirt. Instead of work boots, he wore what looked like hiking shoes, but they were clean and maybe even…new! His face was void of the usual scruff, and his hair was actually in place, although a few errant strands stuck out adorably. He still had the rugged good looks that she was drawn to, but he had neatened up—for her!

"Wow," Damian said approvingly. "Love the dress."

Kelly sent a silent thank you to Brett and then said, "Thanks. You're looking pretty spiffy yourself."

"Spiffy?" He quirked his eyebrows at her.

"Well, you know what I mean. You look…"

"Different. Yeah, I know."

His cockiness was gone, and in its place there was…uncertainty? Kelly placed a hand gently on his forearm. "I like it, Damian. You look good."

He brightened up and gave her a huge grin. "Ok, so let's get going."

Damian held her hand down the three flights of stairs, presumably so that she wouldn't fall, even though she was an expert at walking in heels. Kelly enjoyed the feel of her hand clamped tightly in his, so she kept it there while they walked across the parking lot and when he helped her up into his truck. They had been out to dinner numerous times before, but somehow tonight felt like the first time.

"So, what sounds good? Mexican, Italian, burgers, seafood…?"

Greek! I feel like Greek! "How about Italian?" Greece, Italy—same part of the world, right?

"According to Zack, there's a really good Italian restaurant in Rochester. Do you know it?"

"Bravo."

"Well, thank you, but it wasn't my idea."

Kelly burst out laughing. "No. Bravo is the name of the restaurant!"

"Oh. My bad."

Somehow his expression made her laugh even louder. Here he was, trying to impress her, when he would have easily settled for a carry-out pizza and a beer. She was touched that he was taking her dating idea so seriously, and she had to stop herself from flinging her arms around his neck and kissing him.

When they were seated at a table for two a short time later, Kelly leaned across the table and said, "Thank you for bringing me here."

Damian's face lit up in response, and then he turned his attention back to the menu. "What is all this frou-frou stuff anyway? Where's the spaghetti and meatballs?"

So much for fine dining, Kelly thought. But that was Damian, a man of simple tastes, and she wouldn't want him any other way.

Chapter 12

After their meal of pasta, salad, and bread, Kelly suggested that they walk around the Rochester Village Mall, which was where the Italian restaurant was located. It was an outdoor mall featuring upscale stores, but she wasn't interested in shopping. One, she wanted to walk off their heavy meal, and two, she wasn't ready to go home just yet.

Damian didn't seem in a hurry to leave either, so they strolled side by side down the sidewalk, along with the other shoppers who were out enjoying the glorious late-summer weather.

"So, in the spirit of getting to know each other better, what *are* your parents' names?" Damian asked with a smirk.

"Frank and Maria," she replied, smirking back at him.

"Any siblings?"

"No. My mom had trouble getting pregnant, and she didn't have me until she was forty-two. The doctor discouraged her from trying again after that."

"Plus, how could she top you?"

Kelly darted a look at him to see if he was teasing, but he wore a serious expression.

"So, what was it like growing up as an only child?"

"It was great! I didn't have to share my toys, and I always got my parents' full attention. I know I'm not supposed to say that, but there it is. I never felt like anything was lacking in my life, plus I have tons of cousins, so I always had playmates."

"When did your parents move to Florida?"

"After I graduated from college and got my first 'real' job. My mom wanted to move to a warmer climate, and my dad likes to make my mom happy, so there you have it. They live in Naples now."

Kelly halted in front of a woman's clothing store to admire a beautiful gown in the window. "Oh my gosh. I think that's it. I think that's the one."

Damian looked baffled. "The one?"

"Yes, my maid of honor dress for Emma's wedding."

Damian leaned over her shoulder for a closer look, which momentarily distracted her from the dress. He smelled fresh and clean, with a hint of raw man.

"I would have thought you'd already picked out a dress by now," he said gruffly.

Kelly felt his breath on her neck. If she turned her head slightly, they would have bumped noses. "Emma said that I could pick one out myself as long as it wasn't too sexy. I've been looking, but I haven't found anything yet."

"Why don't you go in and try it on?" Damian suggested.

"Really? I could come back another day so you don't have to wait for me."

He had taken a step back, but he was still standing close enough that she could see the gold flecks in his eyes. "I don't mind," he said.

"Ok."

The minute they walked into the store, a saleswoman approached, and Kelly pointed at the dress in the window. When she gave the woman her size, the woman looked pained. "I'm afraid the only size eight is the one on the mannequin, and we don't typically like to undress them. Perhaps I can order one for you."

Damian spoke up before Kelly could respond. "That's a bunch of crap. Why can't you put another size on the mannequin?"

Kelly watched the saleswoman's face turn crimson, and while she wanted to feel bad for her, she couldn't. Damian had a valid point!

"If you don't want to undress it, I will," he added, and he was about to take the matter into his own hands, literally, when another saleswoman approached.

"Is there a problem here?" she asked, looking down at them through the narrow glasses that were perched at the end of her nose.

Kelly was beginning to feel uncomfortable. She had simply wanted to try on the dress, not make a spectacle of themselves. "No, there's no problem. I was interested in the dress in your display window…"

"But"—Damian glanced down at the first saleswoman's name tag—"Elaine doesn't want to strip the mannequin," he finished.

All three of the women looked startled when he used the word "strip," and then Kelly noticed that the woman with the glasses was trying to suppress a smile.

"I'm sorry for the misunderstanding, sir. If your wife wants to try on the dress, then by all means, we will take it off the mannequin."

Kelly's eyes widened, and she opened her mouth to correct the woman when Damian interrupted again.

"I'm sure my *wife* will be very grateful," he said and shot Kelly a searing grin.

When the two saleswomen left to "strip" the mannequin, Kelly turned to Damian and hissed, "Thanks a lot! That was soooo embarrassing!"

Damian chuckled. "You want to try on the dress, don't you?"

"Yes, but…"

"Then stop complaining and be a grateful wife!"

Kelly didn't have a chance to retort, because the woman with the glasses was heading toward them with the dress draped over her arm. "Let me show you to a fitting room," she said pleasantly. "Sir, if you'd like to come too, there's a chair right outside the fitting room so your wife can model the dress for you."

"That won't be necessary," Kelly said, purposely avoiding eye contact with her *husband.*

Damian peered at the woman's name tag and said, "Thanks, Donna. We appreciate your help."

When Donna had left and Kelly was safely behind the fitting room door, she hurriedly changed into the dress. The sooner this debacle was over with, the better.

"How's it going in there, *dear*?" Damian teased.

"Oh, shut up," she replied. Good thing he couldn't see her trying to stifle a giggle.

"Shit," she said a minute later.

"What?"

"Damn it!"

"Anyone ever tell you that you swear a lot?"

"Yes! Emma tells me all the time. I'm trying to cut back, but right now, I can't reach this damn…zipper!"

"Open the door," Damian demanded.

"No. I'll get it."

"Open the damn door," he said, his voice louder that time.

Since they had already created enough of a scene, Kelly quickly yanked open the door. The look on Damian's face froze her to the spot. He raked his eyes over her like she was a vintage Corvette and he couldn't wait to pop the hood!

Kelly had to admit that she looked good in the dress even without it zipped up! The royal blue color complimented her skin, which was now flushed from Damian's gaze. She had flipped her long, wavy hair over one shoulder while she had tried to work the zipper, and her lower lip was swollen from where she had bitten it in frustration. She was holding the dress tightly across her breasts because it was strapless, and she had removed her bra. The only thing she had on underneath was the tiny thong that she had worn under her sundress.

Apparently, Damian lost his voice, because he motioned with his hand for her to turn around. Once she had her back to him, she let out a breath, relieved to get out from under his intense scrutiny. But then she felt him step in behind her, and his thumb grazed her lower back as he reached for the zipper. She heard his sharp intake of breath when he realized what she was wearing underneath—a whole lot of nothing!

Kelly felt like she was in a tanning booth, her back seared from the heat rolling off him, and she resisted the urge to lean against him. She shook herself, and then she realized that he hadn't moved and the dress was still unzipped.

"Uh, Damian?"

"Yeah?"

The word came out on a whisper that blew against her bare skin and made her weak. "The zipper," she said, hardly recognizing her own breathy voice.

"How's it going back here?" Donna's curt inquiry broke the spell, and Damian quickly yanked up the zipper.

"Good. Really good," he said as he stepped back to let Donna see.

Kelly turned back around and smiled brightly. "I love it," she said.

"It looks gorgeous on you, and I'm sure your husband would agree."

"Gorgeous," he repeated, but his eyes weren't on the dress. They were locked on hers, and they exchanged a silent acknowledgement of what he really meant.

"Who does that?" Kelly exclaimed when they were back in Damian's truck, the dress bag lying on the seat between them. "Why would that woman assume that we were married?"

"I don't know. Maybe it's my outfit," Damian teased.

Kelly had to laugh. "Cargo shorts don't yell *married*, Damian."

"Well, what about the polo shirt? If I would have been wearing my Rolling Stones t-shirt, she might have thought that we were a couple of young hipsters who were dating."

Kelly shook her head. "I don't think your clothes have anything to do with it. I think it's because we're at that age where people assume we'd be married by now."

Damian raised his eyebrows but kept his eyes on the road.

"Not as in you and me specifically, but well, you know what I mean."

"Relax, Kell. I get your point. Actually, I'm a little surprised that you're still single. Seems like you would have been swept off your feet by now."

"Maybe I haven't wanted to be," she replied indignantly.

He glanced over at her and shrugged. "Whatever."

"Well, what about you? We're the same age, so why haven't you tied the knot yet?" The look on Damian's face told the story, and Kelly instantly regretted asking the question. It was obvious that Damian was still affected by his broken engagement whether he wanted to admit or not.

"Marriage and kids aren't really on my radar," he replied, his eyes fixed on the road.

"But you're so good with your nieces. You're like a baby whisperer. Any time you come within five feet of Ava, she stops crying, and Gracie worships the ground you walk on."

Damian's mouth twitched at her description. "I love those girls, but it's not the same as having your own kids. Honestly, it scares the hell out of me."

Kelly raised her eyebrows in surprise. She never would have connected the word "scared" with Damian. The man had confidence in spades, so his admission came as a bit of a shock. "Why's that?"

"It's like this; if I mess something up when I work on a car, I can always fix it. But if you mess up raising your kid—well, there's no fixing that."

"Why would you assume that you'd mess up?"

"I don't know, Kell. In life, there are certain things that you just know that you're good at, and I tend to stick to those."

He took his eyes off the road to shoot her a sly glance, and she understood exactly what he was referring to. "You're terrible," she said while a giggle bubbled up.

"But I'm damn good at it!" he replied.

By the time they reached their apartment complex, it was dark.

"Let me walk you to the door," Damian offered once he had helped her out of the truck.

"It's right there," Kelly pointed. "You can wait here until I get in if you want to."

"Let me walk you up," he repeated, and he grabbed the dress bag out of her hands.

"Ok, fine."

They walked up the three flights of stairs to her apartment, with Kelly leading the way. "Are you looking at my butt?" she called over her shoulder.

"No. Not at all," he said, followed by his gruff laughter.

"Liar."

When they reached her door, she put out her hand to take the dress from him, but he used it to pull her up against his hard-as-a-brick-wall chest. "I'm going to kiss you goodnight now," he warned, right before his lips came crashing down on hers.

Kelly was trapped between her door and his unyielding body, and she melted into his kiss. She felt an intoxicating combination of familiarity and newness because it had been so long—too long—since they'd been this close. She opened her mouth and moaned as his tongue met hers, and her body responded to him with the usual passion. Oh, how she wanted to grab his shirt and pull him into her apartment, but a few seconds later, he abruptly pulled back, and she instantly felt the night chill surround her.

"Goodnight, Kell," he said and handed her the dress bag.

Wait! I'm not done! "Goodnight, Damian," she said before he turned and headed down the stairs.

Chapter 13

She fisted her hand in his shirt and pulled him inside the dark apartment. The dress bag clattered to the floor, but she didn't care. She backed them up until she bumped into the couch, and then tumbled backward, taking him down with her.

His mouth was everywhere—on her lips, on her neck, insistent, demanding. Her body arched into his, and her dress crept up, exposing her bare thighs.

Then his warm, thick hands cupped her face, and he gazed at her with desire burning in his eyes. "Are we doing this?"

And then…

"Rise and shine, metro Detroiters. It's another beautiful day in the Motor City." The radio DJ's voice broke through, and Kelly reached over to shut off the alarm.

The dream came as no surprise this time, especially after the kiss they had shared the night before! Kelly was proud of herself for not inviting

Damian in after that, but boy, how she had wanted to. Damian had kept himself in check too, and she smiled when she thought about how seriously he was taking her rules.

She hummed a tune from the Backstreet Boys during her shower and while she got dressed, and then she headed out to the kitchen in search of breakfast. On her way past the front door, she noticed a piece of paper that had been wedged in the crack. Flyers were often shoved in the apartment doors, so she almost passed it by, but it looked like a plain piece of paper rather than a colorful ad, so she decided to investigate. She yanked the sheet of paper out, opened it up, and read: *Your breakfast is served. Open your door. D.*

He brought me breakfast? Kelly hurriedly pulled open the door, and there, sitting on her doormat, was a bag from the Clarkston bakery. Her mouth watered just looking at the bag, and she brought it up to her nose and inhaled deeply. "Perfection," she said aloud and then glanced around to see if any neighbors were about. *Nobody, thank goodness!*

Kelly carried her treasure into the kitchen and poured herself a cup of coffee, which she had programmed to brew the night before. When she bit into the Bavarian custard donut, she sighed. *What a great way to start the day!* When she was finished, she unplugged her phone from where it had been charging on the kitchen counter and fired it up. She tapped her fingernails on the kitchen table while she thought about what to write, and then she typed: *Thanks for breakfast. What a nice surprise! K.*

She didn't expect Damian to answer right away, because his head was probably under the hood of a car, but a couple minutes later, her phone pinged. *Wish I would have been there to see you eat it.*

Oh boy. She knew what that meant. When she and Damian had been together the first time around, he had often commented on how he liked to watch her eat. Especially when it was something that she loved, like donuts or ice cream. If she recalled correctly, he had said that watching her eat turned him on! She thought for a few minutes and then replied: *Flirting? This early in the morning?*

Seconds later: *There's no wrong time to flirt!*

Kelly glanced at the kitchen clock and realized that she had to go. She hurriedly typed: *Have a good day* and then shoved the phone in her purse.

When she pulled up in front of A New Chapter, there was Mrs. Simmons waiting at the front door, leaning on her cane.

"Hello, Mrs. Simmons," Kelly called as she crossed the parking lot, and then she unlocked the door.

Mrs. Simmons skipped the pleasantries. "I'm on my way to the senior center, and I want to give the ladies a date for our book club meeting. You've had plenty of time, missy, so what's it going to be?"

Kelly knew that she couldn't put it off any longer, and she had given the book selection a lot of thought. She pulled the book out from behind the counter and held it up. "What would your friends think about a tale of forbidden love?"

"Keep talking," Mrs. Simmons replied, looking intrigued.

"This is a story about an executive who falls in love with his assistant, although he's determined not to act on it."

"But eventually they do act on it, right?"

Kelly giggled. "Yes."

"Is there a happily-ever-after ending?"

"Of course."

"It's perfect. The ladies will love it!"

Kelly was encouraged by Mrs. Simmons's enthusiasm. "How long do you think they'll need to read the book? It has three hundred and fifty pages."

"Ha! That's nothing for us retired folks, but of course, some of us don't see very well, so it might take longer…"

"How about three weeks from now? I'll order the copies today, and they should be here by tomorrow afternoon. That will give everyone enough time to read, don't you think?"

"Yes, dear. Now, I know some of the ladies love to bake. Is it alright if we bring snacks?"

"We usually provide the snacks, but if you'd rather ask your friends, that's fine by me."

"Oh, if I know Irene, she will definitely volunteer, along with a few others. These women are fierce about their baking!"

Kelly laughed again as Mrs. Simmons turned and shuffled toward the door. "Goodbye. Let me know how it goes," Kelly said.

"Oh, I will," said Mrs. Simmons.

Kelly spent the rest of the day handling her usual duties and waiting on customers who drifted in and out of the store. They weren't as busy during the warm-weather months, but fall would be here soon, and business would pick up. Toward the end of her shift, Kelly realized that she hadn't told Emma about her maid of honor dress, so she picked up the store phone and dialed the bride-to-be.

"Hi, Kell," Emma answered, sounding out of breath.

"Hey. What's going on over there? You sound like you just ran a marathon."

"I feel like I have. For some reason, Ava's really fussy today, and I've been pacing the floors trying to soothe her."

Not having much experience with such things, Kelly asked, "Is she sick?"

"I don't think so. She doesn't have a fever or anything. She just can't seem to get settled."

"Sounds like a job for the baby whisperer."

"Huh?"

Kelly giggled. "I nicknamed Damian the baby whisperer, because it seems like, whenever he's around Ava, she quiets down."

As if on cue, Ava whimpered in the background. "He does have a way with kids, but he's at work, so that's not going to help me."

"How about if I stop by and give you a break. Besides, I have something to show you."

"Sure. I could use the distraction."

Kelly swung by the apartment after work to collect her dress, and then she rushed off to Emma's house. She noticed that Damian wasn't home yet and wondered if he was working late or if he had stopped by the Tap for a beer. They hadn't discussed when they would see each other again, outside of passing each other by in the parking lot, and Kelly smiled as she envisioned their next encounter. Maybe there would be another goodnight kiss…

When Emma answered the door, she looked fatigued, but the house was quiet.

"Where's the little troublemaker?" Kelly asked, peering around.

"Shh. I finally got her to sleep in her swing. Let's go into Zack's office so we don't wake her up." Emma immediately slumped down in Zack's leather office chair, and Kelly took the seat across from her.

"Ava's wearing you out, huh?"

"She did today, but some days are smooth as silk. Being a mother is exhausting, but I love it," Emma said with a smile.

Kelly briefly wondered what she would be like as a mother, but then Emma pointed to the dress bag inquisitively, bringing her back to the present. "Oh, yeah. I wanted to show you my maid of honor dress!"

"You found one?"

"Yep. Last night." Kelly pulled the dress out of the bag and held it up for Emma to see.

"Wow, Kell. It's gorgeous."

"That's what Damian said too."

Emma's eyes widened. "Damian already saw it?"

"Yeah. He was with me when I tried it on. Wait until I tell you what he did." Kelly proceeded to regale Emma with the story about the mannequin and the persnickety saleswoman.

Emma giggled at Kelly's dramatization, and then she said, "I love it, Kelly. I'm sure you looked gorgeous in it, just as Damian said. Speaking of Damian, he and Zack need to go for a tuxedo fitting soon. Do you want to come with us when we go? You know, to provide another opinion," she added.

Kelly smirked at her friend. "I know what you're up to, Em. You and Zack are trying to push Damian and me together, but you can stop. I think we're doing just fine all on our own."

Emma raised her eyebrows. "Does that mean what I think it means? Are you back to being…intimate again?"

"You still can't say it, can you?"

"Say what?"

"Sex," Kelly said, giggling. "S…E…X, sex!"

"Did somebody say sex?" Zack had pushed the door open without them hearing, and he poked his head into the room. He wiggled his eyebrows up and down and got a laugh from both of them—the charmer!

Emma grinned at her soon-to-be husband and waved him inside. "Kelly was just talking about Damian," she said and fanned her face with a magazine from Zack's desk.

"Ah, I see. My brother the stud." He looked pointedly at Kelly.

"You know what? I'm outta here! I'm going to go back to my apartment and leave you two lovebirds alone."

"Say hi to Damian for us," Zack teased as she turned and fled.

Chapter 14

When Kelly pulled into her apartment complex, she was humming the Backstreet Boys song that was still stuck in her head from earlier, and she was feeling optimistic about her life. She had a job that she loved, great friends, and she was dating her hot neighbor. Life was good. Until a few minutes later when her heart sank like a stone.

She had rounded the corner where Damian's building came into sight when she saw him, and she quickly stepped on the brake so that he wouldn't see her. He stood in the doorway of his apartment with his arms around a woman—a very attractive, leggy blonde, from what Kelly could see of her. They hugged each other for a minute, but to Kelly, it felt like forever, and then Damian backed into his apartment and closed the door.

Kelly sat frozen in her car, scowling at the stranger, who walked confidently and gracefully down the stairs in her short skirt and heels and then strode to the Mercedes that was parked two spaces away from Damian's truck. The woman was even more attractive from the front—the kind of woman Kelly would have been jealous of in her younger days, before she had learned to embrace her ethnicity. All that long, straight blonde hair that framed the woman's lightly tanned face, those expressive blue eyes, and that smile full of perfectly aligned white teeth. Yes, the woman was *smiling* as she unlocked the door to her Mercedes and slid inside.

Kelly managed to pull off to the side of the road so that the woman could get by, and they made eye contact as she drove past. The floozy even had the audacity to give Kelly a friendly wave, which Kelly did not return. Her blood was boiling when she pulled into her parking space and shut off the engine. She considered barging into Damian's apartment and demanding an explanation, but she decided that she should probably try to simmer down first. Instead, she marched up the stairs to her apartment and slammed the door behind her. If Damian had been peeking out his window, he might have seen her display of aggression and realize that he'd been caught.

"UGH!" Kelly yelled and threw her purse at the couch. "You idiot!" She wasn't sure if she meant him or her, but she decided to focus her anger on him for the moment. She was just about to let loose with a stream of swear words when her phone rang from inside her purse. Kelly dug it out, and when she saw Damian's name on the display, she tossed the phone back on the couch.

"Oh no you don't, mister! You don't get to cheat with Blondie and then turn around and call me up like nothing happened! You can just go to…"

The sound indicating that a voicemail message had been left interrupted her rant. She picked up her phone and pressed the button to listen to his message.

Hey, Kell. I can see your car, so why won't you pick up? I have something to ask you, so give me a call.

"In your dreams!" she yelled and stomped off to her bedroom to change clothes. It was the perfect time to don her MSU sweats, since she planned on staying in—alone. She gathered her hair up in a messy ponytail and scrubbed off her makeup. When she was finished, she realized that she might have scrubbed too hard, because she had ugly red streaks on her cheeks and forehead. *Oh well. Nobody's going to see me tonight anyway!*

Kelly was still riled up when she realized that she hadn't eaten dinner yet. She shuffled into the kitchen and had stuck her head in the refrigerator when the doorbell rang.

"Shit." There was a small kitchen window above her sink that looked out on the front doorstep. Kelly stuck her head up just enough to peer outside, and sure enough, it was him. She stood there quietly, hoping that Damian would give up and go away, but the doorbell rang again, and it sounded more insistent that time.

Kelly waited a few beats and then stuck her head up again, but this time, Damian's face stared right back at her. She was so startled that she let out a little screech and was met with Damian's hearty laughter.

Kelly scowled at him and turned away from the window. *Just great!* Now that he had seen her, she felt like she had no choice but to open the door. She unlocked the door and yanked it open, but she immediately turned around and huffed off to the living room.

Damian closed the door behind him and followed her. "Is there a problem?" he asked, sounding genuinely confused.

"Yes. There's a problem," she said through gritted teeth, her arms crossed defensively.

"Care to enlighten me?"

Damian looked more concerned than guilty, but that was probably because he didn't know that he'd been caught. "It didn't take you very long, did it?" she spat.

"I have no idea what you're talking about."

"So, did you get tired of waiting for me and decide to have some fun on the side?"

Damian's eyebrows furrowed, and he took a step toward her. "What exactly are you accusing me of?"

Suddenly Damian loomed very large in her tiny living room, but Kelly stood her ground. "I saw her, Damian. I saw that woman coming out of your apartment, so don't even try to deny it."

Damian relaxed his stance immediately and gave a sigh of…relief? "You mean Rachel? Tall, blonde, attractive?"

"OH MY GOD! So, you're admitting it?"

Damian took another step forward, but Kelly backed up. He threw his hands in the air and said, "Guilty as charged. Rachel was in my apartment because she brought me a housewarming gift."

Kelly glared at him. "So, you must know her pretty well, huh?"

"Yes, Kelly. I know her very well, because she's my cousin's wife!"

While Kelly took time out to digest this, Damian continued. "In my family, people look for any excuse to feed someone. Rachel kindly brought me a homemade cherry pie as a housewarming gift, and I'm sure some of my other family members will follow suit."

Kelly tried to hold on to her dignity for a smidge longer. "If she's your *relative*, then how come I don't remember meeting her at Thanksgiving or Christmas last year?"

"That's because they were in Colorado for the holidays. Rachel's family lives there, and they alternate the holidays each year."

Kelly dropped her arms to her sides and gave a defeated sigh. "Well, don't I feel like an idiot?"

Damian chuckled and shoved his hands through his hair. "Jesus, Kelly. You must not think very highly of me."

Now it was her turn to look confused. "What do you mean?"

"How dumb would I have to be to have a fling right under your nose?"

She giggled nervously. "Sorry?"

"I know how you can make it up to me."

Uh-oh, there's that look again. "How?"

"Come across the street and eat a slice of cherry pie with me."

"Really? You're going to let me get off that easy?"

Damian quirked his eyebrows. "Nobody said anything about getting off."

Kelly followed his gaze down to her MSU t-shirt, where her traitorous nipples were jutting out as if trying to escape. She quickly crossed her arms over her chest again. "Very funny," she said.

"Well, what's it going to be? Cherry pie or some other favor?"

"Ok, fine. Let me change, and I'll be over in a minute."

"Oh no you don't," he said and grabbed her hand. "You're coming over just like you are."

"But Damian, I'm not dressed properly," she protested as he practically dragged her to the door.

"You're dressed perfectly fine for eating cherry pie," he scoffed. "Here, put these on," he added and handed her a pair of flip flops that she had discarded near the front door.

"But what if someone sees me like this?" She purposely glanced down at her sheer t-shirt and back up into his eyes.

"Walk close behind me," he ordered and pulled her out the door.

They passed a young couple walking a Pomeranian, but the couple just gave them a friendly nod. If they thought it was strange that Kelly was practically smashed up against Damian's back as they crossed the street, the couple didn't show it. As soon as they were safely inside, Kelly leaned back against his door and breathed a sigh of relief, which caused her breasts to thrust forward enticingly—not exactly what she had intended.

Damian scratched the back of his head and looked around the room as if trying to remember what they were there for.

Kelly cleared her throat and said, "Cherry pie?"

"Right."

She took a seat at his new kitchen table and observed while Damian extracted plates and forks and dished out two hearty slices of pie.

"I don't suppose you have any vanilla ice cream to go with this?" Kelly asked, remembering that she still hadn't eaten dinner.

"You're in luck! I happened to pick some up the other day. I was saving it for my special guests."

"Guests, plural?" She tried to sound flippant, but she was still smarting from what she had seen earlier, before she had found out that Rachel was a relative. Just the idea of Damian with his arms around another woman made her heart hurt.

Damian plopped a generous scoop of ice cream on her plate and then leaned down until his face was just inches from hers. "You're the special guest, Kell. Just you. No one else."

They gazed at each other for a few seconds before Damian turned his attention back to scooping ice cream.

"Ok," she said softly and relaxed into the chair, content with the knowledge that she was the only woman visiting his apartment. At least the only one who wasn't a relative!

"So, what did you want to ask me?" she said as she scraped up the last morsel of cherry pie from her plate. Kelly would have to give her compliments to the chef if she ever saw Rachel again; even though it wasn't fair for the woman to be gorgeous and bake such a fabulous pie!

"I have two questions for you. First, what are you doing on Labor Day?"

Kelly had almost forgotten that the coming weekend was the last hurrah of summer. "Well, the store is closed on Labor Day, so I'm available. Why?"

"Alex invited us over for a barbecue with Zack, Emma, and the kids. Interested?"

"Sure. That sounds fun. Any other attractive female relatives going to be there?"

Damian chuckled. "No, it's just us. If the weather cooperates, we can take the boat out."

"So, I'll need to bring a bathing suit."

"Oh yeah," he said and smiled wide.

Kelly smiled back. "A conservative one-piece bathing suit, since your family will be there." Right after she said it, Kelly realized that she didn't even own such a thing. Her bathing suit collection consisted of skimpy bikinis and an assortment of revealing cover-ups.

"No. One-piece swimsuits aren't allowed. Only bikinis," Damian teased.

Kelly rolled her eyes at him. "What was your second question?"

"I wondered when you can start helping me with some marketing stuff? Jim plans on leaving by the end of the year, so I need to come up with a plan to attract business."

Kelly perked right up at the idea of helping Damian and at the thought of spending more time with him. There was only one problem. How would she fit it in around her job at the bookstore? "I'd love to help, but I need to talk to Emma first. I'm sure she won't mind, but I'll have to work around my bookstore schedule."

"That's no problem. We can always get together in the evenings."

Kelly raised her eyebrows. "Do you really think that's such a good idea?"

"Kelly, you're over here right now, and I haven't touched you. Even though…" He glanced down at her t-shirt for the umpteenth time since she'd been there.

Somewhere along the way, Kelly had given up on trying to cover herself, and now she crossed her arms over her chest again. "Damian…" she warned.

"Sorry, but you're sitting there looking all…touchable, yet I'm exercising complete control."

Suddenly Kelly wished that he wasn't, and she decided to drop her guard and have some fun. "You have been a pretty good boy, haven't you?" She scraped the kitchen chair back and slowly stood up.

His eyes widened, but he just nodded his head as she stalked toward him.

"I should probably reward you for good behavior."

Damian nodded more vigorously and made a motion to stand up, but Kelly placed her hands on his shoulders to keep him in place. Then, in a move that obviously surprised him, she straddled him on the chair.

Damian's arms immediately wrapped around her waist, and hers coiled around his neck. "Oh God, Kell. This feels so good."

"Kiss me, Damian," she demanded.

His lips were warm and sweet, and she tasted the remnants of cherry pie on his tongue. As the kiss intensified, she felt him grow hard beneath her, and she rocked against him just a little bit, but enough to make him emit a low moan. His hands were on her bare back now, and her spine tingled as he slid them up and down. When his lips trailed down from her mouth to her neck, her head fell back, and it was her turn to moan. He knew right where to kiss her on the most sensitive spot between her neck and shoulder that shot sensations straight to her core.

Damian started to move his hands around to the front of her shirt, but he halted. "Is this ok?"

His words melted her heart, and part of her wanted to tear off her clothes and beg him to take her. But he was following her rules, and they were taking it slow. Still, a few touches couldn't hurt. "Yes," she said.

His hands were on her breasts before she could change her mind, but why would she want to? He cupped them gently at first and then rasped his thumbs over her nipples, causing another shot of adrenaline to rush right to her center. He had ceased kissing her and now stared intently at the movement of his hands beneath her shirt and her reaction to his ministrations.

It was all so good, the heat between their bodies, his rough yet gentle hands on her bare skin, their connection that was so much more than just physical, but still, Kelly wanted to wait. Almost as if he sensed it, Damian pulled his hands out from under her shirt, and planted them on her waist. She leaned forward and kissed him lightly on the lips, one, two, three times, and then pulled back.

"I like eating cherry pie with you," he said, his voice a little raspy.

"Me too," Kelly said and removed herself from his lap.

"I'll walk you home."

She didn't bother arguing.

When they stopped outside of her door, he leaned in and kissed her cheek. "Sweet dreams, Kell."

Of that, she was certain!

Chapter 15

"Open wide," Damian said with a spoonful of cherry pie poised in mid-air.

Kelly opened her mouth wide and relished the mix of flavors from the tart cherries, the flaky crust, and the cold vanilla ice cream. "Umm…so good," she said and licked her lips with satisfaction.

"Again," he demanded, and she immediately complied.

Suddenly this seemed less like eating pie and more like a seductive dance. After the third bite, Kelly licked her lips more slowly and observed Damian as his eyes glazed over with desire.

"I want you to lick me like that," he said, dropping the spoon with a clatter.

"I want that too," she said. The next thing she knew, she was being lifted off the chair and into Damian's muscular arms. She flung her arms around his neck and let him carry her into his bedroom. He laid her down gently in the middle of the luxurious mattress that they had picked out together and

placed his hands on the hem of his t-shirt. Before he pulled it over his head, Damian said, "We're not stopping this time…"

But then, the familiar blast of her radio woke Kelly up, and she rolled over to shut it off just like she did every morning. "When am I going to finish this dream?" she whined to her empty bedroom.

The rest of the week flew by, and Kelly didn't see much of Damian, although they had texted back and forth a few times. He had explained that he was working extra hours because Jim was going out of town for the long holiday weekend. Damian was going to be handling the shop by himself over the weekend, so he wouldn't be freed up until Labor Day.

That was fine with Kelly, because she was busy at the bookstore preparing for her first romance book club meeting, and since Jill was also going out of town, Kelly had to cover her hours too. Being a native Michigander, it was expected that just about anyone who could would travel Up North for the long holiday weekend. The coastal towns and beaches would be packed, and the hotels would have been booked months in advance.

Kelly had made the annual trek Up North many times herself, but not as often in recent years. There was nothing like the crisp, pine-scented air of upper Michigan, and she made herself a promise to visit again soon. She allowed herself to daydream about what it would be like to travel there with Damian. What kind of traveler would he be? Would he want to be active all day and night, or would he be content to simply sit by the water and enjoy the scenery? Surely, someone who had lived in Southern California would enjoy the sun and the sand, right?

Thinking about sun-drenched days on the beach reminded Kelly that she hadn't spoken to her parents in a few weeks. She had been so wrapped up with work and with Damian that she hadn't made her customary weekly call. The bookstore was particularly slow on Sunday, so she sat down and dialed her parents' number.

"Hello, my beautiful daughter," her mother answered cheerfully.

Her mom sounded happy every time she answered the phone, and Kelly thought that it was no wonder given where she lived. Her parents lived in Naples, just a few short blocks from the ocean. They often took their daily walks on the beach, and Kelly could picture the beautiful scenery in her mind's eye.

"Hey, Mom. How's everything?"

"Everything's good. Your father went to the doctor last week, and he checked out fine."

Last fall, her father had suffered some health problems that were directly attributed to him having been a smoker for so many years. He had ditched the habit, but he occasionally experienced shortness of breath. Kelly was relieved to hear that he was doing well.

"When are you going to come down and visit?" Maria asked.

Her mom asked the same question every time they spoke, but this time, Kelly came up with an answer. "How about over Thanksgiving?"

"Oh, we would love that," her mom enthused. "But what about Emma's wedding? Isn't that cutting it close?"

"The wedding isn't until the first weekend in December. The details will be wrapped up well before Thanksgiving."

"Ok, then. What's new with you, sweetie?"

Kelly hesitated for a moment. She could tell her mom some benign stories about work, or she could fill her in on Damian. There was no contest! "I'm dating someone," she blurted.

"Well, that's not really new…"

"No, Mom. I meant that I'm dating someone special."

"Oh. Then tell me all about him."

Kelly gave her mom a summary, purposefully omitting certain details, and ended with, "I think that you and Dad would really like him."

She should have known that her mom would jump all over that one, and sure enough, Maria said, "Well, then why don't you bring him down for Thanksgiving."

"Um… I don't know, Mom. I'll think about it."

"Whatever you decide. Just let us know."

They talked for a little while longer, and then Kelly spoke to her dad for a few minutes too. When she hung up, she thought more about asking Damian to join her in Florida for Thanksgiving. True, she had already been around his parents plenty of times, but initially it was because of Emma and Zack. If Kelly asked Damian to go with her to Florida, he might get spooked. He might feel like that was too serious a step, or even worse, it might remind him of his broken engagement. Surely, he had formed ties with his fiancée's family, but where were they now? Kelly was still contemplating the idea when the store phone rang, and she saw Emma's name on the display.

"Hey, Em."

"Hey. How's business today?"

"Dead, as expected."

"That's what I figured. Why don't you close up, and take the rest of the day off."

"Really?"

"Yeah. I feel bad about you sitting there when it's such a beautiful day outside. You should be out enjoying it along with a certain handsome Greek man."

"Too bad Zack is taken," Kelly teased.

"I was talking about the other one!"

"Unfortunately, he had to work today too."

"Well, why don't you stop by his shop and surprise him? Maybe you can convince him to kick off early too."

"Now that's an excellent idea."

"I'm full of them."

"You're full of something!"

"Hey! Maybe I should rethink giving you the afternoon off."

"Don't you dare. I'm outta here. See you tomorrow at the barbecue." Kelly hung up the phone without saying goodbye. She had a tall, hunky Greek man to go see, and she couldn't close the store fast enough!

A short time later, armed with bags of sandwiches, chips, and sodas from Rudy's Market, Kelly entered Damian's shop. The front door was propped open, so the bell didn't ring to announce her arrival. Kelly set the bags down on the front desk and peeked her head into the shop itself. A radio blasted out Def Leopard's "Pour Some Sugar on Me" while Kelly peered around for Damian.

A slight movement caught her eye, and there, sticking out from underneath a bright orange 1969 Pontiac GTO, were Damian's scuffed work boots. Kelly smiled at the sight of them, and just as the song ended, she called out, "Anybody home?"

Damian rolled himself out from underneath the car and sat up on the creeper. Even though his face and clothes were smeared with grease and his hair was rumpled from lying down, he looked absolutely delicious. His grin said that he was happy to see her too, and she felt the air crackle around them.

"Hey. Didn't expect to see you here."

"The store was dead, so Emma let me close early. I brought lunch."

"Awesome. Let me wash up, and I'll join you in the office."

Kelly returned to the office area and set up a makeshift picnic with the food and drinks. It didn't have quite the same ambience as a picnic in the park or on a beach, but there was something romantic about it all the same. It was them, she decided when Damian strolled into the space. Their chemistry is what made any place electric.

"Wow, Kell. This is great. I didn't realize how hungry I was until now."

"Well, dig in. I got you a Reuben, because I remembered that you liked it before…"

Damian shot her a look that told her he remembered too. The last time they'd had Rudy's sandwiches had been after a particularly vigorous lovemaking session that had left them both famished.

Kelly averted her eyes and tucked into her own sandwich. "So, I see you have a new car to work on."

"Yep, and she's a beauty."

"You said that about the Corvette too."

Damian shrugged. "What can I say? I'm a car whore."

Kelly giggled. "It looks like business is good."

"It is right now because the weather is still warm. Things will slow down once winter comes."

"I've been thinking about some advertising ideas for when you become the owner."

"Hit me."

"For one, I think you need to have a grand reopening party. You can invite all of Jim's previous customers but also make it open to the public so they can stop by and check you out. You should also have some giveaways, like coffee mugs, pens, hats, that sort of thing. People love freebies!"

Damian set his sandwich down and looked at her with awe. "That's a great idea. I never would have thought of it."

"That's because you just want to work on cars, which is understandable, but you need to build customer relations too."

"See, that's why I need you."

Kelly had just taken a hefty bite of her turkey club, and it lodged in her throat, making her cough and sputter. She quickly reached for her Dr. Pepper and took a long slug.

"You ok?" Damian asked.

"Yeah, I'm fine. Too big a bite."

"What other ideas do you have?"

"Well, I think we should run ads in all the local papers and put up flyers in the auto supply stores around here. We have to get your name out there so that people start to recognize it."

"Speaking of names, I'm not sure what to call the place. I want something with pizazz, but I haven't come up with anything yet."

"Don't worry. We'll come up with something." Kelly realized that she had been using the word "we" an awful lot, but Damian didn't appear to mind. On the contrary, he seemed to welcome her advice, and in his words, he "needed" her. It warmed her insides to hear that he needed her in more than just one way, and she was more than happy to lend her services.

After they polished off the rest of their lunch, Damian said, "So, what's on your agenda for the rest of the day?"

"You know what? I think I'm going to lounge at the pool and read a book." The apartment complex contained a decent-sized pool that Kelly rarely used because it was usually teeming with kids. But since it was a holiday weekend, the pool would probably be quiet.

"Sounds great. Wish I could join you, but I have some work to finish up."

"Yeah, I figured," she replied, unable to mask her disappointment.

"Maybe we could get together later," Damian suggested.

Just the thought of it made Kelly's toes tingle. "Sure. Give me a call when you get home."

"Count on it," he said and then leaned over and kissed her cheek. "Thanks for lunch."

Why was it that such simple words and such a simple gesture had her heart thumping like crazy? "See you later," she said, and she hurried out the door before she was tempted to fist her hands in his shirt and pull him in for a deeper kiss.

Kelly chuckled as she drove away. While some women would have been repelled by the smell of oil and grease on a man, she had been turned on by it! She would take a dirty Damian over a sharp-dressed businessman any day!

When Kelly pulled into the apartment complex, she noted the lack of cars and drove past her building to where the pool area was. She was in luck—completely empty! Twenty minutes later, Kelly was leaning back in a lounge chair in her bright red bikini, her hair in a messy bun atop her head. She had already slathered on sunscreen and donned her oversized sunglasses, so now she could kick back and read.

She had chosen to reread the novel that would be featured at her book club meeting, just to refamiliarize herself with the plot and the characters, although there really wasn't all that much to the story. A hot millionaire falls for his equally hot secretary (or, in modern times, administrative assistant), and they have several lusty encounters in the office, on his desk, in the supply room, and so on. Kelly cringed a little when she read some of the sex scenes, wondering how Mrs. Simmons's friends would react, but then she got caught up in the story and her worries faded away.

She must have faded away also, because the next thing she knew, she was awakened by a loud whistle of appreciation. Her eyes snapped open, and there was Damian, staring down at her with the widest grin that she had ever seen.

"Now that's what I call a bathing suit," he said.

Kelly sat up and blinked her eyes a few times. *Am I dreaming again?* "What are you doing here?"

"Couldn't stand the thought of you out here all alone. Plus, it's hot out, and I could use a swim."

Kelly's eyes had finally adjusted to the bright sunshine, and she eyed Damian from head to toe. He was bare-chested, his shirt having been discarded on the chair next to hers. Her eyes followed the smattering of dark chest hair over his defined pecs, down the middle of his muscular abs, and further south, where it disappeared into his swim trunks. When she redirected her gaze to the lightning bolt tattoo on his right upper arm, she swallowed hard and was met with a deep chuckle.

"You done yet?"

"Oops. Sorry," she muttered.

"Hey, I got no problem with it. You can check me out anytime." Damian removed his sunglasses and set them on top of his shirt. "Meet ya in the pool," he said and then turned and dove right in.

Kelly wiped the water droplets off the cover of her book, placed her bookmark inside, and carefully set it on the table next to her chair. "Hey, you got my book wet," she scolded.

"Just get in here," he called.

Damian had seen her butt-naked numerous times, but why did she feel even more exposed with her bathing suit on? Maybe it was because of the way he was staring at her like she was a ripe red apple that he couldn't wait to sink his teeth into!

She stood up, walked over to the edge of the pool where he was waiting, and daintily dipped a red polished toe in the water.

"What are you doing?"

"I'm testing it," she said.

"You're testing it alright!" With that, Damian reached out of the pool, grabbed her around both ankles, and lifted her into the water.

The cool water felt heavenly against her heated skin, but not as good as Damian's hard chest that she was now smashed up against. "I was going to get in," she snapped.

"I ran out of patience," he said.

Damian's hands were still on her waist, and Kelly wondered if his words held a double meaning. She wouldn't blame him if he was running out of patience with her. Hell, she was running out of patience with her too!

"You wanted to swim, so let's swim," she said, her eyes issuing him a challenge.

"You want to race?"

"Sure, but I have to warn you that I was on the swim team," she said haughtily.

"When?"

"In high school."

Damian tipped his head back and laughed. "That was what? Twelve years ago?"

Kelly tried to put her hands on her hips under the water, but the gesture was slowed down by the water pressure, and Damian laughed even louder. "Are you going to race me or not?"

"Yes. Freestyle or breaststroke?"

"Let's go with breaststroke."

"That's my favorite kind," Damian teased.

They took their positions at the shallow end of the pool. "Down and back, and whoever touches the wall first wins," Kelly said.

"Got it. On the count of three. One…two…three!"

Kelly drew a gulp of air into her lungs and took off. She was amazed at how good it felt to move her limbs through the water again. She tried not to pay attention to Damian and just focused on her strokes and her breathing, and before she knew it, she was back where they had started. She popped her head out of the water to see Damian smiling down at her. He had obviously beaten her, but she felt good about her performance anyway.

"Not bad," he said, clearly impressed.

"See? You're learning new things about me every day," she said triumphantly.

"How about if you teach me some more things tonight—over dinner?"

She recognized the look in his eyes and hesitated for a moment.

"I promise to be a good student," he said, and he held up three fingers to simulate a Boy Scout pledge.

Kelly giggled, and said, "Ok."

They climbed out of the pool and wrapped themselves in towels.

"How long do you need to get ready?" Damian asked.

"That depends. Are we going out or staying in?"

"I vote for staying in."

"Ok. Give me a half hour and then you can come over."

As they walked down the sidewalk from the pool area to their apartments, Damian said, "Why do you even need that long? You're gorgeous just like you are."

He said it so matter-of-factly that Kelly knew that it wasn't a line. Plus, Damian wasn't one to waste words. "Thank you," she said when they stopped in front of her building.

"But you're still going to take a half-hour, right?"

Kelly nodded, and smiled up at him.

"Then what are you standing here for, woman? Go. Get ready!" He placed his hands on her bare shoulders and practically pushed her toward the stairs.

Chapter 16

When Damian arrived exactly thirty minutes later, Kelly was in the kitchen, rummaging in her cupboards for something to eat. She held up a box of spaghetti noodles and a bag from the freezer that contained all the ingredients for a chicken stir-fry. "Either of these sound appealing?"

Damian glanced from one to the other and said, "Or we could just order a pizza."

Kelly couldn't locate the carry-out menu fast enough, and after she called in their order, they moved into the living room. Damian made himself comfortable on one end of the couch, and she took the opposite end, tucking her bare feet underneath her. Kelly had changed into a simple knit skirt and a tank top, and because she hadn't had much time, she had thrown her hair into a high ponytail. She felt comfortable and relaxed, and it was obvious that Damian did too.

"So, what do you want to do?" Damian asked, keeping his expression neutral for a change.

"I thought we could play some games," she answered.

"What kind of games?"

"Some 'get to know each other better' games."

Damian looked at her suspiciously. "Such as?"

"Have you ever played Would You Rather?"

"Is it a dirty game?"

"No!"

"Well, then I probably haven't played it."

"That was my idea, so if you don't like it, why don't you suggest something?"

"Ok. I'd *rather* just have us ask each other whatever we want to know. There's no reason to play a game."

"Fine. You can start."

"Question one. Where is your ideal vacation destination and why?"

"Wow, that's a good one! Are you sure you haven't played this kind of game before?"

"Just answer the question."

"I would choose Hawaii, because I've never been there and the pictures make it look so beautiful. Plus, I love warm weather and beaches, so it would be the perfect place for me."

"Noted. Your turn."

"Since that was such an excellent question, I'll ask you the same thing."

"Easy. Alaska, because I like wide open spaces with plenty of places to get lost in."

"Hmm."

"Surprised?"

"Maybe a little. Did San Diego have places like that?"

It looked like a curtain had closed over Damian's face, but he quickly collected himself. "I lived near the city there, but it was surrounded by mountains, so yeah."

"So, no surfing for you?"

"Nah. Wasn't my thing. I would rather hike through the mountains any day."

"Hiking, huh?"

"I take it that doesn't sound very appealing to you, what with the lack of beaches and all."

"Well, I haven't really done it before."

"What? You're kidding."

"No, unless easy strolls down a sandy beach count?"

Damian threw back his head and laughed. "No. That's not the kind of hiking I'm talking about."

"So, you're talking about the full-on, backpack-and-hiking-boots kind of hiking."

"Yep. Nothing like it."

"Well, I guess I'll have to try it sometime."

Just then, the doorbell rang, announcing their pizza delivery.

"I've got this," Damian said, and he rushed to the door before Kelly could open her purse.

She should have known that Damian wouldn't let her pay. He never had when they were *dating* the first time either. She liked that he looked like a tough alpha-male, but inside, he was a real gentleman. Not that he would want anyone to know it!

They ate pepperoni pizza and drank beer in her living room, and it felt just like old times. Only, in those days, dinner would have been followed by…

"So, whose turn is it to ask a question?" Damian said after they had cleaned up.

Since they were on the topic of traveling, Kelly decided to take a risk. "I think it's my turn."

"Hit me."

"I was wondering…uh, I was going to ask you…"

"Out with it, Kell."

"Ok. Would you consider going with me to Florida for Thanksgiving?" Her palms were sweaty, and her heart pounded rapidly, while she waited for his response. He looked at her intently, but when he didn't answer, Kelly felt compelled to fill the silence. "I mean, it's no big deal either way, so don't feel obligated. In fact, you can take some time to think about it. I don't need an answer right now. It's just that…"

"Yes. I'll go with you," he said with a serious expression on his face.

Kelly didn't think first; she simply launched herself off her end of the couch and into his lap. She wrapped her arms around his neck, gave him a loud smacker on the lips, and then leaned back and said, "Thank you!"

Damian didn't speak, but the look in his gold-flecked eyes said it all. She was still in his lap, and his arms were around her waist, and everything felt so wonderful that Kelly leaned in for another kiss.

This one was different though. This one had substance, and they melted into each other's arms like they had never been apart. While their tongues tangled, Damian scooted them down so they were lying on the couch with Kelly on top of him. His hands began to roam, and they were warm and slightly rough, but she welcomed his touch, basked in it. His body felt so hard and strong beneath her, and she held on to it, used it as an anchor to keep herself from floating away.

He smelled like pizza and beer, and the intoxicating scent of Damian. When his hands moved up the back of her skirt and cupped her bare bottom, he groaned. When Kelly had put the thong on earlier, it had been to avoid panty lines, but now it served another purpose, and she was glad she had chosen it.

Suddenly Damian pulled his lips away and gazed up at her with fire blazing in his eyes. "What are we doing, Kell? What do you want?"

"I want you, Damian," she admitted. "So, so much…but…"

He rolled them onto their sides so that she was trapped between the couch and his body. "But you still want to wait," he finished.

Kelly laid her hands on his chest and felt the rapid beat of his heart. "Are you mad?"

Damian shook his head. "Not mad, but maybe a little frustrated," he said, glancing down at the straining bulge in his jeans.

"I'm sorry. I don't mean to be a tease."

"It's ok. I'm handling it, if you get my meaning." He broke out with a huge grin.

Kelly giggled, but then an image of Damian pleasuring himself flashed through her brain and made her squirm.

"What about you? Are you *handling* it too?" he asked.

Kelly's hands were moving back and forth across his pecs, seemingly of their own volition. "Let's just say that I have a very active dream life these days."

"Well, then let me give you some more material." He bent his head down and kissed her again, with more restraint this time. The urgency had tapered off, but in its place was tenderness. He cupped her face in his hands and placed a series of soft kisses on her lips, nose, and forehead. Just because he had downshifted, it didn't mean that Kelly was any less turned on. She felt the dampness between her legs and squeezed them tightly together as if to stop her juices from flowing.

"Is this ok?" he whispered.

"Um-hmm."

Damian trailed his lips under her chin and then into the crook of her neck, where he knew that she was the most sensitive.

Kelly whimpered. She couldn't help it.

"Still doing ok?"

"Um-hmm."

Damian dipped his head down further and placed a smattering of gentle kisses on the exposed part of her chest, which wasn't much because she had chosen one of her more conservative tank tops. His left hand reached up and squeezed her breast, which shot another surge of adrenaline straight to her core.

"Continue?" he asked, his breath warm against her skin.

"Um-hmm."

Damian tugged down the front of her tank top to expose her bra. He glanced up at Kelly, who was staring down at him through hooded eyes. She nodded her head slightly, and then he pulled down the bra cup to expose her nipple. When he drew it into his mouth, she whimpered again, with a little more volume that time. He rolled his tongue around her nipple in lazy circles until she felt like she would burst, and then he carefully tucked her breast away and crawled back up her body until they were face to face.

"Ok. I think I've given you plenty of dream material for tonight. It's time for me to go."

Damian heaved himself off the couch, and Kelly sat up in a stupor. "Do you really have to go right now? It's still early," she complained.

"Yes. I need to leave," Damian said, and he pointed down at his jeans.

It was obvious that she wasn't the only one who was completely aroused! Resigned, she said, "Ok. I'll walk you to the door."

"The barbecue is at noon tomorrow. Drive with me?"

"Of course."

Damian had turned away, and his hand was on the doorknob when Kelly said, "How about a kiss goodbye?"

He turned back around and smirked at her. "Haven't you had enough kisses for one night?"

"No," she replied, and then she pushed up on her tiptoes and entwined her arms around his neck.

He kissed her briefly and then set her firmly back on her feet. "Noon tomorrow," he repeated and then hurried out the door.

When Kelly crawled into bed that night, she anticipated a dream with a different ending than what had happened on the couch with Damian. She read a couple of chapters in her romance novel for added fuel (even though she didn't really need it!), turned off the light, and waited for the dream to begin…

"What do you want, Kell?" he asked, his voice husky in the darkened room.

"I want you. All of you," she replied, her own voice breathy with need.

They had been making out like teenagers, lying on her couch, side by side, still fully clothed. But now Damian slid his hand up the front of her skirt and made contact with her damp center. He ran his index finger back and forth over her panties, and she eagerly thrust her hips forward.

Damian's head was buried in her neck, where he sucked and nibbled, sending shivers down her spine. When he finally pulled aside the material of her panties and dipped a finger inside, she moaned. She was so taut with need at that point that it didn't take long at all for her to tip over the edge. Her body pulsated beneath his nimble fingers, and she clung to him, her own fingers digging into his shoulders, while she rode out wave after wave of intense pleasure.

When her body stopped quivering, she opened her eyes and met Damian's self-satisfied smile.

"Better?" he asked.

"Not quite," she said. "Now it's your turn."

Chapter 17

When Kelly peeked out her window and saw Damian walk out of his apartment the next day just before noon, she went out to meet him.

"Hey," she called.

"Hey," Damian said, and he gave her an appreciative once-over. "What's in the container?"

"Homemade chocolate-chip cookies," she said proudly. "I didn't want to show up empty handed." While Kelly didn't like to cook, she did enjoy baking and had often made treats for the two of them.

As they drove away, Damian asked, "Did you bring your bathing suit?"

"No. You never said anything about swimming."

"I mentioned the boat, remember?"

"Oh, that's right. Well, the thing is, I don't own a bathing suit that would be appropriate for a family gathering."

Damian chuckled and shook his head. "This isn't the 1800s, Kell. The bathing suit you wore yesterday would have been fine."

Kelly scowled. "If we go out on the boat, I'll just have to stay dry, that's all."

A few minutes later, they pulled down the long driveway that led to Damian's childhood home and parked next to Zack's Range Rover. Kelly heard Gracie's squeal of delight as she raced toward them from the side of the house.

"Uncle Damian! Aunt Kelly! You're here!" she yelled.

Damian held out his arms to her, and Gracie leapt into them. She flung her arms around his neck and kissed his cheek repeatedly.

Watching them gave Kelly a flicker of longing that surprised her and made her feel off-kilter. While she loved Emma's children, she hadn't really given much thought to having her own. She had been too busy playing the field and enjoying the single life to concern herself with marriage and children. But seeing how natural Damian was with his nieces tugged at her, and then… Gracie lunged at Kelly's legs, almost toppling her to the ground.

Kelly giggled at Gracie's exuberance and hugged her tight. "Where is everyone?" she asked once Gracie let go.

"In the backyard. C'mon."

Damian shot Kelly a smile, and they followed Gracie around to the back of the house. Kelly took in the idyllic scene and was instantly glad she came. Zack and Emma sat close together on white Adirondack chairs, cooing at Ava, who wore a floral sundress and matching sunhat. The baby was only one month old, but she already had an extensive wardrobe, thanks in part to *Aunt* Kelly!

Joe Kostas was manning a large stainless-steel grill that had smoke rising from it and that emitted the mouth-watering scents of hamburgers and hot dogs. A long knotty pine picnic table set with a red and white checked tablecloth was covered with side dishes that Alex had probably been preparing for hours.

Just then, the hostess made an appearance, bustling out of the patio door carrying red-white-and-blue themed paper plates, cups, and napkins.

"Here, Mom. Let me help you with that," Damian said, and he rushed to her aid.

"Suck-up," Zack teased.

Alex frowned. "Language," she scolded. And then she turned to Kelly. "Hello, dear. You're looking lovely as always." Alex kissed her on both cheeks with her usual flair.

"Thanks. I brought cookies," Kelly said and handed Alex the container.

"Good thing, Kelly, because we might not have enough food," Joe said, and he winked at her.

The Kostas family loved to rib each other, and they especially liked to tease Alex about the mountains of food that she always prepared.

"Oh, shush," Alex said to Joe on her way back into the house.

Kelly and Damian made their way over to Emma and Zack and took the two matching chairs across from them. *What a perfect day*, Kelly reflected as she glanced out at the lake. The temperature was near eighty degrees, and there was a mix of sun and clouds with a slight breeze—typical Labor Day weather for

Michigan. She pulled up on the hem of her tank dress to get some sun on her legs and caught Damian's sideways glance.

Apparently, Zack noticed too, and he didn't pass up the opportunity to needle his younger brother. "Dude, you're so obvious."

"Whatever," Damian muttered.

Emma smiled and handed Ava off to Zack. "So, how's everything going with you two?" she asked, feigning innocence. Everyone knew that Emma and Kelly told each other just about everything, except…

"Damian's coming with me to Florida for Thanksgiving," Kelly blurted. There was a brief moment of silence, and Damian shifted uncomfortably in his chair.

"Wow, bro. That's a big step for you," Zack said, grinning broadly.

Damian shrugged. "She asked, and I said yes."

Kelly instantly regretted her outburst, but luckily, Emma jumped in to save her. "I have some news too," she said.

"You changed your mind about marrying my doofus brother?" Damian goaded.

"Absolutely not. I'm going back to work, starting next week."

"Really?" Kelly said. "Are you sure you're ready?"

Emma nodded. "Alex and my mom are going to take turns watching Ava, but I'm only going to work a few days a week. I don't think I could stand to be away from her for much longer than that."

Zack gave his soon-to-be wife's hand a squeeze and gazed at her adoringly. Kelly loved the way that the two of them interacted. It was obvious how much they loved each other, but they also truly liked each other, which she found to be a rare combination. Kelly snuck a glance at Damian, and their eyes met briefly before he looked away.

"So," Emma continued. "I thought that this would be good news for you, Kell, since you won't have to work as many hours. Plus, that will free you up to help Damian with the marketing for his shop."

When Kelly had quit her job with a marketing company and had gone to work for Emma at the bookstore, she had taken a significant pay cut. To supplement her income, Kelly had taken side jobs as a marketing consultant, with Emma's full support. So far, it had worked out wonderfully, and Kelly was grateful to her friend for always looking out for her.

"That sounds great," Kelly said, but when she turned toward Damian, he was already halfway across the lawn. "I wonder what's up with him? I thought he'd be happy," Kelly said.

"Do you want my opinion?" Zack asked, and when Kelly nodded, he leaned forward conspiratorially. "My brother's in love, and it scares the shit out of him."

Kelly stared at him with disbelief. "No. I don't think so."

"I think Zack's right, Kell, and I'm not just saying that because he's almost my husband."

Kelly looked away from her smiling friends to where Damian stood next to his dad at the grill. "Well, if he's in love, he sure has a sh…crappy way of showing it!"

Zack chuckled. "Give him time, Kell. He'll come around."

Kelly was about to ask Zack about Damian's broken engagement when Alex swooped out of the house and announced, "Lunch is served!"

They all gathered around the picnic table, and Gracie proclaimed, "I get to say grace."

The adults exchanged nervous glances, and then Zack said, "Ok, Gracie. Go ahead."

"Dear God. Thank you that I didn't have to go to school today. And thank you that Uncle Damian lives in Michigan now. Also, I want a baby cousin. Amen."

There was an awkward pause while everyone's eyes zeroed in on Damian and Kelly. They had all been holding hands, but Damian dropped Kelly's hand like it had burned him. Damian opened his mouth to speak, but Zack beat him to it.

"Gracie, you just got a baby sister. I think you should be happy with that for right now."

"Yeah, but Robby has four cousins, and he gets to play with them all of the time."

"I'm sure you'll have cousins someday too, Gracie," Alex stated. "Now, let's eat, everyone, before it gets cold."

After that, they busied themselves with passing the plates of food, and the conversation turned to something else. Kelly purposely ignored Damian and tuned into Alex's and Emma's discussion about the wedding. The men started talking football, and the awkward moment was all but forgotten, except that Kelly couldn't forget the way that Damian's body had tensed up at the mention of a baby cousin or how earlier he had stalked off like he was disturbed about her helping him with his marketing plan.

Kelly tried to focus on Emma's description of the wedding cake that they had ordered, but her thoughts kept returning to the stoic man sitting beside her. Why was it that when they were alone, he was caring and easy with his affection, but when they were around his family, he became closed off and distant? Maybe it wasn't just his family. Maybe he would act the same way around her family too. She knew that he valued his privacy, but that was no excuse for acting the way he did. She hadn't pushed him to do anything. In fact, she was the one who had advocated for them to take it slow. The more she thought about it, the madder she became, but she had no outlet for her anger. They were at a family picnic, and they were supposed to be having fun, damn it!

When they had finished eating, Emma offered to help Alex clean up, and Kelly jumped up too. She wasn't going to spend another tense moment sitting next to *him* when she could be enjoying time with the ladies. As the women gathered up the dirty dishes, Kelly felt Damian's eyes boring into her, but she wouldn't give him the satisfaction of a glance. Instead, she followed Alex and Emma into the house and breathed a sigh of relief as soon as *he* was out of sight.

After their kitchen duties were done, Alex, Emma, and Kelly sat around the kitchen table, sipping iced tea.

"That Gracie, huh?" Alex said and smiled across the table at Kelly.

Kelly smiled in return, but she wondered where Alex was going with this. It was no secret that she was all for Damian and Kelly being together, and Kelly recognized that light in her eyes. "Yes, she's adorable," Kelly admitted.

"As for Damian. Well, you know that I love my son very much, but…"

"Mrs. Kostas…"

"No, dear. Let me finish. But sometimes Damian can be stubborn."

"I won't argue with that," Kelly said, and she looked over at Emma, who was trying to suppress a laugh.

"But that doesn't mean that he doesn't feel things," Alex continued. "When he loves, he loves deeply. Whatever he does, he puts his whole heart into it. He may be a man of few words, but still waters…"

"Run deep," Kelly finished.

"I'm not trying to make excuses for him. I'm just trying to give you some insight into who he is."

Kelly found it endearing that Alex was advocating for her son, but that didn't stop her from being irritated with him. And then, speak of the devil…

"Hey," Damian said, and he glanced around the table warily. "Kell, do you want to go out on the boat now?

He sounded apologetic and hopeful, and Kelly felt some of her anger slip away. "Ok," she said and stood up from the table.

"Have fun you two," Alex called as Kelly followed Damian out of the room.

When they were back outside, Kelly looked out at the dock, where Joe and Zack stood by the boat. Kelly stopped in her tracks and put her hand on Damian's arm to get his attention. "Um, is that the boat you were talking about?"

He gave her an amused grin. "Yep. Is there a problem?"

Kelly peered around him at the dinky aluminum rowboat and said, "Well, when you mentioned a boat, I was picturing something a bit…"

"Bigger?"

"Or at least sturdier. That thing looks like a dented tin can!"

"It's seen better days, but don't worry. You'll be in good hands."

It wasn't his hands she was worried about. "I swore that I heard you and Zack talk about zipping around the lake on a speed boat."

"That was when we still lived at home. Mom and Dad didn't use it much after we moved out, so they sold it."

"Hey, you two, are you going out or what?" Zack called from the dock.

"What's it going to be, Kell?"

With the three Kostas men staring at her, Kelly felt like she had no choice. "Ok, fine."

Damian climbed in first and then reached out to help Kelly get in while Joe and Zack kept the boat in place. Kelly wobbled for a few seconds until Damian steadied her and sat her on the hard metal seat. He took the seat facing her and grabbed the oars that were attached to the sides of the boat.

Joe and Zack shoved the boat away from the dock, and they were off.

"Don't tip," Zack warned as Damian rowed away, his laughter drifting out across the water.

"Jerk," Damian hissed, but only loud enough for Kelly to hear.

The further away from shore they went, the more relaxed Kelly felt. She leaned her head back and soaked up the sun's rays while Damian rowed them into deeper water. She must have closed her eyes for a few seconds, and when she opened them, Damian was eyeing her intently. When they had first started out, he'd had on a t-shirt and swim trunks, but now he had peeled off the shirt, and she was treated to a view of his magnificent bare chest.

"What?" she asked, trying not to stare.

"Just glad to see that you're enjoying yourself."

"Um-hmm. It's so peaceful out here. I love it."

"Even in a dinky old rowboat?"

She giggled. "Yes," she admitted and gave him a genuine smile.

He rowed them out to the opposite end of the lake from his parent's house, into a marshy area where long grasses stuck up from the water. It was quieter here where the speedboats didn't venture, and all Kelly heard was the sound of some birds chattering in the nearby trees.

Damian pulled the oars up so they just drifted, the water gently lapping against the sides of the boat.

"Kell…"

"Damian…"

"You first," Damian said.

"Why do you treat me one way when we're alone and another way when we're with your family?"

She had always believed the direct approach to be the best, and Damian had once told her that he admired that about her.

He shoved his hands in his hair and looked down at his feet. "I don't know, Kell. I guess I just don't like everyone up in my business."

Kelly suspected that that was part of it, but she wasn't completely satisfied with his answer. "And…"

"And what?"

"C'mon, Damian. There's got to be more to it than that."

He raised his eyes to meet hers, and she waited.

"And I guess it makes me a little…nervous. This…us…you and me. You know?"

Kelly's heart lodged in her throat. All at once, she sensed his vulnerability, and it rocked her to the core. Big bad Damian really did have a soft spot for her, but would it be too optimistic to think that it could be love? Kelly's romantic brain often overrode her logical one, but it couldn't hurt to hope. She had an overwhelming urge to kiss him, and in her excitement, she started to stand up in the boat.

Damian tried to warn her, but it was too late. "Kelly. NO! DON'T!" were the last words she heard before the boat tipped and dumped them unceremoniously into the water.

She came up sputtering and coughing, her dress clinging to her body and her hair matted against her head. The water was deep enough that they couldn't touch the bottom, and Damian quickly grabbed her around the waist and pulled her against him.

"You ok?" he asked, searching her face for any signs of injury.

The only damage that was done, was to my pride! "Yes, I'm fine," she muttered.

"Hop on my back and hang on," he ordered, and then she realized that the boat had drifted some distance away. She did as he asked, knowing that it would be quicker than her trying to swim in a dress and sandals, but she cursed herself for not having worn a swimsuit!

Damian's powerful body cut through the water with ease, and they reached the rowboat too soon. Kelly had thoroughly enjoyed being given a *ride*, clinging to his back, with her arms looped around his neck and her breasts smashed against him. She reluctantly let go and tread water while Damian grabbed hold of the boat.

"Now for the fun part," he said. "Getting back in."

"And how do you propose we do that?"

"Climb up on my shoulders and step in while I hold the boat steady."

Kelly looked at him like he was nuts, but what did she know? After all, she was the one who had caused them to capsize in the first place. "Ok," she said skeptically and braced her hands on his broad shoulders. Somehow, she managed to boost herself up to kneel on them, but now her soggy water-laden dress covered his eyes. For some reason, the sight of Damian with her dress hanging over his face caused her to break out in hysterics, and he fought to keep her steady atop his shoulders while she laughed uncontrollably.

When her laughter started to dissipate, he asked, "You done yet?" which only set off a second giggling fit. That time, his deep laugh mixed with hers, and she felt their discord from earlier fade away. By the time they finally made it back into the boat, they were both smiling like fools.

"Well, that was fun," Damian said as he rowed them back toward his parents' house.

"I agree, although, look at me. I'm a wreck!"

Damian did look at her, and thoroughly, from her long brown hair that was plastered against her head to the dress that clung to her curves like a second skin, down to her red-painted toes that peeked out from her wet sandals. "I think you look beautiful," he said.

And those were the sweetest words that she'd heard all day.

Chapter 18

When they pulled up to the dock, the backyard was deserted.

"Why don't you go in and say our goodbyes, and I'll wait in your truck," Kelly suggested, tugging her dress away from her breasts.

"No way. You're not getting into my truck soaking wet. We'll go in and dry off, and I'll find you some other clothes to wear."

Kelly opened her mouth to argue, but then Alex came out through the patio door to greet them.

"Oh dear, what happened to you?" Alex said.

"We accidentally fell in. Do you have anything that Kelly can wear for the drive home?"

"Of course. I have a closet full of clothes in the spare room that I haven't worn in years. Follow me, dear."

When they entered the house, Kelly expected to see Emma and Zack, but it was dead quiet.
"Where did everybody go?" Kelly asked.

"Ava was getting fussy, so Zack and Emma took the girls home, and Joe was getting fussy too, so he went down for a nap." Amused at her own description, Alex laughed loudly, and Kelly couldn't help but join in.

Damian disappeared into the bathroom to change, and Kelly followed Alex into the spare room. When Alex opened up the closet doors, Kelly's hands flew to her mouth. She had never seen such a vivid display of color in one place before! While she had admired Alex's unique eye for fashion, nothing in this closet even came close to Kelly's style. *Oh well, beggars can't be choosers*, she thought as she perused her options.

"What about this?" Alex suggested, holding up a purple and blue paisley printed robe.

Even with the swirls of color, the robe was one of the least *loud* items in the closet. "Sure, that will be fine," Kelly said.

Alex led her to the bathroom that Damian had vacated and said, "There are fresh towels on the shelf, and I'll get you a plastic bag to put your wet clothes in."

"Thank you so much," Kelly said before Alex fluttered away.

Kelly couldn't wait to get out of her wet clothes and into the dry robe, even though the pattern hurt her eyes to look at! She finger-combed her hair and then opened the bathroom door. Damian and Alex were nearby, talking in hushed tones, but as soon as they saw Kelly, their conversation ceased.

"Here you go, honey. Good as new," Alex said and handed her a plastic bag.

Kelly shoved her wet clothes inside and gave them her best smile. She was embarrassed by the entire incident, but she tried not to show it.

Damian smiled at her and then held out his hand. "Ready to go?"

Hmm…why is he suddenly being so nice? "Yes," she said and slipped her hand in his.

Alex walked them to the door, kissed them both, and said to Kelly, "Don't worry about returning the robe. You can keep it."

When they were pulling out of the driveway, Damian glanced at her robe and busted out laughing.

"Go ahead. Laugh all you want. It's your mom's robe, not mine."

"Yeah, but now you get to keep it," Damian said and laughed some more. Then suddenly his laughter died down, and he peered at the bag of wet clothes at her feet.

Kelly smirked as understanding dawned in his eyes.

"You don't have anything on under there, do you?"

Kelly shook her head. "Nope. Not a thing."

Damian swallowed hard, his Adam's apple bobbing in his throat.

"Not so funny anymore, is it?" Kelly said smugly.

Damian was quiet for the rest of the short drive, until they pulled into the apartment complex. "Can I walk you up?" he asked once they had parked.

"No, thanks."

"Are you sure? You have a lot of things to carry."

Kelly stepped out of the truck and gathered her bag of clothes and the Tupperware container with the leftover chocolate-chip cookies. "I got it."

They stood together alongside the Chevy and stared at each other for a few beats.

"You're killing me here. You know that, right?"

"I've got the idea," she said and boldly glanced down at the bulge in his shorts.

"Well, what are you going to do for the rest of the night? It's still early."

"I don't know yet, but I'm going to start out by taking a warm shower. I smell like lake water."

Damian swallowed hard again. "Ok. When you're done…if you want to get together…I mean…"

"I know where you live," Kelly said and then leaned forward to kiss his cheek. "Thanks for a fun day," she called over her shoulder, and then she sashayed away without a backward glance. When she got into her apartment, she leaned her back against the door and breathed a heavy sigh.

Kelly argued with herself while she took a shower, re-dressed in a tank top and loose knit shorts, and assembled her hair in a messy bun. What would be the harm in inviting him over? They could play some more "getting to know you" games. *Ha! Remember what happened the last time?* But Damian was right—it was still early. Too early to get in bed, unless…*no, don't go there!*

Kelly was walking from her bathroom to the living room when she heard the first rumble of thunder. She peered out her front window and eyed the line of dark clouds that was headed their way. So much for the perfect weather from earlier. *Typical Michigan*, she thought and went into the kitchen to dig up a snack. Her head was buried in the refrigerator when the next roar of thunder came, and that time, it shook the floor beneath her.

"*You're ok, you're ok*," she chanted, and peered out the window again. She saw the bolt of lightning flash in the sky and decided that was it! She picked up her phone from the kitchen counter, but before she could dial, it rang.

"Hello?" she answered in as calm a voice as she could muster under the circumstances.

"Guess what's on TV tonight?"

"Tell me."

"*Die Hard*!"

BOOM! There went the thunder again.

"Well, what are you waiting for? Come on over."

"Really?"

"Yes. Right now!" she said urgently as the wind rattled her window pane.

"Ok, ok. I'll be there in a sec."

She watched for him out the window, and he made it across the road just before the sky broke open and let out a deluge of rain. His feet were barely in the door when she launched herself into his arms.

"Whoa, I didn't expect this. Not that I mind…" Damian said and hugged her tight. After another minute of her clinging to him, without speaking, Damian pulled back. "Kell? What's wrong?"

"I'm kinda…sorta…afraid of storms," she admitted with a grimace.

Damian pulled her back into his arms. "Well, this one sounds like a doozy, so you better hold on to me a while longer," he said, nuzzling her neck.

This time, she pulled back. "Nice try. You came over to watch *Die Hard*, remember?"

"Oh, yeah, that's right." Damian stepped around her and picked up the TV remote from her coffee table. "Got any popcorn?"

"Only the microwavable kind."

"That'll have to do."

Kelly went into the kitchen to prepare the popcorn while Damian cued up the movie. When she joined him a few minutes later, he had turned off the living room lights and closed the curtains.

"To create the true movie-theater experience," Damian explained when she raised her eyebrows at him.

She settled in on the couch but placed the bowl of popcorn firmly between them. *Some barrier!*

They munched on popcorn and watched the movie in silence for a while, and Kelly became more relaxed as time went by without any hanky-panky. She got so engrossed in the movie, in fact, that she didn't notice when Damian transferred the empty popcorn bowl from the couch to the coffee table and moved a little closer to her. It was only when he placed his warm hand on her bare thigh that she sat up and took notice. Instead of removing his hand like she should have, she watched, mesmerized, while he rubbed his thumb back and forth against her skin.

Suddenly she felt very warm, even though she wasn't wearing that many clothes. She peered at Damian's profile and realized that he was genuinely engrossed in the movie and probably wasn't even aware of what he was doing. Kelly's legs were cocked to one side, and she was starting to get a cramp, but she didn't dare move. Instead, she kept a close watch on Damian's hand and tried to keep her breathing steady.

After a few more minutes of this, Kelly had to stretch her legs. She started to move, which caused Damian to look up from the TV screen. "Uncomfortable?" he asked.

"My legs. I need to stretch them out," she said, but the words came out in a raspy whisper. She stood up for a moment to shake her legs out, and Damian took the opportunity to stretch out himself, as in across the entire couch.

"Ahh. Much better," he said and crossed his arms behind his head.

"Hey, wait. What about me?"

He scooted himself against the back of the couch as far as he could go and patted the empty space beside him.

Kelly looked down at him and warred with herself for about two seconds before lying down on her side with her back to him.

"There," Damian said and placed a hand casually on her hip. "Now, stop interrupting the movie!"

Kelly rolled her eyes, even though he couldn't see her, and then redirected her attention to the TV screen. It was an intense scene, where Bruce Willis was being chased by the bad guys, and Damian's hand tightened on her hip as if he were in the scene too! Kelly had to admit that this was nice. Lying here with Damian, touching but not touching, on a dark stormy night, just the two of them...and then, there went his hand again, drifting, just barely, under the hem of her tank top, his fingers tracing lazy patterns across her skin.

Her nerve endings were on high alert, and she willed his hand to move just a little bit up or down. Either way would do. *There we go. That's the ticket.* His hand travelled up, slowly but surely, and her heart started to pound double time. She stayed perfectly still, not encouraging but not discouraging either. And now he had reached her bra. He stopped for a moment, as if waiting for her reproach, but when none came, he continued, gently squeezing, first one breast and then the other.

Oh my God! She was burning up. *It's got a front hook—easy access*, she told him in her mind, and somehow he got the message. The click of the bra clasp opening sounded extremely loud to her ears, even with the noise of the movie in the background. And when he twisted her nipple between his thumb and index finger, she moaned. He plucked and played with her for a few more minutes before she turned into his arms and threw her arms around his neck.

How does he always know exactly what I need? she wondered, right before his lips crashed down on hers. It was spontaneous combustion, and they went at it like two teenagers exploring each other on the couch, fully clothed, and unable or unwilling to stop. Damian hooked her right leg over his hip and pressed his erection against her center. As their kissing intensified, so did their movements below, and it felt almost as good as if they were naked. In fact, they were both coiled so tight and the friction was so perfect that…

"Kelly, I think I'm going to…"

"Me too."

Then his tongue was back in her mouth, and he was thrusting, and her hips were arching to meet him. Kelly wrapped her legs around his waist, opening herself up to feel even more, and a few minutes later, Damian groaned against her lips, and his whole body shuddered. She was right on his heels, her fingers digging into his biceps as she writhed beneath him.

Damian buried his face in her neck and kissed her softly as she floated back down. And then he popped his head up and searched her eyes, for what, she wasn't sure. She wasn't angry. How could she be? She had been just as eager as he had been, maybe even more! Kelly reached her hand up and cupped his face, that rugged face that she loved to touch, and smiled softly.

"It's ok," she whispered.

"We're good?"

"We're *very* good."

"I was trying not to break the rules, but technically, we still had our clothes on."

Kelly giggled. "True."

"I kind of need to clean up," he said, and when she nodded, he heaved himself off the couch. "Be right back."

Kelly pulled on the cozy fleece blanket that was draped over the back of the couch and snuggled beneath it. *I'll just close my eyes for a minute*, she thought. The next thing she knew, she was being lifted, very gently, into Damian's arms.

"Where are you taking me?" she asked sleepily.

"To bed," he replied.

In the past, that would have meant one thing, but now he simply tucked her under the covers—alone. He leaned down and placed a brief kiss on her lips. "Sleep well, beautiful."

And she did.

Chapter 19

"So, what's the final count for the book club meeting?" Emma asked.

Kelly couldn't believe that it was already the end of September and the book club meeting was only one day away. The last few weeks had flown by, between work and seeing Damian, and dreaming about Damian…

"Kell?"

"Oh, sorry. There are twelve confirmed and two maybes."

"What about Sam and Nikki?"

"They're confirmed."

"Yay! I can't wait to see them."

Sam (short for Samantha) Sullivan was an elementary school librarian who frequented the store on the weekends when she was looking for something "adult" to read. Kelly and Emma had taken an instant liking to her and had even met her for a ladies' night out on occasion. Sam was married to Jason, a much younger man, and they had two beautiful children, one boy and one girl. Jason had come into the store with Sam a few times, and not only was he young, but he was charming and obviously head-over-heels for Sam.

Nikki (short for Nicole) Branson was a well-known and respected real estate broker in town who was also an avid reader. She split her time between Clarkston and Los Angeles, as she was married to Nate Collins, a famous Hollywood actor and heartthrob. Kelly and Emma didn't get to see Nikki very often, but whenever she came into the store, they chatted about books and the latest Hollywood gossip. Kelly and Emma had met Nate once, when they had run into Nate and Nikki at a local restaurant, and even though Nate was *incognito*, they found him to be warm and friendly.

"Are you nervous?" Emma asked.

"You know, I was at the beginning, but now I'm looking forward to it."

"Me too!"

"You're going to be there for sure, right?"

"Of course. I wouldn't miss it."

"Damian told me that he's going over to your house to help Zack with the girls."

"I know. I love how close he and Zack have become. And of course, the girls adore Uncle Damian."

"That makes three of us," Kelly said and then covered her mouth with both hands.

"It's ok, Kell. It's me you're talking to. I already know that you're crazy about him."

"Yeah, well…"

"And the feeling is mutual. I'm sure of it."

"How can you be sure if I'm not?"

Emma raised her eyebrows. "Really, Kell? Don't you see the way he looks at you?"

"That could just be pent-up lust."

Emma burst out laughing. "Well, that's your own fault for imposing all those rules."

"I know. How stupid am I?"

Emma placed a hand on her arm. "You're not stupid. You're going slow this time, and I think it's admirable."

"That's one word for it, but frustrating might be a better one."

"Just think about how great it will be when you two finally get together."

"Oh, I do, believe me. I only hope that Damian can wait that long."

"He's waited this long, hasn't he?"

Kelly decided to skip the story about the episode on the couch. "Technically, yes."

Emma didn't ask any follow-up questions. Instead, she glanced at her watch and said, "Since I'm here and it's kind of slow today, why don't you go and surprise Damian at his shop?"

"I don't know, Em."

"Why not?"

"I'll be seeing him this weekend when we go for the tuxedo fitting, and then we're meeting on Monday to work up a marketing plan. Things are going well right now, and I don't want him to get spooked."

"I hardly think that stopping by his shop to say hello is going to spook him, but I suppose you know him better than I do."

"That's just it. Sometimes I think I know him, but then he shuts down on me. Did Zack ever tell you that Damian was engaged?"

"He mentioned it, but he didn't go into detail. Anyway, that was a long time ago. I'm sure Damian's over it by now."

I'm not so sure, Kelly thought. And then it struck her that Damian's fiancée had abandoned him, in a way, and probably had made it difficult for him to believe that another woman wouldn't do the same. That was why he retreated at times. That was why it had been easy for him to walk away from Kelly the first time around. Well, she wouldn't make it so easy for him to walk away this time. She would show him that she wasn't going to abandon him, or tire of him, or do whatever it was that *that woman* had done to him.

"You know what, Em? I think I will pop in on Damian. Thanks for the idea!" Kelly hurriedly grabbed her purse from the office and headed out the door.

"You're welcome," Emma called.

When Kelly pulled into the parking lot of the auto shop, there was another car parked alongside Damian's truck. *It's probably Jim's*, Kelly thought and then questioned her decision to stop by. She didn't have a legitimate reason to be there, and Damian was working after all. Kelly glanced at her watch and realized that it was almost noon. *Perfect! I'll ask him out to lunch.*

When she entered the front door of the shop, a bell chimed to announce her presence, and she waited to see if Jim or Damian would arrive to greet her. Her face fell when a gorgeous young blonde girl came around the corner instead.

"May I help you?" the young blonde asked.

Kelly guessed the girl's age to be in the low twenties—not quite old enough to be considered a woman, although she had the body of one. Slightly taller than Kelly, she was busty, and her t-shirt with Jim's Custom Cars printed across the front stretched tightly across her breasts. She wore snug skinny jeans and Converse sneakers (another sign of her age), and her long blonde hair fell in soft waves to the middle of her back. What struck Kelly the most was the girl's confident, almost arrogant demeanor. It was if she were well aware of how striking she was and used it to her advantage—probably to make men fall on their knees and to make women (like Kelly) bristle with envy. Kelly could usually hold her own around such women, but with Damian in the picture, she felt the sharp prick of jealousy at the base of her spine.

"Yes. I'm here to see Damian Kostas," Kelly replied.

The girl sized Kelly up too and, with a look that said she found Kelly lacking, asked, "And you are?"

"His girlfriend. Kelly Cruise." That was the first time that Kelly had pulled out the girlfriend card, and she decided that she liked the sound of it. A lot. She gave blondie a smug smile.

"Huh. Funny, he never mentioned you before."

"I could say the same about you. And you are?"

"Lexie Farrell. I'm the owner's niece."

She said the last part proudly, as if Kelly should be impressed that her uncle owned the shop. *Ha! Silly girl!*

Before Kelly could respond, Damian stuck his head around the corner, and seeing Kelly there, he broke into a wide smile.

"Hey," he said, and then he must have felt the tension in the small space because he added, "I see you've met Lexie."

"Yes. We were just getting to know each other," Kelly said with a forced smile on her face.

"You never mentioned that you had a girlfriend," Lexie accused.

Kelly caught the flash of disappointment on Lexie's face while they both awaited Damian's response.

He shot his brows up at Kelly and then shoved his hands in his jeans pockets, a telltale sign of nervousness if ever there was one. "Well, I, uh…"

"Damian likes to keep his private life private," Kelly said and then took a step closer to him. "Right, sweetie?"

"That's right," he muttered and looked back and forth between them as if he were trapped between two venomous snakes.

Kelly decided that he'd suffered enough—for now. "I came to see if you could get away for lunch."

Damian glanced up at the wall clock and looked relieved. "Lunch sounds great. I'll go wash up and meet you outside." He scurried back into the shop before Kelly could reply, which left the two cobras alone.

He may have wanted Kelly to wait outside, but her job wasn't done yet. "So, Lexie, what are you going to do for work when your uncle retires?"

Lexie narrowed her eyes at her opponent. "I was planning on asking Damian if I could stay on until I find a *real* job. I'm graduating from college in December, but it might take me a while to find something."

"What field?"

"Human Resources."

Figures, Kelly thought, *a fluff job!* Although some people said the same thing about her marketing degree.

"You ready?" Damian asked, reentering the room with a look of surprise that Kelly was still standing there.

"Yes," Kelly said distractedly.

As they walked toward the door, Lexie called out, "Don't forget about your one o'clock appointment, Damian."

He just nodded and practically shoved Kelly out the door.

Kelly didn't speak until they were a half a mile down the road. "Is A&W ok?"

"Sure."

There was an old-fashioned drive-up A&W nearby, and Kelly pulled up next to the speaker and shut off her car. She placed their order for Coney dogs, fries, and root beer and then turned sideways to face Damian.

"Just curious. How come you never mentioned your *co-worker* before?"

"Kell…"

"Just answer the question."

"I don't really think of her as my co-worker. She's Jim's niece, and she only works part time. I didn't think it was important."

"Just like you didn't think that it was important to mention me to her?"

"Kell…are you…jealous?"

"Ha! Right! Jealous of a teeny bopper? No way!"

"She's not a teenager; she's twenty-two years old." At her scowl, he added, "Not that it matters."

"Did you know that she wants to stay on after she graduates?"

"No."

"Well, you better break the news to her soon."

"What news?"

"That she won't be staying. As your marketing consultant, I would highly recommend against it."

Damian tilted his head back and burst out laughing. When his laughter subsided, he said, "And that advice would have nothing to do with jealousy?"

"I just don't think it would be a wise business decision. You need to portray a professional image to your customers, so the front desk person should probably be an older, more mature person, and preferably a male."

Damian laughed again. "I'll take that under advisement."

The carhop roller-skated over to deliver their order, which put a temporary halt to their conversation. As they tucked into their food, Damian kept shooting her glances until she finally said, "What?"

"I never figured you for the jealous type. I'm learning new things about you every day."

Kelly wiped a glob of mustard from the corner of her mouth and replied, "Well, ordinarily I'm not. However, I could tell by the way that *girl* looked at you that she'd like to rev your engine."

"That's too bad, because there's only one woman who does that for me."

They faced each other again, and Kelly melted under his gaze. "Me?" she asked hopefully but with a fair amount of confidence.

"You," he confirmed.

It was difficult to finish eating after that because Kelly had a large lump in her throat. Her man of few words always managed to captivate her with just one. When they pulled up in front of the auto shop a short time later, Lexie's face was there through the window, as if she had been anxiously awaiting Damian's return.

"Instead of me *telling* Lexie that you're my girlfriend, why don't we just show her?" Damian said with a sparkle in his eyes.

"Great idea," Kelly said.

He leaned across the console and pressed his lips to hers. At first, Kelly thought they would exchange a few chaste kisses, but when he pried her mouth open with his tongue, she suddenly forgot all about their performance. She moaned against his lips and flung her arms around his neck to pull him closer. The kiss only lasted for a minute or so, but when they pulled apart, they were both panting. When Kelly finally remembered their audience, she glanced over at the window. Lexie glared at her for a second and then turned on her heel and disappeared behind the counter.

Damian kissed her again, a quick peck this time, and said, “See you tonight?”

She nodded and watched him walk away, admiring his broad shoulders, narrow waist, and fine backside. Oh no, she wasn’t going to let Lexie or any other woman get their hands on him. She was going to be the only one to *rev his engine*, and she smiled as she drove away, because, according to him, she was!

Chapter 20

Kelly found him in the shop standing next to a long creamy white car with tailfins.

His head swiveled around when he heard the click of her heels on the cement floor, and he broke out with a huge smile.

So sexy, *Kelly thought as she approached him. "She's a beauty," she said, adopting the language he used when he referred to cars.*

"That she is. A vintage 1965 Cadillac Eldorado."

Kelly walked around the car and peeked into the windows. "Wow, the backseat is huge!"

"Hop inside and test it out."

"What? No, that's ok."

"Oh, come on." Damian opened the back door and motioned for Kelly to get inside. She hesitated for a second but then slid across the creamy leather seat, and he climbed in after her, shutting the door firmly behind him. Suddenly, the roomy interior felt very intimate with Damian's large frame beside her.

He patted the seat and said, "Perfect for making out, huh?"

Kelly's eyes locked on his, and she read his intent. "This is someone else's car," she protested as he slid closer to her.

"They'll never know," he said, and he buried his head in her neck.

Kelly's head automatically tipped back to allow him greater access, and with each kiss, she forgot that they were in a stranger's car in the shop, where someone might come upon them at any moment.

And then his hand grazed her thigh and disappeared beneath her skirt. "Damian…not here…we shouldn't…"

He muffled her protests with his lips and tongue and then slipped a finger inside her panties.

"You're the one, Kell. You're the only one who revs my engine," he repeated over and over and over until…

"Damn," Kelly groaned as she slammed her hand down on the alarm clock. "Just when I was getting to the good part!"

"What was your favorite part of the story and why? Who wants to start?" Kelly asked. The romance book club meeting was in full swing, and Kelly was enjoying herself immensely. It was an eclectic group of women, ranging in age from twenty-five to eighty-five, but they all had one thing in common—they loved to read romance novels!

Mrs. Simmons's friend Irene raised her hand enthusiastically. "The sex," she stated to an appreciative round of laughter from the group.

Another hand shot up—this time from Samantha Grant, who was there with her friend Leslie. "The sex scenes were juicy. However, it was the chemistry between the main characters that made it so good."

"I agree," added Nikki Collins, who had brought her assistant, Rosa. "To me, that's the most important aspect of a romance novel. It's not the sex itself, but the rapport between the characters that makes it so enjoyable."

"That goes for real life too," said Elizabeth, another friend of Mrs. Simmons. The women laughed again and nodded their agreement.

"How did you feel about the theme of forbidden love?" Kelly prodded.

Jenna, the youngest member of the group, raised her hand. "I liked the theme of forbidden love because I can relate to it. I have a serious crush on my boss, but I know that he's off limits."

"Why? Is he married?" asked a middle-aged woman in the back row.

"No. It's just because he's my boss, and I wouldn't want to compromise his job or mine because of a crush," Jenna replied.

"Smart girl. There are plenty of other fish in the sea," Mrs. Simmons said adamantly.

"But I can't help but wonder if he has feelings for me too," Jenna said with a faraway look in her eyes. "Sometimes, the way he looks at me..."

The women gave a collective sigh, lost in their own tales of love, until Samantha's hand shot up. "I experienced a kind of forbidden love too," she admitted, twisting her hands together as if to gather courage. "I fell in love with a man who was seventeen years younger than me. He was still in college when I first met him."

The room went quiet, and Leslie squeezed Sam's hand reassuringly.

"What happened?" Irene asked.

"I married him, and now we have two beautiful children."

A few women clapped, and more than a few teared up. Kelly started to wonder if the meeting was becoming too personal, but then she realized that none of the women seemed to mind. Everyone in the room had experienced love in some form or another, and they related to one another no matter their age or status.

"Why do we read romance novels, and why do we love them so much?" Kelly asked, scanning the room.

"Because they make us feel things," Jenna ventured.

"You can say that again," shouted Irene while she fanned her face with the book.

When the round of chuckles died down, Nikki's hand went up. "Because they give us hope," she said. "And they remind us that there is a special someone out there for each of us." Rosa smiled proudly at her boss, and there were murmurs of agreement among the group.

Damian's face flashed through Kelly's mind, and the image was so clear, so vivid, that it was almost as if he were standing right before her. The room went silent, and that's when Kelly realized that he actually was standing there, leaning against a bookshelf just a few feet away, watching her.

Kelly quickly collected herself and said, "Well, ladies, I think we've exceeded our time limit, but I'd like to thank you all very much for coming. If you'd like to vote on the book for next month's meeting, please send me an email. I'll contact everyone once the selection has been made, and I'll let you know when the next meeting will be."

As the women rose and shuffled toward the door, they all glanced at Damian as they passed by. Mrs. Simmons even stopped, laid her bony hand on his arm, and whispered something in his ear, to which he smiled and nodded.

After the last person left, Kelly and Emma began cleaning up, and Damian pitched in by stacking up the folding chairs. "Didn't mean to interrupt your meeting, but it was after nine, and Zack started to panic. He asked me to come and check on you two."

Emma giggled. "That sounds like him. Has he always been this overprotective?"

"Pretty much. Especially when we were kids, but then I got bigger than him, and he didn't need to protect me anymore."

Kelly shot an appreciative glance at Damian's muscled physique, but then she wondered about his heart. *Who's protecting that?*

"I better get home before he calls the police," Emma teased. "Can you two finish closing up?"

"Sure. We got this," Damian said.

Kelly walked Emma to the door. "You did a great job tonight," Emma said.

"You really think so?"

"Yes. Everyone seemed to be having a good time, and you kept the discussion moving."

"I was surprised when some of the women shared their personal stories," Kelly said, and she glanced back at Damian, who was taking down the snack table.

"Everyone has their own love story, although some are still being written," Emma said, and then she pulled her friend in for a goodbye hug.

"See you tomorrow," Kelly said and then locked the door behind her. When Kelly turned around, she didn't see Damian's head over the bookshelves, so she went toward the back of the store to investigate. She found him sitting in one of the beanbag chairs in the children's section, with the book club romance novel open in his hands. His eyes were glued to the page, and he didn't even look up when she came and stood before him.

"Holy shit! This book is hot!" he said, flipping to the next page.

Kelly giggled. "I wouldn't peg you for a romance reader," she teased.

Damian put his thumb in the book to keep his place and peered up at her. "Why not?"

"Well, because you're not really the mushy, gushy type."

"From what I've read so far, neither is this guy, but that's not stopping him from getting lucky!"

Kelly put her hands on her hips and cocked her head at him. "You've only read a few pages. There's a lot more to the story besides that."

"Oh," he said, looking disappointed.

Kelly shook her head and started to take the book away from him, but he clasped her wrist in his tight grip. "You don't think I can be romantic?" he asked, a hint of challenge in his voice.

"I didn't say that…"

"But that's what you think."

"No. Not exactly."

"So, leaving donuts on your doorstep isn't romantic? Saving you from drowning isn't romantic?"

Kelly laughed. "I wasn't drowning. Besides, I could have swum to shore if I had to. I was a swimmer, remember?"

"IN HIGH SCHOOL!" he shouted.

"Never mind," she said and started to turn her back on him.

Damian still had a grip on her wrist, and he spun her back around. "Grand gestures. Is that what you want? Am I supposed to ride up on a white horse and whisk you off into the sunset?"

"No, Damian. I don't need grand gestures."

They were both frustrated now, and Kelly wasn't sure how their conversation had turned from playful to inflamed in a matter of minutes.

"What do you need, Kelly? Tell me, because I feel like I'm operating under a serious disadvantage here."

I need to know how you truly feel about me. I need to know that you want me for more than just sex. But the words wouldn't come out. They were stuck. They were trapped under the hurt, under the pain of her many failed relationships. They were buried under the memory of him leaving her once before, when he had walked out of her life without so much as a look back, like what they had shared was meaningless. She hadn't been important enough to warrant a phone call, a text, an email, nothing. She had been easy to leave behind, and why should she think it would be any different now?

Damian had let go of her wrist, but he was still clutching the book in his left hand. "You know what? You think about it and let me know. I'm outta here." With that, he turned and stalked to the front of the store. He fumbled with the lock for a second and then jerked the door open, cursing loudly on his way out.

Kelly watched him peel out of the parking lot, and amidst the jumble of emotions that flooded her brain, something else registered. "That idiot stole my book!"

When Kelly pulled up in front of her apartment a short time later, she noticed that Damian's truck was parked in its usual spot and a light was on in his apartment. She sat in her parked car for a few minutes, debating about whether to have it out with him right away or sleep on it. Feeling as keyed up as she was, she knew she wouldn't get any sleep, so she settled on the first option. Kelly gathered her courage as she walked up the three flights of stairs to his apartment and rang the doorbell.

It took a few minutes for him to answer, and she was just about to turn away when he flung open the door. The sight of him took her breath away. He was shirtless, wearing only a pair of gray sweats that hung low on his hips. His thick, dark hair was still damp from a shower, and it curled up enticingly at the ends. He must have dried off in a hurry, because there were still water droplets on his shoulders and upper arms. Kelly's eyes naturally honed in on his lightning bolt tattoo, and she swallowed hard. Oh, how she had loved to trace the design with her fingertips before, during, and after their lovemaking.

Damian's expression was neutral as he stared back at her, but then he softened a little when he stepped back and said, "Come on in."

Kelly followed him into the living room and took a seat on the couch while he sat in the lounge chair across from her. "You stole my book," she began. Facts were always an easy place to start!

He quirked his eyebrows, but his lips remained in a tight line. "I didn't steal it. I borrowed it. Figured I might be able to gain some tips."

"Hmm…"

"Did you stop by just for the book, or is there something else on your mind?" Damian asked, his expression a cross between trepidatious and hopeful.

Kelly entwined her hands in her lap and sighed. "You asked me what I needed, and I'm here to tell you."

Damian leaned forward and rested his chin on his hands. "Tell me."

"I need to know why you never contacted me after you returned to California, and I want the truth. All of it."

Damian studied her for what felt like an interminable amount of time before he spoke. "I needed some time to figure some stuff out. I had to get my shit together before I saw you again."

It was something, but it still wasn't enough. "Figure out what exactly?" she asked, careful to keep her voice steady—determined to stay calm.

"I had to decide if I was ready to do this again. This meaning us. Having a relationship."

Now they were getting somewhere, but she wanted more details. "So, what we had before…"

"Was fun and easy. My usual M.O., but when I left, I wasn't satisfied. I felt like I wanted…more."

Kelly's eyes widened at his admission, but she didn't dare speak. She wanted him to tell her at his own pace.

"The problem was that I hadn't felt that way in so long. Not since…well, you know. And it knocked me on my ass. At first, I tried to ignore my feelings, but they wouldn't go away. They *never* went away."

Kelly's breath caught, and she felt a tear prick the corner of her eye.

"I thought about you every day after I left, but I fought it, and I didn't think that it was fair to you for me to call until I was ready. Really ready."

"But what if…"

"You had been with someone else? It killed me to think about that, but I shielded myself from finding out. I didn't ask Zack or Emma about you because I didn't want to hear that there was someone else. I took a chance, and it was probably foolish, but I didn't want you to put your life on hold for me. Honestly, I thought you deserved better than me anyway."

Kelly felt the tears drip out of one eye, but she ignored them. "But you came back. You came back…"

"Yes, and at first, I used the excuse that my big brother was getting married and that Jim was selling the shop, but those weren't the real reasons."

"You came back for me," she said, almost disbelieving.

Damian nodded and crossed the room to pull her into his arms. She buried her face in his chest and let the tears flow freely, watching as they dripped onto his bare chest. He ran his hands soothingly up and down her arms until she stopped crying.

"I'm not perfect, Kell. Far from it. And I still have commitment issues, but I want this to work between us, and I'm willing to do whatever it takes."

Which was why he had been agreeable to forgoing sex. Suddenly Kelly realized that she had all the answers she needed and that she had punished them both long enough. She placed her hands in his and looked deep into his eyes, finding further confirmation there.

"There is one more thing that I need from you."

"Name it."

"I need you to make love to me."

Chapter 21

Damian sucked in a breath. "But you said…"

"I know what I said, and I changed my mind. It's a woman's right, you know."

Damian chuckled and then swiped his thumb across her tear-stained cheek. "Is that what you really want?"

"Yes," Kelly said. "Don't make me ask you again."

With that, Damian lifted her into his arms and carried her down the short hall to his bedroom. He laid her gently on his new bed and kneeled over her, staring at her reverently.

"Don't you want to tear my clothes off or something?" Kelly asked, placing her palms on his bare chest.

Damian's mouth curled up with an amused grin, but he shook his head. "If I do, it'll be over in a few minutes. I'd rather take my time."

Kelly squirmed when he placed his hands on the hem of her dress, which fell to just above her knees.

"I do want to see more of you though." Damian tugged her dress upward, and she felt a whoosh of cool air as he lifted it over her head and tossed it aside. "That's better," he said as he ran his eyes over her from head to toe and back again. He wasn't even touching her, but her body was on fire, her nerves prickly with desire.

Like the rest of her wardrobe, Kelly had an extensive lingerie collection, which had served her well in the past and was having the desired effect now. Damian's eyes glazed over as he zeroed in on her sheer pink bra, especially where her nipples poked assertively at the fabric, begging to be released. He ran a fingertip down the middle of her chest and over her belly button until he reached the edge of her matching pink sheer panties. There was nothing left to the imagination there either—just a thin piece of material pressed against her damp skin.

Damian's Adam's apple bobbed as he swallowed roughly. "Do you know how many times I've dreamed of this? Do you have any idea how tempting you are?"

"Tell me," she whispered, her voice strained with emotion.

"Twice as tempting as before. Even more than that. I wanted you from the first time I met you, but now, now…"

"Show me, Damian. Show me how much."

He bent over her then and sucked her bottom lip between his, drawing gently at first. And then he traced her lips with his tongue, and she arched her back, begging for more contact. He braced himself on his forearms, and his magnificent biceps strained with the effort. Kelly gripped them tightly and parted her lips for him, inviting him to take more of her.

Suddenly he flipped onto his back, pulling her over on top of him. Kelly smiled down at him seductively, because they both knew that she liked to be in the driver's seat. They had discovered that it was one of their favorite positions and had practiced it often in the past.

Kelly seated herself on his hips and wiggled against his thick erection. "Still want to take it slow?" she teased.

"Um-hmm." He laced his hands behind his head and watched as she moved her hands around her back to unhook her bra. The sound of it coming undone caused Damian to buck underneath her, and she relished the feel of him—so strong, so powerful. Kelly slid the bra straps off her shoulders one at a time, slowly, just for him, until she revealed her ample breasts.

Damian reached out for them automatically, cupping and squeezing, just the way she liked. Kelly realized that she was grinding against him now, eager for more, but Damian seemed content as he plucked her nipples almost to the point of pain.

Since she was still in the driver's seat, Kelly pulled back, just out of reach, and laid her hands on the tie of his sweats. Damian lifted himself up so that Kelly could bare him, and as she did, she drew in a ragged breath. First of all, he was sans underwear, so his glory sprang forth immediately. Secondly, she had almost forgotten just how glorious he was! Long and thick, straight and proud, throbbing with need, and all for her.

Once his sweats were discarded, she took him in her hands and glided them up and down, rhythmically, her memory returning as he groaned beneath her. *Just like riding a bike*, she thought, smiling softly. It was too dark for her to see the look on Damian's face, but his sounds were like music to her ears.

He gripped her wrists just as she felt him getting close. "I need to be inside you," he stated.

Kelly wriggled out of her panties while Damian leaned over and extracted a condom from his bedside table. She was in the passenger seat now, spread out and waiting for him as he straddled her.

"You ready?" he asked, dipping a finger inside her at the same time.

She didn't need to answer. They both knew that she was more than ready. Damian glided in easily, and Kelly sighed as he filled her completely. She threw her arms around his broad back and wrapped her legs around his hips, and as they moved, she said, "You're home. You're finally home."

Afterwards, she curled up next to him with her head against his chest and traced the pattern of his tattoo. "Tell me again about what this symbolizes to the Greeks," she said, always interested to learn about his heritage.

Damian gave her a squeeze. "You like to hear stories, don't you?"

"Um-hmm. It reminds me of when I was a kid and my parents would read me a story before bed."

"My parents did that too, although they didn't always read from a book. Sometimes they told stories from our family history or from Greek mythology."

"So, the lightning bolt," she prompted.

"According to legend, Zeus was responsible for throwing lightning bolts. Since he was the most powerful of all the Greek gods, the lightning bolt became a symbol of that power, although there are other meanings for it as well."

"Such as?"

"Some saw it as a symbol of fertility and masculinity."

Kelly giggled. "Seems fitting, although there's no proof of your fertility running around somewhere, is there?"

Damian laughed. "Not that I'm aware of."

"So, you got the tattoo done on a dare, right?"

"Yep. Dumb reason, I know. I was on spring break in Mexico, during my senior year of high school. Me and my buddies were goofing around one night, and there may have been some drinking involved, and the next thing you know, we were at a tattoo parlor."

"But you were the only one who went through with it," she finished. "Any regrets?"

"No. Not about that. Getting a tattoo is not a big deal in the scheme of life, Kell."

She glanced up to see that his expression had turned serious. "It sounds like you might have other regrets."

He ran his hand down the back of her long hair and placed a tender kiss on her forehead. "I think that most people have some, but I try not to dwell on past mistakes. What about you? Any regrets?"

"Just one." She crawled over on top of him and buried her hands in his hair. "I regret making us wait so long to do this..." She bent her head down and nibbled on his bottom lip. They were still naked, and she felt his erection press into her belly.

Damian cupped her bottom as she peppered him with kisses along his stubbled jaw, on the tip of his nose, and on the slight indention in his chin. When she blew into his ear, he groaned, and when she reached between them to grab his manhood, the groan turned into a growl.

"Then let's make up for lost time," he said and flipped her onto her back. As Damian kissed his way down her body, Kelly marveled at how wonderful it felt to make love with him again. There was comfort in knowing each other's bodies, but there was a newness to it as well. Their sex had been explosive before, lust-fueled and driven, and even though she still felt those things, there was something else now. This time, she wasn't just giving him her body. She was giving him her heart, which was terrifying and exhilarating at the same time. She wondered for a moment if Damian felt it too, but then he was stroking her center and licking her neck simultaneously in the perfect spots. The orgasm ripped through her before she knew it, and she clung to him, pulsating and rocking, until she slowly drifted back down, safe in the comfort of his arms.

Afterwards, she loved on Damian with her hands and her mouth, and then they lay together in the dark, him spooning her from behind.

"Stay with me tonight," he whispered.

Kelly glanced at his bedside clock, and she was shocked to see that it was after midnight. She had to work the next day, but right then, it didn't matter. Nothing else mattered but being with Damian. "Ok," she agreed, "but I have to set an alarm for work tomorrow."

"It's already set for six o'clock."

She flipped around to face him. "Are you crazy? Why do you need to get up that early?"

"Because I want to go into the shop for a while before our date tomorrow night."

What with all the sex, Kelly had almost forgotten that they were double dating with Emma and Zack. "I don't think I like this early rising habit of yours."

"Well, we can't just stay in bed all day. We wouldn't get anything done."

Kelly wiggled closer to him. "I'd say there's plenty we could get done."

And they went at it again until they were so exhausted that they finally agreed to sleep. Neither one bothered with clothes. They simply cocooned themselves under the covers and drifted off into a dreamless sleep.

Kelly barely registered the alarm ringing at six o'clock, nor the kiss that Damian placed on her forehead before he left for work. When the alarm woke her at eight, she realized that Damian must have reset it for her, and she smiled. She stretched her arms above her head and luxuriated in the cloud-like mattress for a little while longer, delaying the inevitable. When she finally made her way into the bathroom, she smiled again at the note that he had left her.

Breakfast on the table. Walk, don't run.

Kelly practically skipped into the kitchen, crossing her fingers in hopes of what might be there. "YES!" she yelled when she saw the bag from the Clarkston bakery and another note.

Coffee in the microwave. You're welcome!

After Kelly had warmed up the coffee and bit into the Bavarian custard donut, she sighed with contentment. She thought back to their conversation just yesterday and recalled Damian accusing her of wanting grand gestures. She would have to reassure him later that the simple things were what mattered to her. The night they had just spent together, the way that he had opened up to her—that was what was important. The sharing, the listening, the laughter, the need to satisfy each other, and his promise to "do whatever it takes" to make their relationship work. The donuts and coffee didn't hurt either! Those were the romantic gestures that she needed, and if she wasn't in love with him before, well, then she certainly was now.

Luckily, the walk of shame across the parking lot in the clothes that she had worn yesterday was short, and no one was outside anyway. Kelly found herself humming as she took a shower, dressed, and then hopped in her car. She connected her phone to Bluetooth and called Damian as she drove to work.

"You woke up," Damian teased.

"It must have been the smell of donuts wafting down the hallway. Thank you, by the way. Nothing like sugar and caffeine to get the body moving."

"You're welcome."

"So, do you have a lot to do today?"

"Yeah. Jim will be here soon, and then we're going to meet with some suppliers this afternoon. But I'll be home in time for our date tonight."

Kelly was still floating from the night before, and the words "our date" sounded particularly promising. She didn't want to get ahead of herself though, so she simply replied, "Sounds good. I'll see you later."

She was about to hang up when Damian said, "Hey, Kell?"

"Yeah?"

"Wear that black one-piece thingy under your clothes tonight. You know the one."

Kelly squirmed with anticipation, and it was only ten o'clock in the morning! *How am I going to make it through the entire day?*

"Kell? You still there?"

"Yes, I'm here, and yes, I'll wear it." Kelly wondered if the air waves between their cell phones were crackling the way her entire body was.

"Can't wait," Damian said, his voice husky.

"Me neither," Kelly said and then squeaked out a quick goodbye.

Somehow, Kelly made it through the day without bursting into a ball of flames. In between waiting on customers and her other bookstore duties, she thought about Damian. Images from the night before flashed through her mind, along with the sweet words that he had spoken. Even though Kelly felt positive about the future of their relationship, she recalled him warning her that he still had "issues."

She was fairly certain that he was referring to his broken engagement, but she wondered if there was more to it than that. She felt too buoyant to dwell on it, although she made a mental note to dig a little deeper.

Just before the end of the day, Kelly received an email from a college friend of her and Emma's inviting them and their *significant others* to a Halloween party in a few weeks' time. Beth Thompson had lived in the dorm room across the hall from Kelly and Emma at Michigan State, and she had made it a point to have a college friends get-together at least once a year. Kelly read the email twice, noting that costumes were "optional" and that the party would be taking place at Beth's house in Rochester.

"Hmm. I wonder if Damian would go with me?" Kelly mused aloud. And then she began to visualize Damian dressed up in various costumes. It would have to be something masculine and strong, just like him. Batman, perhaps? A pirate, a police officer, a fireman…a Greek warrior? Kelly was still daydreaming when Emma called.

"Hi, Em," Kelly answered cheerfully.

"Hi. Just calling to remind you about tonight. The tuxedo fitting is at five-thirty, followed by dinner at the Woodshop."

"I remember. Hey, did you see the email from Beth Thompson?"

"No. I'm a new mom, remember? I barely have time to take a shower, let alone read my emails."

"Well, we're invited to a Halloween party at Beth's house three weeks from now, and boyfriends and husbands-to-be are invited too."

"Interesting. Maybe Zack could go as Superman."

Kelly giggled, since she was in on Emma's fascination with the superhero and Zack's collection of Superman underwear. Zack had no idea that Kelly knew, as she was sworn to secrecy. "That's funny, because I was thinking that Damian would make a good Batman."

"You could be Catwoman, and I could be Wonder Woman! It's perfect!"

If Damian liked her in black lingerie, wait until he got a load of her in a Catwoman suit! "Let's ask the guys at dinner tonight," Kelly said, and she went back to her daydreaming as soon as she hung up the phone.

Chapter 22

"No way!" Damian said a couple of hours later, once they were seated at the Woodshop restaurant in downtown Clarkston.

"Why not?" Kelly implored.

"Because I'm not the kind of guy who wears tights," he said emphatically. "Back me up on this, Zack."

Zack arched his eyebrows at his surly brother. "No can do, bro. I think it sounds like fun to dress up as superheroes."

"You would," Damian replied.

Kelly decided to try another tactic. She placed her hand on Damian's arm and rubbed it gently back and forth. "Wouldn't you like to see me dressed up as Catwoman?" she purred, leaning into him.

He relaxed his shoulders some, but he still didn't look convinced. "Not if it means that I have to wear tights," he said.

Zack interjected. "Your friend said that costumes were optional, right? Well, then the three of us could dress up, and numnuts could just come as himself."

Damian flipped his brother off, but Kelly grabbed his hand and entwined her fingers with his. "Please, Damian. If you do this for me, I'll owe you a favor. A big one!"

That seemed to get his attention. "A favor, huh? Anything I want?"

Uh-oh, this had the potential to backfire on her. "Yes. Within reason," she added.

The sly smile that spread across Damian's face reminded her of the Grinch who stole Christmas! "Ok," he said. "But you guys are my witnesses." He pointed at Emma and Zack, who were giving each other a high five.

"Yay! This will be so much fun!" Emma enthused.

"Let's go costume shopping next weekend," Kelly suggested.

"We'll ask your parents to babysit," Emma said to Zack.

Damian glared at his brother. "This is your fault, you know. You were supposed to back me up, but now we're both going to have to wear tights."

"Hey, I'm not ashamed to show off my package. If you are, that's your own problem," Zack said.

"Damian has a fine package," Kelly said in his defense, and he just shook his head as Zack and Emma erupted with laughter.

Their orders arrived shortly after that, and they all tucked in with gusto. Kelly and Damian split a rack of barbecued spareribs and mashed potatoes, while Emma and Zack split a steak dinner. Kelly had just speared a hefty chunk of meat with her fork when a shadow came over their table. She glanced up, and there stood Ken looking down on her and her forkful of meat. She quickly set down her fork, and said, "Ken. Hi. Where did you come from?"

"Right over there," he said, pointing to the table across the aisle, where two other men were seated.

Damian, Zack, and Emma had all stopped eating to watch the transaction unfold.

"I've been sitting there the whole time, but you obviously didn't see me."

Damian narrowed his eyes at the man, but he kept quiet.

"Um, Ken, this is my…"

"Boyfriend," Damian finished, standing to his full height. "Damian Kostas." He stuck out his hand, which Ken reluctantly shook.

"Oh. I see. Well, sorry to bother you, Kelly. I just wanted to come over and say hello."

"No problem," Damian replied for her, and then Ken hastily retreated to his table.

"That was bordering on rude," Kelly hissed at Damian once he sat back down.

"What are you talking about? I shook the guy's hand."

"Yeah, but you looked like you wanted to kill him."

Emma's eyes went wide, and Zack snickered behind his napkin.

"Well, that's what Batman does. He eliminates his enemies," Damian said drily, and then he picked up a sparerib with his bare hands, tore off a chunk with his teeth, and gnawed on it like a dog with a bone.

Kelly couldn't help it. She busted out in hysterical laughter intermingled with snorting and coughing. Emma joined in, and before long, Damian and Zack were laughing too. They were causing quite a commotion, and the waitress hurried over under the guise of refilling their water glasses, though her true aim was to get them to pipe down.

"Can I get you anything else?" the waitress asked with cool politeness.

"No. Just have the valet pull my Batmobile around," Damian replied, setting off another round of hysterics.

The waitress left, shaking her head, and Kelly ventured a glance at Ken's table. He and his friends had stood up and were getting ready to leave. Ken gave Kelly a brief head nod and then walked away looking baffled.

"I feel kind of sorry for him," Kelly said after they had calmed down. "He's not a bad guy."

"Yeah, but you've got Batman. Besides, it never would have worked," Emma said, pointing to the demolished plate of spareribs.

Damian and Zack exchanged a look of confusion.

"Ken's a vegetarian," Emma explained.

"He's not a vegetarian. He's just into healthy eating," Kelly said.

Damian smiled broadly and threw his arm around Kelly. "Emma's right. That never would have worked!"

Later that night, Catwoman brought Batman to his knees when she stripped down to her lacy black teddy.

Damian had walked Kelly up to her apartment and didn't want for an invitation to come in. He slammed the door behind him, hauled her into his arms, and carried her off to the bedroom. "I can't wait to see what you've got on under there," he growled before ordering her to strip.

Once their clothes were puddled on the floor, they attacked each other with the same vigor as they had their rib dinner, and afterward, they lay sweaty and breathless in each other's arms.

"Do you have to work tomorrow?" Damian asked as he fiddled with a strand of her hair.

"No. Brett's on the schedule. Why?"

"I thought we could spend the day together."

Kelly turned on her side to face him. "What do you have in mind?"

"Well, how about going to the Henry Ford Museum?"

Kelly idly traced his lightning bolt tattoo. "Hmm. I haven't been there since I was a kid. I think it was on a sixth-grade field trip."

"We don't have to go there. It was just an idea."

"No. It's a good idea, especially since you agreed to dress up as Batman for me."

He gently tugged on the strand of hair he had been playing with. "Exactly. And then next weekend, you can choose what we do."

Kelly warmed at the idea of her and Damian making plans together. The thought of there even being a "next weekend" with him was a welcome relief from eight months ago, when she had wondered if she would ever see him again. "I like that plan."

"Good. Now how about this plan? I stay here tonight, and we make love until the wee hours of the morning."

Kelly wiggled against him. "I like that plan too, as long as we can sleep in."

"Um-hmm," Damian mumbled, his head already buried in her neck.

"And you have to go out and buy donuts for us in the morning," she added.

"Consider it done," Damian said, dipping his head down to her breasts. He drew a nipple into his mouth and made a loud popping sound when he released it.

"Any other requests?"

"Do that to the other one," she said and pointed to her other breast.

"Your wish is my command."

And so it went… First, it was Kelly's turn to make requests (or demands, depending on her tone of voice), and then it was Damian's turn. They spent the next few hours rediscovering each other—exploring, playing, laughing, and loving, even if *loving* wasn't what they were officially calling it yet. But to Kelly, that was exactly what it was, and when it was time to sleep, she snuggled up against him and drifted off, happy and content.

For the next few weeks, that feeling of contentment continued. Kelly and Damian spent every free moment together, and they had even begun to work together in preparation for Damian's takeover of Jim's Custom Cars.

Kelly preferred to come into his shop on the days that Lexie wasn't working, but occasionally the women crossed paths, only to exchange cool greetings and relieved goodbyes. Damian had broken the news to Lexie that he wouldn't be keeping her on after graduation, which Lexie quite obviously blamed on Kelly. Kelly had promised Damian to help find a replacement, and she had begun putting out ads for an experienced front-desk clerk. Damian also put Kelly in charge of the initial interview process so she only introduced him to candidates that she felt were qualified for the job. Therefore, all young, attractive women were out of the running from the minute they walked in the door! Kelly thought that she had been pulling the wool over his eyes until, one day, he walked in on her interviewing an attractive, long-legged brunette.

The brunette, who had been a very dull interviewee, perked up considerably when Damian came strutting into the front office.

"Are you here about the job?" Damian asked politely.

"I am," the leggy brunette purred. "Would you be my boss?"

Kelly rolled her eyes, but Leggy didn't notice. She was too busy perusing Damian from head to toe.

"If you were hired, then yes," he replied, shooting Kelly an amused look.

"Well, after I'm done here, I'd be happy to sit down and discuss my credentials with you," Leggy said.

I just bet you would! Kelly thought. *Too bad you're not going to get that chance!*

"I trust my assistant to do all the *legwork* for me," Damian said drily. "But good luck."

When he turned and sauntered away, Leggy stared right at his butt, and Kelly immediately terminated the interview.

A few minutes later, Kelly huffed into the shop, where Damian was polishing the chrome on a '57 Chevy, and cleared her throat loudly to get his attention.

He shoved the rag into the back pocket of his ripped jeans and said, "Yes, princess?"

Damian had bestowed the nickname on her after he had been repeatedly asked to deliver her favorite breakfast in the mornings before he left for work. Most of the time, she didn't mind the moniker, but at that moment, it irked her. "You flirted with that woman right in front of me," she accused, hands on hips.

"I did not," Damian replied, frowning.

"You did too! You purposely pointed out her legs. Don't tell me that you didn't notice them."

Leggy had shown up for the interview in a short denim skirt, which had been the first strike against her. *Everyone knows that's not how you dress for an interview!*

Damian took a few steps closer, but Kelly shot out a hand to warn him to keep his distance. "I noticed, but I just wanted to rile you up," he said. "And look, it worked!"

Kelly sputtered, her ire rising even higher. "But why? Why would you want to do that?"

"Because you're fun to tease," he said and grabbed her by the wrist.

The next thing she knew, Kelly's back was pressed against the side of the '57 Chevy, and Damian's mouth was on her. After a thorough kiss, he broke away and said, "You're the only one I want, princess. Don't forget it."

Two weeks later, Kelly found the perfect replacement for Lexie. Brian Winters was a retired employee of General Motors who had decided that being retired wasn't exactly what it was cracked up to be. He and his wife had been arguing a lot, and they had reached the conclusion that their relationship was better when he had been working. Kelly took an instant liking to the soft-spoken gray-haired man, and she wanted to hire him on the spot. After Damian met Brian, he agreed, and the man was hired. Since Brian had experience in the auto industry, he would not only man the front desk, but he would be able to help Damian in the shop as well. It was the perfect solution, and Kelly was especially relieved that the interview process was over.

With that job done, Kelly turned her attention to planning a grand reopening celebration for January, although they were still trying to decide on a name for Damian's shop. They mulled it over during lunches, dinners, and donuts, and yes, even when they were in bed, and that's where it finally struck her. Kelly was tracing Damian's lightning bolt tattoo when she sat up straight and declared, "I've got it! Lightning Fast Autos!"

Damian repeated the name a few times and then said, "Lightning Fast Autos, it is!"

In between helping Damian, Kelly continued her work at the bookstore and started planning the next romance book club meeting. She had received nothing but positive feedback from the attendees of the first meeting, and a few more participants had jumped on board for the next meeting.

Kelly was sharing the news with Damian over dinner one night while he listened intently, a quality that she loved about him. When she had finished talking, Damian set his beer down and said, "I have an idea."

"About the book club?"

"Yeah. What about including a man's perspective?"

Kelly cocked an eyebrow at him. "Go on."

"I finished that book that you lent me. The one with the rich boss and the sexy assistant…"

"You mean the book you *stole* from me?"

"Borrowed. Anyway, I could come to your next meeting to represent the male point of view."

Kelly chewed on the inside of her cheek while she considered his proposal. "Are you serious about this?"

"Sure. Why not? You've got enough estrogen in the club—why not add a little testosterone?"

"A *little* testosterone?"

Damian shrugged. "Ok. A lot. But I bet the ladies would love it! How many men do you know that read romance novels?"

"I didn't know any until I discovered that *my* man reads them!"

"I'll admit it. When I first started reading, I thought it was going to suck, but then I really got into it. I was actually rooting for Hudson and Lacey to get together!"

Kelly almost spit out the slug of beer that she had just taken. "You even remembered their names?"

"Yeah. Who has names like that anyway?"

"This ought to be interesting."

"So, is that a yes?"

"It's a maybe. I need to give it some more thought. Besides, I'm still in shock that you would actually consider doing this."

"Anything for you, princess," he said and clinked his beer bottle against hers.

And the funny thing was, she was starting to believe him.

Chapter 23

Kelly should have known that the blissful feelings that she had been experiencing wouldn't last. Just like a storm that suddenly gathers in the sky, she hadn't seen it coming. She never could have predicted what happened at the Halloween party and how it would be connected to the conversation that she and Damian had had the night before.

They had just finished eating dinner at her apartment and were sitting on her couch, flipping through the television channels, trying to find something worth watching. After a few minutes, they gave up, and Kelly suggested that they just talk. She had learned so much more about Damian since they had been spending so much time together, but there were still some major topics that they hadn't delved into, and one of them was money.

It had dawned on her that Damian would have needed a sizable amount of money in order to buy the auto shop, and she wondered where it had come from. Damian wasn't a big spender, but he always offered to pay whenever they went out, and he never seemed concerned about his finances. Kelly hesitated to bring up the topic, thinking that it was really none of her business. However, if they were going to have a future together…

"Did you know that money is one of the top three topics that couples fight over?" she ventured.

"I've heard that. What are the other two?"

"Sex and parenting."

"Hmm. Well, at least we can cross sex off our list," Damian said, shooting her a toothy grin.

"Yes, we seem to have a handle on that one."

Damian leaned in to kiss her, but Kelly pulled back. "Not yet. We're still talking."

"Oh," he replied, sitting up straighter. "What is it that you want to know, Kell?"

"I was thinking that it had to have taken a lot of money to buy the shop, and I was wondering…"

"Where I got it from," he finished.

"Yes," she replied, relieved that he didn't seem put out by her question.

"Well, I have my grandparents to thank for most of it. When my dad's dad died around six years ago, he left Zack and me a generous amount of money, with the stipulation that we use it for something worthwhile. He didn't want us to squander it."

Kelly nodded, encouraging him to continue.

"Zack was engaged to Alicia at the time, so he used his money to put a down payment on their house in Ann Arbor. Since I was single and didn't have any debts to pay off, I invested mine."

"Ah, I see," Kelly said.

Damian shifted his body to face her. "The thing is, most of my money is tied up in this business, so until I start to turn a profit, things will be a little…tight."

"But I'm confident that the business will be successful. Aren't you?" she asked, suddenly feeling nervous for him.

"That's the goal, but there's also some risk involved. When I started out on this venture, I didn't have anyone else to take care of. It's only been me for such a long time, and I wasn't worried. I don't need a lot of 'stuff' to be happy, Kell. Give me a roof over my head, a decent car to drive, and some food in my belly, and I'm content."

Kelly took a moment to digest his answer while Damian studied her. "Just say it, Kell."

"I guess I'm pretty content too, although I don't plan on living in this apartment forever. I'd eventually like to own a home and have some money left over to do some extra things, like travel. Don't you want those things too?"

Damian shoved his hands through his hair and looked at her with an unreadable expression. "Yeah, I do, but it's going to take a while for me to get there. I'm not like Zack. I didn't have my life all mapped out like he did, with the nice house in the 'burbs, and the fancy car, and the money to fly off somewhere on a whim. I can't give you what Zack and Emma have. At least, not right now."

Kelly wasn't sure if he was referring to their "stuff" or their lifestyle, but she didn't like Damian's implication. "What's wrong with wanting the things that I mentioned?"

"Nothing, except that I can't give them to you," he repeated.

"I'm not asking you to *give* me anything, Damian. I've worked hard all of my adult life to support myself, and I will continue to do so. I'm not looking for someone to take care of me." *At least, not financially.*

"How did we get on this shitty topic anyway?" he asked, still exasperated.

"I brought it up, but I can see that it was a mistake."

Damian stood up and shoved his hands in his pockets. "It's not your fault. I think I'm just overtired. Why don't we finish this conversation another time?"

Kelly stood up too and wrapped her arms around his waist. "I'm sorry," she whispered. "I didn't mean to cause an argument."

Damian just held her close and rubbed his hands up and down her back. Kelly thought about pulling him into the bedroom, but the air was still fraught with tension, and she was filled with uncertainty. Her fear was confirmed when Damian let go and said, "I should probably get going."

On previous Friday nights, Damian would have stayed over, or at least stayed late, but it was only ten o'clock. "You're not staying?" Kelly asked, but she saw the answer in his eyes. He had begun to shut down, and there was nothing she could do but wait it out.

"Like I said, I'm really tired, and we have to work tomorrow. Plus, we have the Halloween party tomorrow night."

Excuses, all of them, but Kelly didn't have the energy to argue anymore. "Ok. I guess I'll see you tomorrow, then."

Damian was already at the door, lacing up his boots. When he stood up, she was right in front of him, and she willed him to put his arms around her, but he didn't. He simply leaned over and kissed her forehead, and then he turned abruptly and rushed out the door.

That night, Kelly lay in bed, staring up at the ceiling, searching for answers that wouldn't come. Money was obviously a hot-button topic for Damian, but why? And why did he sound almost accusatory when she told him about her goals for the future? Then there was the reference to Zack and Emma, whose lifestyle was comfortable but not extravagant. Damian seemed to be hung up on the idea that he had to provide for Kelly even after she had tried to convince him otherwise. Maybe it was his sense of pride that had caused such a negative reaction.

Kelly racked her brain, trying to figure out if she had ever given him any indication that she wanted to be taken care of, but she came up blank. Finally, her eyes started to droop, and her body began to relax, but then another thought popped into her mind. *Maybe this has nothing to do with me. Maybe it was her, the mysterious ex-fiancée, who made Damian feel inadequate. Does this woman still have a hold on him after all these years?*

Somehow Kelly got to sleep, because, the next thing she knew, her alarm was going off. She reached over and shut it off, and then burrowed back under her covers. She wasn't worried about falling back asleep, because her mind was busy replaying last night's conversation with Damian, and then a knock sounded at her door.

Excited at the prospect that it was him, she shoved the blankets aside and rushed toward the door. Her hair was sticking out in every direction, and she still had sleep in her eyes, but she didn't care. She just wanted to see him and be assured that everything was all right. She heard the rumble of his truck and spied the note sticking through her door crack at the same time. "Damn," she muttered, frustrated that she had missed him.

Curious, she extracted the note and read…

Sorry about last night. I brought a little something that I hope will make you smile. Looking forward to tonight. Batman

Kelly shook her head, because she was smiling already! She swung the door open, and there was the bag in its usual spot with a steaming cup of coffee next to it. "And he thinks I need a lot of *stuff* to be happy!" Kelly scoffed as she hurried into the kitchen with her treasures. Before she gave into temptation, she picked up her phone and sent him a text.

Catwoman thanks you, and I will thank you in person later! xoxo

She set her phone down, thinking that he wouldn't be able to text her until he got to work, but she was wrong.

Batman is seriously looking forward to that! xoxo

Satisfied that their argument was behind them, Kelly dug into the donut bag. She hesitated before biting into the second donut, considering that she had to get into her Catwoman costume that night, but then she decided, "Ah, what the hell?"

It wasn't until later, when she was actually squeezing into the costume, that she regretted her earlier indulgence. Once the suit was on and she had surveyed herself from all angles, she was pleased. When Kelly and Damian had gone to the costume shop a couple weeks earlier, they had agreed not to show each other their costumes until the night of the party. Now Kelly was anxious for him to see her, and vice versa.

She slipped the eye mask into place and unzipped the black catsuit a touch further to provide Damian with a peek of her cleavage. Black elbow-length gloves and four-inch high-heeled boots completed the costume, and her long dark hair lay smooth and sleek down her back. She swiped a deep red lipstick across her lips and declared herself ready.

And she was just in time, because the doorbell rang, announcing Batman's arrival. "Your Batmobile awaits," Damian said from outside the door.

Kelly giggled and swung the door open to find the best-looking Batman she had ever seen standing before her. "Holy smokes, Batman!"

Damian was also cloaked in black from head to toe, and all that she could see of him were his sparkling brown eyes and his chiseled jaw. The suit fit his muscular body to a T, and underneath the exaggerated contours of the costume, Kelly knew that the real thing was even better! His pose made him look dark and menacing, but the smile he gave her showed the true Damian, the man with the soft heart underneath all that muscle.

"Do you know what that outfit makes me want to do?" he asked.

"Tell me," she teased.

He ran a gloved fingertip down the middle of her chest until it landed on the zipper. He gave the zipper a little tug to reveal even more cleavage, and she squirmed under his penetrating gaze. "It makes me want to strip you out of it, because I can tell that you don't have a stitch of clothes on underneath."

"Ha! I could barely zip this thing up as it was," she said. "There's definitely no room for anything else under here."

Damian leaned in, his eyes darker than they were just a minute ago. "I think there's room for my hand or my tongue," he said, and he flicked his tongue out at her.

Kelly swatted him on the arm, which he obviously didn't feel because of the bulkiness of the costume. "As enticing as that sounds, we have to go. Emma and Zack are expecting us in five minutes."

Kelly took a step forward, but Batman blocked her way. "Uh-uh. First, we zip you back up. I don't want anyone else getting a peek at the goods." Damian zipped her suit back up to her neck and said, "There, that's better."

Kelly was about to argue but thought better of it. The last thing she wanted was another disagreement between them. Besides, tonight was all about having fun.

They pulled up to Zack's house a few minutes later, and Kelly spotted Gracie waiting expectantly at the front door. Emma had asked them to meet there so Gracie could see all of them in costume. The plan was for Zack and Emma to drive separately in case Emma was overtaken with the urge to leave the party early. Even though Mrs. Kostas was babysitting, Emma was still a new mom who occasionally suffered from separation anxiety, as she liked to remind everyone on a regular basis.

When Damian and Kelly stepped out of the car and approached the house, Gracie's hands flew to her mouth, and her eyes grew wide. "Uncle Damian? Is that you?" she asked, peering up at him.

"No, it's Batman!" he said and picked her up while she squealed with delight.

Once he set Gracie back down, she looked at Kelly and giggled. "You look like a pretty cat," she said.

"Well, thank you, sweetheart."

"Come in and see Mommy and Daddy!"

It struck Kelly that Gracie had referred to her soon-to-be stepmom as "Mommy," and Kelly felt a twinge of envy. And it wasn't because of the well-appointed two-story house or the nice cars sitting out in the driveway. No, it was much more basic than that. It was because Emma was truly loved—by Zack, and Gracie, and baby Ava, and…

"Catwoman? You ok?" Damian asked.

"Yeah. I'm fine," she said and took his hand as he pulled her into the living room.

Emma and Zack, a.k.a. Wonder Woman and Superman, were posed in front of the fireplace, and Alex Kostas was rapidly snapping pictures of them while chatting incessantly.

"Look who's here!" Gracie exclaimed as Kelly and Damian entered the room. Everyone exchanged enthusiastic greetings and appraisals of each other's costumes before Alex demanded that Kelly and Damian pose for pictures too. The four of them had fun hamming it up for the camera until Zack announced that it was time to go.

"If we don't leave now, Ava will wake up, and I won't be able to get Emma out the door," he explained.

"Good thinking, Clark," Kelly said to a round of laughter.

Alex and Gracie walked the four of them to the door, and the superheroes were treated to hugs and kisses all around before Zack ushered them out.

"This ought to be a riot," Emma said to Kelly as they teetered down the sidewalk in their heels.

Kelly would think back on those words later and wonder how a night that had started out so wonderfully had turned into a complete disaster.

Chapter 24

Beth Thompson lived in a Tudor-style home in an upscale neighborhood of Rochester, a prosperous community with a thriving downtown district. When Kelly and Damian pulled up to the house, there were already several cars there, and the front porch was decorated with flashing black and orange lights. Damian parked his truck behind Zack's Range Rover, and they all headed for the door together.

"We don't have to stay long," Kelly whispered to Damian as he tugged on his costume.

"I'll stay as long as you want to, princess," he said and took her hand.

Beth greeted them at the door in a 1950s style poodle skirt and tight sweater, with her blonde hair pouffed out in a bouffant. She took turns hugging Kelly and Emma and then asked to be introduced to their dates.

"There's plenty of food and drinks in the kitchen, so help yourself!" she said before flouncing off to greet some other guests.

The foursome made their way to the kitchen, stopping along the way for Kelly and Emma to say hello to some of their friends. There were a lot of people in the house already, but it was hard to tell who was who behind the costumes. The superheroes received a lot of appreciative glances from the men and the women alike, but when one guy, who was dressed like a police officer, paid a little too much attention to Kelly, Damian quickly gathered her to his side.

"Maybe this wasn't such a good idea," Damian whispered. "I don't like the way the men are ogling you in that getup."

Kelly put her arm around his waist and squeezed. "I only have eyes for Batman," she said, which seemed to settle him down, at least for the time being.

After they had filled their plates with appetizers and grabbed some beers to drink, the four of them made their way into the sprawling living room, where most of the guests were congregated. They ate and drank in between chatting with Kelly's and Emma's friends and their dates, and the time passed quickly.

"See, dressing up wasn't so bad after all, was it?" Kelly said, directing her question at Damian.

"Ok, I'll admit it. I kind of don't mind being Batman."

After another round of beers, some of the men broke off to play pool and darts in the Thompsons's finished basement. Damian and Zack joined them after some convincing from Kelly and Emma.

"We'll be fine," Emma said, used to Zack's overprotective nature. "These are our friends. Go on and have fun!"

Damian made an uncharacteristic show of kissing Kelly on the lips before they departed.

"What was that about?" she asked, even though she didn't mind in the least.

"I wanted all the dudes to see who you're with, and now they'll know better than to mess with Batman."

Kelly giggled. "I'm pretty sure they know who I'm with, since you haven't left my side all night. Go on, play pool and let me hang out with the ladies."

After the men left, Emma turned to Kelly and said, "It looks like everything's going well with you and Damian. I think it's sweet how attentive he's being with you tonight."

"Maybe it's because we had a little argument yesterday and he's trying to make up to me."

"Oh really? Want to talk about it?"

Kelly was about to share when Beth came over, dragging a woman with her who was dressed up as Daisy Duke from the old television show *The Dukes of Hazzard.* She wore extremely short denim shorts, a red and black checked shirt that was knotted under her breasts, and fire-engine red high heels. Her chestnut brown hair cascaded down her back in soft waves, just like the character from the show.

She makes a perfect Daisy Duke, Kelly thought as she studied the woman's face.

"Hey, Kelly, Emma. Do you remember Amanda Jennings? She lived in our dorm, a few floors below us. We went to a few parties together, remember?"

Kelly and Emma exchanged a confused glance, because neither of them recognized Amanda.

"That's ok. My hair was a lot shorter back then, and it may have even been a shade or two lighter," Amanda said and laughed.

"Now that you say that, you do look kind of familiar," Emma said.

"It was a long time ago. No worries," Amanda said. "Anyway, I'm Amanda Russo now, but I'm flying solo tonight. My husband is out of town on business."

Kelly kept trying to place her as they chatted, but it was to no avail. After a few more minutes of general chitchat, Amanda excused herself to join another group.

Beth stayed behind and leaned in toward Kelly and Emma conspiratorially. "Amanda lucked out in the husband department. Jake is an executive with a plastics company, and they have beaucoup bucks!"

Looking around the house, Kelly thought that Beth wasn't doing too bad either, but she didn't comment. Kelly was suddenly very glad that Damian wasn't around to hear Beth prattle on about how much money people made.

Emma seemed to have tired of the conversation too, and she suggested that she and Kelly "go check on the boys."

They grabbed a couple more beers as they passed through the kitchen, and then they carefully walked downstairs in their high-heeled boots. The basement was just as impressive as the rest of the house, boasting a game room, a workout room, and a large in-home theater system. *Beth has thought of everything*, Kelly mused as they walked by the giant flat screen television where *The Addams Family* movie was playing.

Damian and Zack were huddled around the pool table, chuckling about something with the rest of the guys, but when Kelly and Emma entered the room, all eyes shifted toward them. Kelly warmed under Damian's intense gaze, and Emma was getting the same treatment from Zack.

"Aww…you ladies couldn't stand to be away from us," Zack teased.

"Just thought we'd check in on you," Kelly said as she handed a beer to Damian.

"Glad you did," he said. When the rest of the men went back to their game, he added, "You almost ready to get out of here?"

"No rush. Go ahead and finish your game," she replied, even though part of her was ready to have Batman all to herself.

"I've had my fill of 'girl time,'" Emma said to Zack. "I'm ready to be alone with Superman."

"Let them finish their game," Kelly said, and then she grabbed Emma's arm to pull her away.

"Ugh. You and Zack are too adorable together, and you make it look so easy," Kelly whined once the men were out of earshot.

"Kelly, things aren't perfect for us, believe me, but at the end of the day, Zack is the one that I want to spend my life with. Even with all his little quirks, I can't imagine being with anyone else."

Kelly giggled. "His quirks? What about yours?"

"Well, we all have them, but the person who can see past that and loves you unconditionally, he's the keeper."

That's how I feel about Damian, but does he feel the same about me?

When they reentered the kitchen, Amanda was standing there talking with Lisa, a woman that Kelly and Emma knew well, so they went over to say hello. All four of them were chatting when Kelly heard Damian's and Zack's voices as they clomped up the stairs.

"That sounds like our men. We'll have to introduce you to them," Emma said.

Zack came over and slung his arm around Emma's shoulder immediately, but Damian hung back, and Kelly turned to see what he was up to. The look on his face instantly told her that something was wrong, but she had no idea what it could be until…

"Amanda and Lisa, meet our dates, Zack and Damian Kostas," Emma said proudly.

Amanda's face fell, and suddenly the light bulb kicked on for Kelly. She glanced from Amanda to Damian to Zack, who now wore a similar expression of recognition.

"Am I missing something here?" Emma asked nervously.

"Damian? Is that really you under there?" Amanda ventured, her voice somewhat shaky.

"Hello, Amanda," he said tightly.

Kelly felt her blood pressure rise, and the catsuit suddenly felt unbearably constricting. She wasn't sure where to look—the tension in the room was palpable.

"You two know each other?" Emma said, and Zack tugged on her arm as if to warn her of impending disaster.

"Yes. We used to…we were…" Amanda stuttered.

"Engaged," Damian finished, his voice sounding unnaturally harsh.

At that moment, Kelly wished that they had the superpower to disappear. She had no idea what to do or say, yet she felt rooted to the spot as the scene unfolded.

"That was a long time ago," Amanda said with a strained smile.

"Yes, it was. So, where's your *husband*?" Damian asked.

"He's on a business trip," Amanda said. She looked just as uncomfortable as the rest of them, but it was as if they were all actors in a play, and the scene wasn't over yet.

"Ahh…I see. So, you married some rich guy who's at work more than he's at home. But hey, at least he can provide you with the lifestyle that you always wanted."

Kelly reached out and placed a hand on Damian's arm, but he didn't even glance her way. "Don't," she hissed.

Amanda's discomfort had morphed into anger, and she placed her hands on her hips and said, "He makes good money, but that's not why I married him."

"Oh, so you married him for love? Yeah, right!"

"Damian, I think we should leave," Zack piped up, but his suggestion fell on deaf ears.

"What do you know about love anyway? You've never truly loved anyone other than yourself," Amanda accused, her voice rising with each word.

Kelly had been so focused on Amanda and Damian, that she had failed to notice the small crowd that had gathered near the entrance to the kitchen. She noticed now, and she wanted to scream at them to go away and mind their own business. Beth's face stuck out of the crowd, and she wore an expression of consternation mixed with amusement, which made Kelly want to slap her.

"I think you have that the wrong way around, sweetheart," Damian hissed.

"Damian, we're leaving. NOW!" Zack said, and he moved to stand alongside his brother.

"So, this is your girlfriend? Kelly?" Amanda spat. When Damian nodded, she took a step toward Kelly and said, "Good luck with him. You're going to need it!" And with that, she turned on her red heels and stomped out of the kitchen. The people crowded around the doorway were forced to separate as she shoved her way through.

Zack locked his hands on Damian's shoulders and forcibly turned him toward the door. "We'll wait for you ladies outside," he muttered as he led Damian away.

Kelly and Emma had set their purses down in the den, which meant that they would have to traverse the crowded living room to retrieve them.

"Stay right here," Emma demanded. "I'll get our purses."

Kelly didn't think that she could move even if she had wanted to. She forced herself to take several deep breaths before she would have to face Damian, and as she was doing so, Beth came into the kitchen.

"I'm so sorry, Kelly. I had no idea that Amanda used to be engaged to your boyfriend. If I'd have known, I wouldn't have invited her."

For some reason, Kelly doubted Beth's sincerity. It seemed like she was more interested in gossiping than worrying about Kelly's feelings. Before she could respond, Emma rushed back into the room and handed Kelly her purse.

"It's not your fault, Beth. How would you have known? Anyway, we're the ones who are sorry. We didn't mean to disrupt your party."

Leave it to Emma to smooth things over, Kelly thought gratefully. A minute later, Kelly and Emma were outside, and Kelly welcomed the crisp fall air into her lungs. As they walked down the driveway toward their vehicles, Kelly noticed that Zack and Damian were sitting inside Damian's truck, but Zack was behind the wheel. Emma held her hand tightly as they approached the driver's side.

"I'm going to drive Damian home. Emma, you can take Kelly and meet me in the parking lot of their apartment complex," Zack said, leaving no room for argument.

Kelly sought out Damian's face, but he was turned the other way, and the set of his shoulders told her that he was in no mood to talk. On the drive home, Emma attempted to make Kelly feel better, but it didn't work. The ugly scene kept replaying in her head, and the soundtrack was stuck on Amanda snarling, "Good luck with him." As Kelly thought about it, she realized that she and Damian had what could be described as a tumultuous relationship, and she wondered if, or when, things would smooth out. She wanted to believe it was because they were two passionate people who felt strongly and loved deeply, but was that really the case? It disturbed Kelly that Amanda had accused Damian of being incapable of love. He may not have said the words yet, but Kelly felt his love in so many ways and saw it there in his eyes even when he was trying to hide it. She knew how much he loved his nieces and his family, maybe not so much by his words, but by his actions, and that was what was important to her. Still, it would be nice to hear the words someday…

"Kell, do you want to stay over at our house tonight?" Emma said, breaking through her tangled-up thoughts.

"No. I'll be fine once I get over the shock. When Damian told me that his ex went to MSU, I thought it was a possibility that I might know her, but he never told me her name, and I didn't ask. Even if he would have, I obviously didn't remember her."

"Me neither. She must not have made a big impression on us," Emma said and reached over to squeeze Kelly's hand.

"It was just so ugly, wasn't it? The words they flung at each other and everyone staring. I don't know if I'll ever be able to show my face in front of those people again."

"It was probably a bigger deal to us than to them. I bet everyone will forget about it after tonight."

"Maybe, but I won't, and Damian won't either. Do you think that he's still in love with her?"

"Absolutely not. From what Zack said, Amanda broke up with Damian over the phone, and they never really had it out. He's probably carried that anger with him all this time, and when he saw her tonight, he lashed out. It probably didn't help that he had been drinking too."

Kelly hadn't kept track of how many beers Damian had had, but she doubted that he was drunk. Besides, she had seen him intoxicated before, and he had never acted like that. "Well, I'm going to ask him about it when he decides to talk to me."

"Just give him some time, Kelly. I'm sure he'll explain everything once he simmers down."

When they pulled into the apartment complex, Zack was leaned against Damian's truck waiting for them—alone. Emma pulled into the space next to him, and Kelly got out.

Zack immediately pulled her in for a hug and said, "I apologize on my brother's behalf. I'm sure he'll apologize himself once he gets his shit together."

"Yeah, I might have heard that once or twice before," she said and sighed.

"Do you want me to walk you up to your apartment?" Zack asked.

"No. I'm fine, but thank you," Kelly replied, grateful for how calmly Zack had handled the situation.

Emma and Zack waited in the car until she made it safely inside her apartment, and as they drove off, she couldn't help but feel envious. They were going home together, happily in love, while she and Damian lived across the street from each other, yet it felt like they were a million miles apart.

Chapter 25

"Let's get you out of this thing," Damian said in her darkened bedroom. He took hold of the zipper on the Catwoman costume and slowly eased it down to just past her navel. His fingertips were warm as they brushed the bare sliver of skin that he had revealed. "I couldn't wait to be alone with you," he said, his voice muted because of the pounding in her ears.

"I'm burning up in here. Hurry up and take it off," she said.

He chuckled as he peeled the fabric away from her breasts and off her shoulders, but then he stopped and bent his head down to pull a nipple into his mouth. Kelly's arms were still trapped in the tight costume, and she was helpless against the onslaught of his warm tongue as he swirled it around first one nipple and then the other.

Finally, he pulled back, and with his help, she wiggled out of the costume. Damian lifted her into his arms and laid her on the bed. He gazed down at her and said, "I love you, Kelly."

"No, he doesn't," said a woman's voice. "He'll never love you. He only loves himself, himself, himself…"

The incessant buzz of the alarm clock broke through her sleep-muddled brain, and Kelly bolted upright. She was sweating, and her breath came in short pants.

"It was just a dream," she said repeatedly until her heart rate returned to normal. And then the events of the previous evening came flooding back, and she realized that the woman's voice in her dream was Amanda's.

Kelly hadn't heard a word from Damian after Emma had dropped her off, and she hadn't really expected to. Even though she wanted to confront him, she forced herself not to, and she had even turned off her phone so she wouldn't be tempted to call him. If he could be stubborn, then so could she! Besides, this time, none of it was her fault. As Zack had said, Damian owed her an apology, and she would make herself wait for it.

It was Sunday, and since Brett had asked for the day off, Kelly had to work. She was glad that she wouldn't be sitting around her apartment stewing over Damian all day, and she decided that she might even go in early.

Kelly showered, dressed, and ate breakfast, and she purposely ignored her phone until she was ready to leave. Not surprisingly, there were no texts or missed calls from Damian. There was only one lengthy voicemail from Emma telling her not to worry—that Damian would come around.

When Kelly opened her front door to a cool, overcast fall day, she noticed that Damian's truck was already gone. Like her, he had probably gone off to work, with the hopes of escaping his troubles for a little while.

A couple hours later, Kelly was at the bookstore, responding to emails about the next book club meeting, when Mrs. Simmons hobbled in.

"Just the lady I wanted to see," Kelly said. "The votes are in for our next romance book."

"First things first," said Mrs. Simmons. "How did the Halloween party go last night? Do you have any pictures?"

Ugh. Kelly had forgotten that she had told Mrs. Simmons about the party, but the spry old woman didn't forget a thing! "Well…" She must have hesitated for too long, and Mrs. Simmons jumped on it.

"That boy better be treating you right. I warned him the other day…"

"What? You warned him?"

"Yes. At our first book club meeting. I told him that you were special and that he better treat you right or some other man would."

Kelly threw her head back and laughed. "And what did he say to that?"

"He promised that he would."

"I don't know what it is, Mrs. Simmons, but with Damian, I feel like I'm constantly on a rollercoaster ride. First, we're up, then we're down… sometimes I think that I would rather ride the merry-go-round."

"Ha! Merry-go-rounds are boring. Rollercoasters are a lot more fun! Believe me."

Suddenly Kelly realized that she didn't know that much about Mrs. Simmons's personal life outside of their shared interest in romance novels. "Is that what your life was like with Mr. Simmons?" she ventured.

Mrs. Simmons's face lit up with a sweet smile. "We had our share of ups and downs, that's for sure, but I loved him right up until the day he died. Still do, as a matter of fact."

"I hope that I get to experience that kind of love someday," Kelly said wistfully.

"Perhaps you already have, but your Adonis is too mule-headed to admit it. Sometimes men need a swift kick in the…"

"Mrs. Simmons," Kelly warned, cutting her off just as a male customer walked in.

"Sorry dear," she said and wandered off to the romance section.

The man walked right up to the counter. "How can I help you?" Kelly asked, trying not to stare. He was shorter than Damian and leaner, and his eyes were the most extraordinary bluish-green color that she had ever seen. His light brown hair was close-cropped, and he sported a smattering of facial hair, but it was those eyes that really drew her in. He was exactly the type of man she would have been attracted to in the past. *Damn you, Damian, for spoiling me for any other man!*

"My name is Luke Donovan, and I'm here to pick up a special order."

"Oh, I spoke to you on the phone last week, when you placed the order. I'm Kelly," she said and reached over the counter to shake his hand. *Old habits die hard.*

Luke looked slightly perplexed, but he graciously shook her hand. "Nice to meet you," he said.

"Your book is right under the counter," Kelly said, and when she handed it to him, her surprise must have been evident. It was a romance novel that she had never heard of, with a rather racy cover. So, Damian wasn't the only guy to read romance after all!

"I don't usually read these types of books, but someone I know wrote it," he said proudly.

It might have been a lie, but for some reason, Kelly believed him. "I have to admit that I've never heard of Kate Stephens," she said, glancing down at the cover again.

"This is her first book, and it just came out a few weeks ago."

"Well, it looks…interesting. I hope you enjoy it."

Luke chuckled. "I think I need to pay you," he said, his bluish-green eyes sparkling.

"Oh, yeah. That's right. I don't know where my head is at today." Kelly quickly rang up his purchase and placed the book in a bag.

"Thanks a lot, Kelly," he said and then turned and strolled out the door.

"Have a good day," she called, but she doubted that he even heard her. The minute he stepped outside, he pulled the book out of the bag and stared at the cover as he walked over to his car. She watched him drive away with a smile on his face and idly wondered what his story was.

Just then, the phone rang, and Emma's name flashed on the display. "Hey, Em."

"Hey. Did he call you yet?"

"No. The jerk."

"Well, if it helps at all, he's avoiding Zack too. Zack's called him at least three times, but he hasn't answered."

"When I left for work this morning, his truck was already gone. I'd guess that he went to the shop, but who knows."

"How are you doing today?"

"Honestly, I'm all over the place. I'm angry and frustrated, but I want to see him, to talk to him. I thought things were going so well, but now it's like we took a giant step backward. I just don't understand what Damian and I have to do with *her*. Why would he let something that happened years ago come between us?"

"I wish I had the answers, Kell, but I guess you'll have to wait to hear it from him."

"Well, he can't avoid me forever. We live right across the parking lot from each other, for Pete's sake!"

"You could always hide behind a tree and ambush him when he comes home."

"I don't think I'll go that far, but it's not a bad idea! Oh, and get this. Some gorgeous guy came in the store today and bought a romance novel! A *romance* novel, Emma."

"Please tell me that you didn't exchange phone numbers."

"No, but in the past, I would have been all over that!"

"Oh, I know. So, what stopped you?"

"A certain pig-headed Greek man, that's who. Oh my God, Emma. What's happened to me?"

"You're in love. I hear it's been going around these days."

"Well, it's kind of hard to be in love when it's one-sided."

"Patience, Kell."

"*Not* my virtue."

They talked for a few more minutes about business matters and then hung up after Kelly promised to let Emma know if Damian contacted her and vice versa. Mrs. Simmons had left while Kelly was on the phone, so now the store was quiet again. Somehow, Kelly kept herself busy until closing time, and as she drove home, she wondered if Damian would be there and if she should confront him or continue to wait.

She was disappointed, but not surprised when she pulled into the parking lot and saw the empty space where his truck was supposed to be. While she went through the routine of eating dinner and cleaning up, she kept her ears open for the rumble of his Chevy, and she peeked out of her front window numerous times throughout the evening. When she crawled into bed that night, her anger had turned into concern, and she checked her phone for the umpteenth time before finally turning it off. Kelly decided that she couldn't take his silence anymore and that if she didn't hear from him tomorrow. she would hunt him down. Having made up her mind, she fell into a troubled sleep, and her head was so full of worrisome thoughts that no dreams would come to her that night.

The next morning, Kelly turned on her phone immediately, only to find a text that Emma had sent late the night before stating that they still hadn't heard from Damian. Kelly flung back the covers and hurried to the front window. Sure enough, his truck wasn't there, and now she questioned whether he had even come home the night before. She had slept so fitfully that surely she would have heard the loud rumble of his truck if he had come home. Now she was beyond worried, and she called Emma right away.

"Hey, Em. Since you're opening the store today, do you mind if I come in later? I can't take the waiting any longer. I want to drive over to Damian's shop and at least make sure he's ok before I kill him."

Emma giggled, but her voice was serious when she said, "That's a good idea. I think Zack's starting to get concerned too."

"Thanks. I'll let you know if I find him."

"Oh, and Kell? Take as long as you need. I'll be at the store all day, and then Brett's coming in this evening. If you don't make it in at all, I'll understand."

"Thanks, Em. I love you."

"I love you too."

I wish it were that easy to share the same sentiment with Damian, Kelly thought when she hung up.

Since she wasn't going to work, she threw on jeans, a sweatshirt, and a pair of sneakers. She put her hair up in a hasty ponytail, swiped on some lip balm, grabbed a jacket, and raced out the door. It was still early when she left, and as she drove north out of Clarkston, she noticed how brown everything had become over the past few weeks. The colorful leaves had already fallen and had long since been raked up, and the last truly warm days were behind them. She usually liked this time of year before winter closed in, but she had been so busy with work and with Damian that she hadn't fully appreciated the fall season. It struck her that today was the first of November, and Thanksgiving was only a few short weeks away. She and Damian had bought their plane tickets to Florida a couple of weeks back, but now, with all that had happened, would he still want to go?

Kelly's mom had called just a few days ago to confirm that they were coming and to express her interest in finally being able to meet the man that Kelly had been raving about. Now Kelly was left wondering if she would be boarding the plane alone, and her heart sank at the thought of it. Her heart sank even more when she pulled up in front of Jim's Custom Cars a few minutes later. There sat Jim's white truck with the auto shop's name printed on the sides, but Damian's truck was nowhere to be seen.

Kelly almost turned around and left, but Jim spotted her through the front window and waved her in. She figured that Damian wouldn't like the idea of her checking up on him like this, but she felt like she had no choice. She stepped out of the car, took a deep breath, and plastered on a smile as she approached the door. After all, there was no need for Jim to know that anything was amiss.

"Hello there," Jim said, his demeanor relaxed and friendly as always, although he looked surprised to see her.

"Hi, Jim. I just stopped by to see Damian. Is he off running an errand?"

Now Jim looked even more confused. "No. Didn't he tell you?"

"Tell me what?" Kelly asked, feeling more anxious by the minute.

Jim scratched the back of his neck and frowned. "I just assumed…"

"Just tell me. Please," she added.

"Well, it seemed like something was bothering him yesterday, and we got to talking, and he said he was thinking about getting away for a few days. So, I offered for him to stay at my cabin—up north."

Kelly's eyes grew wide, but she quickly adopted a neutral expression. "Where up north?"

"Just outside of West Branch."

"Huh."

"I take it he didn't mention it?"

Knowing Jim's character, he had asked out of concern, not nosiness, so Kelly decided to be straight with him. "No. I haven't heard from him for the past couple days, and I came here to make sure that he was all right."

"I assume that he's safely at the cabin, but the phone reception isn't very good up there, so that could be why you haven't heard from him."

Kelly appreciated what Jim was trying to do, but she shook her head. "I think he would have found a way to contact me if he had really wanted to."

Jim gave her an empathetic smile. "Look. It's probably none of my business, but I really like you two. Damian is like the son I never had, and in the short time that I've known you, I can tell that you're good for him. I'd be willing to give you the address of my cabin if you're interested."

His offer hung out there for a minute or two as Kelly mulled it over. On one hand, Damian might be angry that she had infringed on his privacy, but on the other hand…

"Yes, Jim. I would like that very much."

"Now, Damian said he only planned on staying for a few days, so I hope you don't drive all the way there for nothing," Jim said as he jotted down the address.

"I have a feeling that he'll still be there. Besides, West Branch is only two hours away. If nothing else, it will be a pretty drive."

Jim handed her the slip of paper. "Well, I hope everything works out for you two. Damian may not be one to express his feelings easily, but for what it's worth, your name comes up a lot around here. Don't tell him I said that though!"

Kelly genuinely laughed for the first time in two days. "Thanks. Jim. I really appreciate this."

"Go on now. Don't waste your time talking to an old-timer like me. Go get your man."

"I will," she said, and then she left, fueled with determination and optimism once again.

"Damian Kostas—ready or not, here I come!"

Chapter 26

The first thing that Kelly did when she turned out of the parking lot was to call Emma.

"Did you talk to him? What did he say?" Emma asked in a rush.

"He wasn't there, but get this, he went Up North. Apparently, Jim owns a cabin near West Branch, and he loaned it to Damian for a few days."

"So, let me guess, you're on your way to West Branch."

"Yes, assuming my boss will let me have a couple of days off," Kelly said.

"Well, luckily you have an excellent boss!"

"Do you think it's a mistake, Em? What if Damian doesn't want to see me?"

"He can't hide forever, Kell. Being alone together without any outside distractions is probably just what you two need. You'll see."

"I hope you're right. Anyway, I'll give you a call when I'm on my way home, and tell Zack not to worry."

"I'll tell him, but it won't do any good. Worrying is his second job!"

About an hour into her drive, Kelly realized that she didn't have any clothes or toiletries with her, but maybe she wouldn't even need them. Damian could already be on his way home, or they could talk and then drive back home in the evening. Either way, she decided that there were much bigger concerns than not having a toothbrush! For the remainder of the drive, Kelly focused on the road and the scenery, and soon the flat landscape gave way to gently rolling hills and farmlands. It was amazing how quickly one could travel outside of the cities and suburbs, into the Michigan wilderness, and she welcomed it. Hadn't she thought not long ago about wanting to travel Up North? Thanks to Damian, she'd gotten her wish, even though these were less than ideal circumstances.

Kelly kept driving until she came to the West Branch exit, where she stopped for gas and bought a sandwich and a soda. She figured she'd need her energy to confront Damian, and who knew if he had any food at the cabin. She ate and drank while she followed Jim's directions to the cabin. West Branch was a typical Up North town that contained a smattering of shops and restaurants before giving way to widespread homes and the occasional party store. Kelly remembered what Damian had said about getting lost in the mountains, and even though there weren't any mountains here, there were plenty of woods to get lost in.

The directions took her to Clear Lake, and she followed the gravel road around the lake until she spotted Damian's truck parked in front of a tiny log cabin.

This is it. The moment of truth, Kelly thought when she pulled up and shut off her engine. She gathered her courage as she walked up to the front door, took a deep breath, and then knocked. The sound of her knuckles against the wood exploded in her ears compared to the peacefulness around her. Seconds later, Damian opened the door, and she felt like it had been years since she'd seen him last. He looked like he belonged in the rugged surroundings, given his torn jeans, sweatshirt imprinted with the words "Up North," and his two-day beard growth. Neither of them spoke for a long minute, and then they both began at once.

"What are you…?"

"I came to…"

Damian stepped aside and motioned for her to come in. As she brushed past him, she caught the scent of body wash and warm male, and she wanted to fling herself into his arms. Instead, she walked into the dimly lit room and glanced around. It was a typical cabin like many she had stayed in as a child when she had travelled Up North with her parents. Knotty pine walls, scuffed wood floors, and framed prints of bears and lake scenes made up the décor in the sparsely furnished space. It was clean, charming, and rustic, the perfect getaway for a man with simple tastes. Kelly perched herself on the edge of the loveseat while Damian took the chair across from her.

They eyed each other for a few beats before Damian started again. "Ladies first," he said, giving her the floor.

Kelly mentally thumped herself on the head for not having thought ahead about what she would say to him. Surely, that was something that Emma would have done, but Kelly had always been more spontaneous, thus the reason that she was sitting in front of him at that moment. She usually went with her instincts and trusted herself to say whatever was in her heart. Now was no different.

"Why did you react so strongly to Amanda at the Halloween party? And why did you run away instead of talking to me?"

Damian cleared his throat and ran his hands through his already disheveled hair. "God, Kell. There's so much I want to say to you…"

"Well, start talking. I didn't drive all the way up here to play Scrabble!"

Damian's loud laugh filled the room, and his shoulders visibly relaxed. "Good thing, because there's nothing in this place."

"Except you," she said softly.

"Except us," he corrected.

There went the crackle in the air again, but Kelly was not to be deterred. "Talk," she demanded.

"Ok. In answer to your first question, I think that seeing Amanda brought back a lot of the feelings that I had tramped down, and they just came spewing out. When she broke off our engagement, she gave me some really lame excuse about us not having mutual goals. What I translated that to mean is that she was afraid that I wasn't going to amount to much. I worked at a car shop. I didn't go to college. I didn't have my life perfectly mapped out. I think that she was afraid that I couldn't give her the lifestyle that she wanted."

"And that made you feel inadequate," Kelly finished.

"I guess so. Yes."

"Did you try to talk to her about it at the time?"

"I tried calling her a couple of times after the break-up, but she wouldn't take my calls. It wasn't long after that that I left for California."

The puzzle pieces were beginning to fall into place, but she still had a lot of questions. "Didn't Amanda plan on working after you were married? She went to college. Didn't she expect to help out financially?"

"We never really discussed the particulars. We were young, we were in love, or so I thought, and I believed that we would figure everything out. Stupid, right?"

Kelly ignored his question because, frankly, she didn't want to think about Damian being in love with someone else. "So, you were hurt. I get that. But to leave your home and your family? To start over on the opposite side of the country? That, I don't get."

"Maybe that's because you've never been in love," Damian said.

Kelly froze. *Not until now*, she thought, realizing that he spoke the truth.

"Anyway, it was mostly a matter of pride. I couldn't face the pitying stares of my family and friends. I didn't want to have to explain to people why we broke up. What could I say? That she dumped me because I wasn't good enough? That she didn't have enough faith in me to make something of myself?"

Kelly reached her hand out to touch him, but he rose from the chair abruptly and started pacing. "You don't understand, Kell. A man wants to feel like he can provide for his woman, even if he doesn't really have to. Just like the other day, when you said that you didn't need to be taken care of. That you make your own money. Even though I know that, it doesn't stop me from wanting to take care of you. Don't you see?"

Kelly stood now too, and she started to walk toward him, but he held up his hand to stop her. "Don't you know that when you love someone, you want to give them everything? Everything that they want and everything that they deserve."

Her throat caught, but she managed to say, "And don't you know that when you love someone, you're willing to work *with* them to make that happen? Furthermore, when you love someone, what you really want is their heart."

"You already have that," he said, right before she flung herself into his arms.

He held her so tight that she thought she would burst, and she was bursting—with love. Damian let her go just long enough to gaze into her watery eyes and to state clearly, "I love you, Kelly. I love you twice as much as when I knew you before. No, twice doesn't even begin to cover it."

She smiled so wide that her cheeks hurt. "I love you too, Damian, but I need you to do me a favor."

"What's that?" he asked as he scooped her up into his powerful arms.

"Don't *ever* run away from me again. If there's a problem, we stay and work it out. Got it?"

"Got it," he said and carried her down the short hall to the bedroom. "Right now, I'd like to give you something in addition to my heart…"

"I want *that* too," she said.

Damian set her down in the bedroom in front of the window that overlooked the lake, and she looked out while he cleared the bed of his discarded clothes. A few minutes later, he came up behind her and slid his arms around her waist.

"It's beautiful here," she whispered.

"You're beautiful," he said and dipped his head into her neck.

Kelly tilted her head to one side to give him better access and pushed her backside against his pelvis.

"You're all that I've thought of since I came here," he said, his voice thick with desire.

She reached her arm back and wound it around his neck. "I missed you," she said. "I missed us."

Damian continued ravaging her neck as his hands slid up the front of her sweatshirt and cupped her breasts.

She moaned, and he hadn't even touched her bare skin yet.

"I want you so much, Kell. I never stop wanting you."

He moved his hands away from her breasts, and she felt an instant chill as he took a step back. She was about to ask what he was doing, but her head was covered by her sweatshirt as it was being pulled off. Her skin broke out in goosebumps, but she wasn't sure if it was because of the cold temperature in the room or if it was from the anticipation of what came next. When Damian unhooked her bra and was about to slip it off, she recovered enough to say, "We're right in front of the window."

"Who cares? No one can see us, and even if they could…"

Kelly sucked in a breath at his implication. In the past, they'd discussed some of their secret fantasies, and one of hers had to do with being seen having sex. She always thought of it as a fantasy though, and in reality, she wasn't quite so brave.

Damian sensed her hesitation. "We're in the middle of nowhere, Kell. Look out the window and tell me what you see."

She did as he asked and gasped as her bra hit the floor. "I see…" Now his large, work-toughened hands were kneading her bare breasts, and it was hard to concentrate.

"Tell me," he demanded, his fingers pinching her nipples, gently at first and then with more vigor.

"Just…the…lake," she said in between pants.

"And nobody's on it, right?" he said as his hands trailed down her abdomen to the button of her jeans.

"Right," she said, her body taut with need.

Damian unbuttoned and unzipped her jeans, hooked his thumbs into her panties, and slid them both down her legs.

Another whoosh of cool air hit her warm body, and she shivered.

"You cold?" he asked as he rose back up behind her, trailing his fingers up the inside of her thighs.

"No," she said, although she wasn't really cognizant of what she was saying at that point.

When Damian had returned to his full height behind her, he reached his right hand around and cupped her center.

"Ohhh," she moaned.

"No one can see us or hear us, so feel free to scream out my name when you come." With that, Damian inserted a finger deep inside her and used his thumb to stroke her on the outside.

Kelly slapped her palms against the window for support, even though Damian held her firmly in his grasp. Her head fell back against his shoulder, and she gave in to the sensations: his fingers warm and slightly rough, fondling her, probing her; his moist lips on the sensitive part of her neck; his erection pressing into her back through his jeans. While his right hand worked her below, his left hand played with her nipple, and the combination was too much. She tipped over the edge in no time, gyrating her hips into his hand, and then, as he had suggested, she yelled out his name.

Damian kept his hand in place until she floated back down to earth and she had regained her breath. Of all the things that they had done with and to each other, Kelly thought that this might have been one of their most erotic moments. Her legs felt wobbly as she turned in his arms to face him.

"You good?" he asked, even though his smug expression said he already knew the answer.

"I'm great," she replied and kissed his smiling lips.

Damian was about to back them up toward the bed, but she shook her head. "Oh no. If I had to stand in front of the window, then so do you."

He arched his eyebrows at her but stood still, waiting to see what she would do. When she put her hands on the button of his jeans, he whipped off his sweatshirt, presumably to save time. Kelly wet her lips at the sight of his bare chest but went back to work removing his jeans. When his erection sprang free, she wrapped her hands around him and watched his reaction with extreme satisfaction. When she dropped to her knees on the bearskin rug, he groaned.

"You can either look out the window or watch me," she offered, and then she brought the tip of his swollen manhood to her mouth.

Damian chose to watch her, and she gave him quite the show, alternating between licking him like a popsicle and drawing him into her mouth as far as she could take him. His masculine sounds of pleasure filled the room, and before long, he gave her the warning call.

"KELLLLL…"

She nodded, and that was all it took. When his body stopped convulsing, she let go and slowly stood up, unsure if her legs would support her.

Damian immediately wrapped his arms around her and lifted her up, placing her gently on the bed and crawling in next to her. "That was…"

"Fantastic? Spectacular? Stupendous?" she suggested, giggling.

"All of the above," he said, covering them with a plaid blanket.

Kelly snuggled against him and soaked up his warmth. "Is the heat turned on in here?"

Damian chuckled. Finding an acceptable temperature for both of them was an ongoing battle. No matter if they were in each other's apartments or vehicles, they were constantly fighting over the thermostat. "It's set to sixty!"

"Well, it feels more like forty."

"I'll keep you warm," he said gruffly and hauled her in closer.

She idly traced the pattern of his tattoo and then softly whispered, "I love you, Damian."

He gave her a squeeze and smiled broadly. "I love you too, princess."

Chapter 27

They were spooned together, naked, when his hands began to move. He started at her shoulder, brushing just the pads of his fingers down her arm, into the dip of her waist, over her curvy hip, and along her outer thigh. He traced the same path in reverse and repeated the pattern a few more times.

Next, he gathered the bulk of her long hair in one hand and moved it aside so that he could kiss the back of her neck, but he didn't stop there. Following the ridge of her spine, he blazed a trail of soft, warm kisses down her back, all the way to the curve of her butt and back up again.

She felt herself go damp and squeezed her legs tightly together to stave off her reaction. This was only a dream after all. But wait a minute, what was that? The same hand that had been tantalizing her a minute ago had curled around to the front, and it gently stroked her damp folds.

Suddenly Kelly jerked awake and realized that she hadn't been dreaming after all. Damian chuckled against her neck, letting her know that what she had felt was very real.

"Wake up, sleepyhead," he said while continuing to fondle her.

"I can't believe I fell asleep," she mumbled, distracted by what he was doing to her.

"I did too, but only for a few minutes. You slept for half an hour."

Since they'd been talking, Kelly felt Damian grow hard against her back, and she purposely wriggled against him. "This is some wake-up call," she said.

"Um-hmm. I wouldn't mind waking up like this every day."

His words hung in the air for a minute as Kelly soaked up his admission. Suddenly she flipped herself over to face him, bringing a halt to his ministrations. She wrapped her arms around his neck and scooted closer so that they were touching from head to toe. "I love this," she said.

"I love you," he volleyed before his lips claimed hers in a heated kiss.

Their passion flared, as always, and Kelly felt like she couldn't get close enough. She broke away from him and panted, "Condom?"

"In my toiletries bag."

"Go get it," she demanded.

Damian scrambled off the bed in such a rush that she had to laugh. She saw a flash of his muscled backside whiz by as he raced to the bathroom. When he returned, she was on her knees, and she patted the mattress where she wanted him to lay.

Damian's sexy smile lit up the room. "So, you're in charge, huh?"

"Yep," she replied. This was another little game they liked to play—taking turns telling the other what to do. It usually didn't take long before Kelly relinquished her role as the boss though. She had to admit that she preferred when Damian took control. But for now, she waited for him to get comfortable, and then she straddled him.

Kelly slid her core up and down the rigid line of his manhood, teasing him (and herself too), until she glanced up to see Damian watching her through hooded eyes.

"Oh yeah," he groaned, reaching up to fondle her breasts.

Suddenly, Kelly realized that she didn't feel cold anymore, and she was about to get a whole lot warmer! She lifted her hips up and positioned his erection at her entrance. Then, with Damian's hands gripping her waist, she slowly slid down onto him, and when he was fully inserted, she stretched her entire body length against his.

For a moment, neither of them moved, and it was the most exquisite feeling on earth. Kelly's eyes were glossy as she stared into his. She felt as if they were truly seeing each other for the very first time. All of their love, all of their "quirks," all of their insecurities were now laid bare, and she'd never felt closer to him.

Damian reached up and brushed her hair away from her face before gently kissing the tip of her nose and then her lips. Her man of few words had clammed up, but this time, she could see what he was feeling, and she didn't need him to tell her.

Seconds later, they began to move, and it was like a match had been lit. The quiet spell was broken, and their movements became frenzied, their momentum building. Heat encompassed their bodies, every nerve ending on fire, until they exploded, tightening and clenching around each other, milking each other of every ounce of energy until they were completely drained.

Afterward, they were still again until the loud rumble of Kelly's belly broke the silence. "Oops," she said and giggled.

Damian smiled down at her. "I think I need to feed you."

"Do you have any food here?"

"No, we'll have to go out. Let me clean up, and I'll be right back." They parted, somewhat reluctantly, and Kelly admired his backside again as he padded out of the room. While he was gone, she hurriedly donned her clothes, and she was standing on the bearskin rug when he returned—still naked.

"I left my clothes in here," he explained, grinning unabashedly.

"Is this thing for real?" Kelly asked as she rubbed her socked feet against the rug.

Damian's head was covered by his sweatshirt, but his bottom half was still naked. "I was just inside of you, babe. Of course it's real!" came his muffled response.

"Not that! I'm talking about this rug."

"Oh," he said drily while he pulled up his jeans. "Probably. Jim's a hunter, so I wouldn't be surprised. You ready to go?"

"Yes and no," she said, meeting his eyes. "Everything's been so wonderful, I hate to leave this place."

"We're only leaving to eat, Kell, and then we'll come right back."

She perked up. "So, we're staying here tonight?"

"Hell yeah. I didn't plan on leaving until tomorrow anyway, and I don't want you driving home in the dark."

Kelly glanced out the window and noticed that it was already dusk. Now that it was November, the days were getting shorter, and soon winter would arrive. "Good idea," she said and accepted his hand as he led her from the room.

A few minutes later, they were in his truck, bumping down the gravel road. "If I'm going to stay tonight, I'll need to stop at a store after dinner and get a few things," Kelly said.

"Like what?"

"Like fresh underwear and a toothbrush."

Damian tilted his head back and let out a loud chortle. "It's only *one* night, Kell," he said.

"Still, I'm not wearing the same underwear two days in a row! That's just gross. And I absolutely have to have a toothbrush."

Damian chuckled some more. "Why can't you just use mine?"

"What, your underwear or your toothbrush?"

"My toothbrush." When she scrunched up her face, he added, "Your mouth was on my…"

Kelly held up her hand. "I know, I know, but that's not as bad as using somebody's toothbrush."

"I will never understand women."

"Good thing you don't have to, because, from now on, you only have to understand *one* woman, me!"

"Point taken," he said and reached over to clasp her hand. "Ok. After dinner, we'll stop at a store where you can buy underwear and a toothbrush."

"Oh, and while we're there, I might as well buy deodorant too."

Damian shot her a sideways glance, but he didn't argue.

"Well, I didn't come prepared," she explained. "I was in such a hurry to get to you that I didn't take the time to pack a bag. Plus, I wasn't sure that you'd even want me to stay."

Damian swallowed hard. "Man, I was such a jerk. I'm so sorry, Kelly."

Kelly squeezed his hand. "Let's just put it behind us, ok? From now on, let's promise to talk things out, no matter what. No more running off to cabins in the woods, or to California, or to Alaska, or anyplace else, ok?"

"I promise," he said firmly.

They rode in silence for a while after that while continuing to hold hands. As they neared the commercial section of West Branch, Damian asked her what she'd like to eat.

"A big, juicy steak," she responded immediately. "With fries and a side salad. On second thought, skip the salad. Oh, and an ice-cold beer!"

"That's my girl!" he said proudly.

When Damian pulled into the parking lot of Lumberjack Food & Spirits, Kelly smiled. "We're definitely Up North," she said as they walked into the restaurant. The atmosphere was warm and rustic, with the lodge-style décor that was typical of many restaurants in this part of the state.

"I ate here last night, and the food was really good," Damian said.

"I believe you. Everything looks delicious."

They demolished their steak dinners in no time, but declined the waitress's offer of dessert.

"We can have dessert when we get back to the cabin," Damian said.

Kelly knew that he wasn't talking about food, and the thought made her tingle all over. "But first, we have to stop at the store," she reminded him.

They ended up at Walmart, which was just down the street from the restaurant. "Let me grab a shopping cart, just in case," Kelly said.

Damian rolled his eyes, but he simply followed along as she went up and down the aisles, adding things to the cart. Kelly took some time selecting the requisite toothbrush and trial sizes of body wash, shampoo, and deodorant. Once they got to the "intimates" department, Damian perked up considerably. "How about if I pick out your underwear?" he suggested.

The poor man was so bored that she didn't have the heart to argue. He proceeded to make a great show of holding up various lingerie items to see how they would look on her, and they received more than a few curious glances from nearby shoppers. After he had added three pairs of provocative panties, two see-through bras, and a silky red baby-doll set to the cart, Kelly put her hands on her hips in mock exasperation.

"All this for only *one* night?" she chided.

"We only have one more night here, but we're going to have a lot of other nights together. I'm just stocking up."

No argument there! "How about if we check out and go back to the cabin?" she said.

"I thought you'd never ask."

They were mostly quiet on the drive back, each lost in their own thoughts yet hopefully on the same page. Kelly couldn't wait to be alone with Damian again, snuggled up under the warm comforter with no distractions. Emma had been right. This impromptu getaway had turned out to be the best thing for them. Not that there wouldn't be any more bumps in the road, but Kelly felt confident that their future looked much brighter. She had gained a much better understanding of the man beside her, and as long as he didn't retreat from her again, they would be ok.

When they reached the cabin, Damian hauled in the bags containing Kelly's overnight necessities and placed them on the kitchen counter. They had left one lamp on, which cast a dim glow in the dark room. Damian closed the curtains in the kitchen and living room, which were basically one and the same, while Kelly kicked off her shoes and took a seat on the sofa. He tried to hide his look of surprise when he came to sit beside her.

"I thought we could talk a little more first," she explained. "But would you mind putting the heat up? It's freezing in here!"

Damian chuckled as he heaved himself off the couch and went to adjust the thermostat on the wall. "It'll be warmer in a few minutes," he said. He sat back down and flung an arm over her shoulder, tucking her in close to his side. "In the meantime, you can share my body heat."

"Thanks," she said, leaning her head on his broad shoulder.

"So, what did you want to talk about? I could tell that there was something on your mind when we were driving."

"There were a lot of things on my mind. All good," she added when she noticed his look of concern.

Damian kissed the top of her head. "That's a relief."

She traced the outline of the words "Up North" on his sweatshirt, since she couldn't get to his tattoo, and began to speak. "Have I ever told you how proud I am of you?"

Damian had been playing with a strand of her hair, and now he stilled. "Proud?"

"Um-hmm. Owning your own business is a huge undertaking. I know firsthand from working with Emma. A business owner never truly has time off. Even when she's not at the bookstore, Emma is constantly working to keep her business running smoothly."

"You deserve some of the credit for that too," he said.

"I appreciate the compliment, but we're talking about you. I just want you to know that I really respect what you're doing, and I'm confident that your shop will be a success." She glanced up at him then, and even though his face was in the shadows, she saw him swallow hard.

"Thanks, Kell," he said, his voice full of emotion. "That means a lot to me."

"Also, about Amanda, I've known other women like her, women who are more concerned with status and the size of their bank account than more important things like love and family. Please don't ever mistake me for one of those women."

Damian put a finger beneath her chin and tilted her face up. "No, baby. I don't think of you like that."

"Well, the other day, when I mentioned wanting certain things…"

Damian cupped her face with both hands and shook his head vehemently. "There was nothing wrong with what you said, Kell. It was my reaction that was wrong."

Kelly had been trying hard to hold back her tears, but one slipped out and made a slow slide down her cheek.

"Oh, baby. Please don't cry. I love you. Please."

Kelly swiped the tear away, but another one took its place. "I love you too, Damian. And I need you to believe that it's *you* I love and not what you can give me."

"I do know. I can see it in your eyes and in your smile. I can feel it every time you touch me. I just don't understand how I got this lucky. How someone so beautiful, and strong, and intelligent could love someone like me."

Does he still not get it? Kelly had tried telling him with words, but now it was time for a new tactic, one that her man of action would surely understand. "Let me show you. Take me to bed, Damian."

And he did.

Chapter 28

Kelly spent most of the night showing Damian how much she loved him, interspersed with a few short hours of shut-eye. It seemed like just when she was getting into a deep sleep mode, Damian would move or touch her in some way, and she'd become wide awake. And then she would touch him, and they'd end up making love again. At some point, in the wee hours of the morning, they collapsed, and Kelly didn't rouse again until her nostrils were filled with a tantalizing scent.

"Rise and shine, princess. Your breakfast is here."

Kelly's eyes popped open, and she saw that Damian was waving a box of donuts under her nose. She stretched and then threw off the covers before she remembered that she was naked. She hadn't bought any pajamas, nor could they be bothered to put on any clothes last night.

Damian gave her a sultry smile, set the donut box on the bed, and turned around to rifle through his duffle bag. "Here. Throw this on," he said and handed her one of his long-sleeved t-shirts with a car logo on it.

"Is that coffee I smell too?" Kelly asked as she hurriedly donned the shirt.

"Yes, ma'am."

She stood up on the bed and flung her arms around his neck, peppering him with kisses. "Have I told you how much I love you?"

"You're just saying that now because I delivered your breakfast," he teased, and then he lifted her off of the bed. "Let's eat. I'm starved."

A tall, steaming cup of coffee awaited her at the small oak dining table, and Kelly did a little dance of joy before plopping down in a chair.

"Wow! You're unusually perky this morning," Damian said as he sat down beside her.

"Well, why shouldn't I be? I'm with the man I love in a cabin in the woods, and we have donuts! It doesn't get much better than that."

Damian gave her a satisfied grin before biting into an oversized cinnamon roll. "I hate to say this, but we should probably get going pretty soon. I told Jim that I'd be back today, and if we leave soon, I could still get a few hours of work in."

"I know. I need to get back to work too."

"Don't worry, Kell. This won't be our only getaway."

She nodded and drained the rest of the coffee while she looked out over the lake one last time. It wasn't a five-star hotel with all the amenities, but Kelly would never forget this place. Afraid that she was getting too sappy, she changed the subject. "Let's take a shower, and then we'll get on the road."

While Damian cleared the table, Kelly gathered up her new underwear and toiletries, and they went into the bathroom together. "Now, if you're really serious about leaving, there can be no shower sex. We simply wash and get out," she instructed.

"I'll try to restrain myself," he said.

Kelly turned her back to him and reached into the shower stall to turn on the water and adjust the temperature. She then went about lining up her products neatly on the shelf inside the stall. During that time, she heard the thud of Damian's clothes hitting the floor, but she didn't turn around. With her back still to him, she removed his t-shirt, folded it neatly, and placed it on the bathroom counter. Satisfied that the water temperature was to her liking, she stepped inside and immediately tipped her head back into the warm spray. Her eyes were closed when she heard Damian come in, and after her hair was thoroughly wet, she opened her eyes.

Damian was practically on top of her in the tiny stall, and his eyes shone with an intoxicating mix of desire and adoration. She moved her eyes downward, over his muscular chest and tight abs, until she was met with absolute proof of his desire for her. It was enough to make Kelly want to break her own rule, and she started to reach for him…

Damian waggled his index finger in front of her face and said, "You said no shower sex, remember?" And with that, he reached behind her for the bottle of shampoo.

Kelly frowned. "But rules are meant to be broken," she whined.

He simply ignored her and proceeded to suds up his thick crop of dark hair.

To avoid temptation, Kelly turned her back on him again and went about lathering up her own hair, taking extra time to massage the shampoo into her scalp. Next, she poured some strawberry-scented body wash onto her new body pouf and started cleansing herself, moving the pouf in slow circles, starting at her neck and shoulders and working her way down. When she bent over to reach her cherry red painted toes, Damian groaned, but she was determined to ignore him. She may have purposely bumped into him once or twice, and she was assured that his desire for her hadn't waned.

"All set?" she asked after she had finished rinsing.

Damian was so close that she felt his body heat against her damp back.

"For now," he muttered.

Kelly stepped out first and wrapped herself in a towel before handing one to him. *Oh, the games we play*, she thought as she took her sweet time drying herself off. Damian stood next to her in front of the bathroom counter that had a lighted mirror above it. She kept glancing at him in the mirror while he dried off too, but anytime their eyes met, she quickly looked away. Once she was completely dry, she had no choice but to return the towel to the rack, and she took her time arranging it just so, fully aware that Damian's eyes bored into her.

When she turned around, he was naked, his own towel lying in a puddle at his feet. Her eyes darted to the bathroom counter where she had left her pile of clothes, but they were no longer there.

She peered around the hulking man before her and spied them lying neatly on top of the closed toilet lid. Kelly put her hands on her hips and tried to summon a look of reproach as Damian stalked toward her.

"I thought we said no sex this morning," she said, reading the intent in his eyes.

"No. *You* said no shower sex. We're out of the shower now."

The cat and mouse game was up. Damian swooped her up in his arms and set her bare butt on the bathroom counter.

"Here?" She started to protest, but Damian had spread her legs wide and was standing in between them, rubbing himself against her center.

There was no slow and sensual lead-up this time. There was only raw passion, intense heat, and insistence. He took her hard and fast, and sometimes, like now, that was just the way she liked it. He had retrieved a condom from his jeans pocket and had it on in a flash, and afterwards, it dawned on her that he had planned this all along.

After Damian withdrew and cleaned them both off, he lifted her off the counter. He picked up his sports watch from atop his pile of clothes and said, "Look at that. We're still on schedule!"

Kelly playfully swatted his arm and started to get dressed. "You planned that whole thing," she accused.

Damian smirked at her. "It's always good to be prepared," he said.

They spent the next twenty minutes tidying up the cabin and packing up their belongings. When they were done, they stood at the front door together and looked around one last time.

"I really loved it here," Kelly said wistfully.

"I really loved *you* here," Damian replied.

Kelly reached up on her tiptoes and kissed him softly before they turned and walked away.

"Don't forget to call Zack on your way home. He was really worried about you," Kelly said after Damian had loaded up their bags.

"When will my brother realize that I'm not a little kid anymore?"

"You'll always be his little brother, Damian. He loves you, and so do I."

Damian leaned his head into her car window and kissed her goodbye. "I love you too. Be careful driving."

"You'll be right behind me, won't you?"

"Always," he said and patted the roof of her car.

Kelly beamed at him and then slowly drove away. Seconds later, she glanced in her rearview mirror, and there he was, as promised, beaming right back at her.

Kelly waited until they were on the expressway headed south to Clarkston before she used the Bluetooth to call Emma. As she expected, Emma answered right away.

"Where are you? Did you find Damian? Are you two ok?"

"Slow down, Em. You sound like Alex." Mrs. Kostas was notorious for firing off questions in rapid succession without waiting for the answers.

"Well, I am part of the family now, or almost."

With all the recent hub-bub, Kelly had almost forgotten that Emma's wedding was just around the corner. "Yes, we're ok. We're better than ok. We're terrific," she said, glancing in her rearview mirror for the umpteenth time since they had left the cabin. Sure enough, Damian was right behind her, and she saw his mouth moving, so he was probably talking to Zack.

"Whew! Am I glad to hear that!"

"Emma soon-to-be Kostas, are you relieved because you thought that Damian and I might ruin your wedding or because you're truly happy for us?"

Emma giggled. "Maybe a little bit of both," she admitted. "Anyway, tell me everything. Or at least, almost everything."

As close as they were, and as much as they shared, Kelly and Emma had an unspoken agreement that they would always keep a few things to themselves, so Kelly gave her an edited version of what had transpired at the cabin but made sure to include some of the good parts. When Kelly shared that she and Damian had exchanged the "L-word," Emma whooped and hollered.

"Are you at the store right now?" Kelly asked.

"Yes, but nobody's here at the moment."

"Thank God."

"So, what's next for you two?"

"Well, we're leaving for Florida in a couple weeks, and then your wedding is after that."

"That's not exactly what I meant," Emma said, "but ok."

"Oh, you meant about the future, future?"

"Yes, but you don't have to answer, Kell. I just want you to be happy."

"You know what? We don't have everything mapped out, to borrow Damian's words, but I am happy. Very happy." Kelly glanced in the rearview mirror again, and Damian waved at her.

"Has Damian had a chance to call Zack yet? He's been driving me nuts for two days!"

Kelly laughed. "Yes. As a matter of fact, he's on the phone with Zack right now."

"Good. While I have you on the phone, we need to go over a few business items. Namely, the next book club meeting. Mrs. Simmons was in earlier today, and she asked if you had set a date yet."

"No, but that's the first thing on my agenda when I get back. I need to stop by my apartment to change, but I thought I'd come in to work after that."

"Sounds good. I'm leaving soon, but Brett will be here, so you should be able to get your work done."

"Em? Before I forget, are you sure you don't want a bachelorette party? There's still time to get a few of our friends together for a ladies' night out."

"You know what? I'd rather hang out with my best girlfriend, kind of like we used to do before these two overbearing yet undoubtedly gorgeous Greek men came into our lives."

"Sounds good to me! Movie night at my apartment?"

"Yes, and Zack can hang out with Damian that night. I'll ask my parents to babysit."

"It's a date!"

"Do you think Damian will mind? He might not want to be apart from you now that you're officially 'in love.'"

"I'm sure he won't mind. He'll probably be glad to spend some one-on-one time with his brother."

"Oh no. Do I have to?" Damian complained.

Kelly and Damian were in her apartment after work that evening, and she had just broken the news about ladies' night. "I can't believe you wouldn't want to spend some good quality time with your brother!"

"It's just that his idea of a good time differs from mine."

"How so?"

"For example, I could sit and watch a game and not say a word, while he would sit there and talk the entire time! The man's exhausting."

Kelly giggled. "Maybe you two could play cards or something. Don't you have some poker buddies?"

Damian scowled. "I hate playing games. Haven't we already established that?"

"Ok. So, why don't you watch an X-rated movie? Isn't that what guys do at bachelor parties?"

"First of all, I'm not interested in watching porn with my brother. Second, a bachelor party is usually made up of more than two people, and there might even be strippers. Hmm…"

"Oh no you don't. You and Zack should just drink a few beers and watch a gangster movie or something."

"What about you and Emma? What will you two be doing that evening?"

"We're going to make frozen strawberry daiquiris and watch a romantic movie."

They were sitting next to each other on the couch, and Damian got that gleam in his eye. "Will there be a pillow fight?"

"Yes. Yes, there will be. And it starts right now!" Kelly reached behind her for the throw pillow that she had been resting against and flung it at Damian before he could react. This set off a retaliation whereby he pinned her to the couch and pummeled her with said pillow gently yet repeatedly until she cried "uncle."

Damian continued to hold her arms down while she caught her breath. "The truth is that I hate the thought of being away from you for even one night," he said.

Kelly thought about all the time they had spent apart in the past and sent up a silent thank you to God for bringing Damian back into her life. "We don't have to be apart all night. Emma will want to leave at a reasonable time to get back to her girls, and Zack will too. You can come over after they leave."

Damian's features instantly relaxed, and he bent down to kiss her. She opened her mouth wider to accept his tongue, and the match was lit. Kelly tried to keep track of how many times he said "I love you" between kisses, but she lost count somewhere around twenty. After that, it was hard to keep track of anything else.

Chapter 29

Kelly's week was filled up with work, both at the bookstore and at Damian's shop, followed by evenings spent at either her apartment or his. If their neighbors didn't know that they were an "item" before, they certainly did now, what with all the traipsing back and forth across the parking lot.

Kelly set up the next book club meeting for the second Friday in December, and she didn't forget about Damian's offer to be a participant. When she sent an email to the ladies in the group asking for their opinion, the response was an overwhelming yes, they would love to hear a man's perspective at the next meeting. When Kelly reminded Damian of his offer, he first pretended to have forgotten, and then he tried to back out of it.

"But I told all the ladies you'd be there," Kelly said, glaring at him.

Damian smoothed his index finger over her furrowed brow. "I must have agreed to that in the heat of passion," he said. "I probably didn't even realize what I was saying."

"As I recall, we were fully clothed at the time. But our 'passion' will be put on hold unless you do this for me."

Damian chuckled and threw up his arms. "Ok, ok. I'll do it."

There were no complaints after that.

On Saturday evening after work, Kelly donned her MSU sweatpants and a matching hoodie. She put her long hair up in a high ponytail and started to wipe the makeup off her face, but then she decided against it. It was movie night for her and Emma, but she planned on seeing Damian later, so she kept her "face on." Damian had told her countless times that he thought she was beautiful au naturel, but Kelly always felt a little better with a touch of makeup.

Emma showed up promptly at seven o'clock bearing two grocery bags full of snacks and frozen daiquiri mix. When Kelly opened the door for her, she glanced across the street and spotted Zack jogging up the stairs to Damian's apartment. Damian leaned casually against his open door, with his hands stuffed in his jeans pockets, and Kelly swore she could see him roll his eyes from across the street.

"Have fun, ladies," Zack called before disappearing into Damian's apartment. Kelly gave Damian a thumbs up before she ushered Emma inside and firmly closed the door.

"Zack was really looking forward to tonight," Emma said as she unpacked the bags.

"Yeah? Damian too." Kelly said with her fingers crossed behind her back. *A little white lie never hurt, right?*

"So, what all did you bring? This looks like enough food for the entire Kostas family," Kelly teased.

Emma giggled. "I really am adopting some of their habits, aren't I?"

"Yes, you are."

"Well, get used to it, because you might be part of the family someday too."

Emma had been making more and more references like that, and they always made Kelly feel slightly squeamish. Not because she didn't want a future with Damian, but because she was afraid to be too hopeful. She was actually content with the way things were between them right now, and she tried not to look too far ahead.

"Zack mentioned something about Damian looking at a house the other day…" Emma said, but she stopped talking when she saw the shock on Kelly's face.

"A house?"

"Yeah. You know, those rectangular things with windows," Emma teased.

"Funny, he didn't mention that to me," Kelly replied.

"Uh-oh. Maybe I wasn't supposed to say anything."

"Apparently, Damian still likes to keep secrets," Kelly said.

"Maybe he wants to surprise you. Don't say anything, Kell. I mean it. Wait and let him tell you."

Kelly shook her head to clear the thoughts that were zinging around like they were in a pinball machine. "Ok. Let's talk about something other than our men. This is ladies' night after all!"

"You're right. You make the popcorn while I whip up some drinks."

They worked side by side in the tiny kitchen, and their talk turned to other topics. Whenever either of them accidentally mentioned Zack or Damian, they quickly switched gears. They brought out their drinks, bowls of popcorn, and M&M's (chocolate was a must for ladies' night) to the living room and set them all on the coffee table.

"So, which movie do you want to watch, *The Notebook* or *The Lucky One*?" Kelly asked, waving both DVDs in her hands.

"Hmm…that's a tough one. Ryan Gosling or Zac Efron? Who am I in the mood for?"

Kelly waved *The Lucky One* a little more vigorously to indicate her choice.

"You're right. *The Notebook* will just make us cry, but *The Lucky One*…"

"Will make us horny!" Kelly finished.

"Zack and Damian will be glad for that," Emma said and giggled.

Kelly popped in the DVD and settled next to Emma on the couch. "For the rest of the night, the only man we talk about is Zac Efron. Deal?"

"Deal," Emma said and dug her hand into the popcorn bowl.

They were about halfway into the movie, and almost to the really good part with the steamy shower scene, when a knock came at the door.

"Oh no," Kelly said. "I know that knock."

She pressed pause on the remote and put her index finger to her lips. "Maybe if we're really quiet, they'll go away."

"C'mon, Kell. Open up. We know you're in there," Damian called, his voice booming loud and clear through the door.

Emma put her hands over her mouth to prevent her laughter from escaping while Kelly got up and marched over to the door. "What do you want? We're right in the middle of our movie,' she replied without opening the door.

"I have a key, you know."

"Ugh!" Kelly whipped the door open but blocked the entrance as best she could, considering she was one small woman standing in front of two hulking men. Damian smirked at her and held up a six pack of beer.

"We came over to join your party," he said.

Zack peered over Kelly's head, to where his future wife was perched on the edge of the couch. He winked at her and then said, "Look, they have snacks!"

"Hey, I had snacks too," Damian said with mock exasperation.

"Your idea of snacks was a stale bag of pretzels. There's real food over here."

Damian took a step forward, but Kelly placed her palm firmly on his chest. "Where do you think you're going?"

Damian's eyes twinkled down at her. "Please, Kell. Let us join your party."

Emma, ever the peacekeeper, finally piped in. "You two can come in on one condition. You have to let us finish watching the movie."

"Which movie is it?" Damian asked.

"Dude. Who cares? They have snacks," Zack said, and he stepped around Kelly to greet his bride-to-be.

Kelly still had her hand on Damian's chest, but now he covered it with his own. "I promise to let you watch your movie," he said solemnly.

"Ok, fine, you big brute. C'mon in."

The four of them settled on the couch, with Damian on one end, Zack on the other, and the two women in the middle. Zack immediately reached for the bowl of popcorn and placed it on his lap.

Damian glared at him and repeated, "I had snacks."

"Quiet, you two. We're putting the movie back on," Kelly said. Even though she was somewhat miffed at Damian for crashing their party, she couldn't help but lean into him once the movie started. He pulled her in so close that she could feel his body heat searing through her sweats. She glanced over at Emma and saw that she was leaning into Zack too. *So much for ladies' night!*

When it came to the scene where Logan (played by Zac Efron) and Beth (played by Taylor Schilling) had sex in an outdoor shower stall, Zack and Damian were particularly quiet.

After the scene was over, Zack said, "Whoa! This beats eating stale pretzels in Damian's apartment any day!"

"See what I mean? The man never shuts up," Damian said drily, after which the ladies burst into laughter.

After that, Zack and Damian let the ladies watch their movie, and given the hot sex scenes, they seemed to enjoy it too. When it was over, and both bowls of popcorn had been devoured, Damian let out a huge yawn.

"Boy, am I beat," he said, stretching his arms overhead for added effect.

Kelly thumped him on the chest. "Don't be rude. Maybe Zack and Emma want to stay for one more drink."

But both had already stood up and were collecting their belongings. "That's ok, Kell. It's been a long day for us too, right, honey?" Emma said.

"I'm fine, but it's obvious my little brother is trying to be the next *lucky one*, so we can leave," Zack said.

"Classy," Damian muttered.

Emma helped Kelly bring the dirty dishes into the kitchen, and when they were alone, she whispered, "Even though they interrupted, I still had fun, Kell. And even after I'm married, I still want to spend time with you."

Kelly felt herself tear up, and she pulled Emma in for a tight hug. Of course, the men came around the corner right at that instant and stopped in their tracks.

"Not quite a pillow fight, but good enough," Damian teased while Kelly glared at him over Emma's shoulder.

The four of them walked toward the front door, where more hugs were exchanged, but not between the brothers. They chose to thump each other on the back a few times and called it good. Kelly and Damian stood in the doorway and waited until Zack and Emma were safely in their car before Kelly shut the door and turned on Damian.

"Uh-oh," he said, well aware that he was in big trouble.

"I thought we had agreed that this was my night with Emma," she began.

"Yes, but…"

"No buts, Damian. Even though you and I are together, I'm still going to want my girl time. A few hours. That's all I asked for."

Damian took a step toward her, but she scooted around him and started to walk away.

"Where are you going?" he asked.

His voice was strained with remorse or sexual tension, Kelly wasn't sure which, but she was going to stretch out the torture just a touch longer. "To bed," she said. "You said you were tired, remember?"

Kelly went into the bathroom and shut the door firmly behind her, and then she locked it for good measure. She took out her ponytail and brushed her hair until it shone. She heard rustling outside the door as she pulled down her sweatpants.

"Do you want me to leave?" Damian asked through the door.

"I'm still deciding," she said before lifting her hoodie over her head and smoothing her hair back down.

"Would it help if I said I'm sorry?"

She turned on the faucet and squeezed toothpaste onto her toothbrush. "Maybe," she said over the sound of the running water.

"I'm sorry. The next time you and Emma have girl time, I promise not to interrupt."

Kelly finished brushing her teeth and wiped her mouth on the towel. "Ok."

"Ok?" Damian repeated, obviously stunned that it had been that simple.

"Ok," she said and yanked open the door.

Damian's mouth dropped open, and Kelly heated while he drank in the sight of her. Under her sweats, she had purposely worn the red baby-doll lingerie set that Damian had picked out for her when they'd been Up North. It was the first night he had seen it on her, and as she suspected, it made quite the impression.

"Holy…"

"You like it?"

"Hell yeah."

"But you haven't even seen the back yet."

Kelly watched his Adam's apple bob as he swallowed hard, and then she slowly turned around to show him the back. When she turned back to face him, his eyes were ablaze, and he instantly reached for her.

"I thought you were tired," she said, her voice demure, teasing.

"Suddenly I'm wide awake," he said, and there was no mistaking the reason for his gruff voice this time.

She didn't fight him when he picked her up and carried her to the bedroom. Instead, she wrapped her legs tightly around his waist and nipped his earlobe with her teeth. "I should punish you," she whispered.

"Because I've been a bad boy?"

"Yes." *Let the games begin!*

Chapter 30

On the day before they were leaving for Florida, Damian came strolling into the bookstore around lunchtime.

"Mind if I borrow Kelly for a while, Em?" he asked, leaning casually against the front counter.

Kelly watched the transaction with curiosity, because, so far, Damian hadn't even said hello to her!

"Sure. No problem." Emma replied, smiling brightly.

Kelly cleared her throat loudly. "Sorry to interrupt, but nobody asked me," she said, trying to sound irritated. But she had already discovered that it was impossible to stay mad at Damian for long, especially when he looked so scrumptious in his Carhartt jacket, Levi's, and scuffed work boots. He wasn't shaving as often these days, and the extra facial hair added to his rugged masculinity.

Damian bowed. "Oh, I'm sorry, princess. Would you do me the honor of accompanying me to lunch?"

Emma giggled, and Kelly shot her a look that said, *Don't encourage him*!

"That depends. Where are you taking me?"

"It's a surprise. But let's not waste time talking. Yes or no?"

Before she could answer, Emma handed Kelly her coat and purse. "Get out of here, you two. I have work to do."

When they drove out of the parking lot, Kelly tried to get the surprise out of him, but the man was as stubborn as a mule.

"Patience, Kell. You'll see in a few minutes."

When Damian turned off the main road onto a residential street, Kelly was bursting with curiosity. She was very familiar with the area, and there were definitely no restaurants on that road. Damian remained quiet, but a small smile graced his handsome face as they pulled into a gravel driveway that was lined with tall trees.

"Damian?"

The driveway was sloped, and when they climbed over the slight rise, a house came into view. It was a white-sided Cape Cod-style house, with black-shuttered windows and a wraparound porch. There was a two-car attached garage, but Kelly also spotted the roof of a large pole barn poking up from behind the house.

Damian pulled up close to the walkway and shut off the engine. There were no other cars in the driveway, and no one came out to greet them. Kelly opened her mouth to ask more questions, but Damian was already out of the truck and coming around to help her down. He took her hand and started up the brick-paved walkway, but Kelly planted her feet and refused to move.

"What are we doing here? Tell me what's going on, Damian."

"I will, but it's cold out here. Let's talk inside."

He tugged on her hand, and this time, she followed him. When they reached the front door, Damian dug a key out of his jacket pocket and inserted it into the lock. Kelly's heart pounded rapidly in her chest when she realized that this must be the house that Emma had mentioned on ladies' night. But she was still confused, because there wasn't even a for sale sign in the yard.

Once they were inside and standing in the foyer, Damian started talking. "So, I've been restoring an old Mustang for this guy, Ray. Anyway, we got to talking, and he mentioned that he was going to put his house up for sale in the spring."

Kelly's pounding heart was making her feel uncomfortably warm, and she shrugged out of her jacket as Damian continued.

"So, I asked him about it, and he showed me a few pictures on his phone. I told him that I was currently living in an apartment but that my lease was up in the spring…"

"This is Ray's house, then?"

"Yes. And here's the good part… Ray is willing to forego contacting a realtor and will sell it to me himself if I'm interested. We even discussed trading the work I'm doing on his Mustang for a down payment, although by the spring, I should be in a much better financial position, and that might not even be necessary."

Damian usually didn't talk this much unless he was really excited about something or he was in trouble, so Kelly knew that this was important to him, but she still wasn't sure where she fit in.

He must have sensed her confusion, because he locked his hands on her forearms and stared directly into her bewildered eyes. "I brought you here because I wouldn't want to buy a house unless you liked it too."

Kelly swallowed nervously. "I'm not sure what to say, Damian. What exactly are you getting at?"

"Well, the way I see it, why should we keep separate apartments when we spend all our time together anyway? And you said that you didn't want to live in an apartment forever, and neither do I, so…"

"You want us to live together?"

"Eventually. Yes."

Kelly was still in a state of shock, so she didn't immediately reply.

"C'mon. Let's take a look around and see what we think."

Kelly set her purse and jacket on the bench in the foyer and followed Damian through the house. He rattled off some figures to her as they went from room to room, and she tried to take it all in. The house had twenty-five hundred square feet, with three bedrooms on the second floor and two and a half baths. Kelly found the floor plan on the first level particularly appealing, with the living room, dining area, and kitchen all blending together across the entire length of the house. There were also plenty of windows overlooking the wooded backyard, which

Damian said was about five acres in size. Since the trees were now bare, Kelly glimpsed a house in the distance, but there was still plenty of space between them. She liked the home more and more with each room they went through.

When they stepped into the master bedroom with the vaulted ceiling and very generous his and hers walk-in closets, Kelly sighed. "Finally, a space for all my clothes!" The words slipped out without her permission, but Damian just chuckled and dragged her into the attached master bathroom.

"Here's what I like," he said, pointing to the large, jetted tub. "Plenty of room for two!"

The nervousness that Kelly had felt earlier was beginning to morph into excitement, but she still held back. She wanted to be clear about Damian's plans first. After they toured the inside of the house, including the basement and the garage, Damian suggested they walk outside to the pole barn.

Kelly donned her jacket again and held Damian's hand as he led her around to the backyard and down another brick-paved path to the barn. If he was excited before, his enthusiasm rose a few more notches when he unlocked the double doors and slid them open.

"You wanted space for your clothes, and I want space for all my toys," Damian said as he walked around the interior of the barn. The pole barn was large enough to house a car and some additional "toys," such as Ray's riding lawnmower, a motorcycle, and a snowmobile. Shelves lined the walls, and they were filled with tools and gadgets that Kelly could only guess at the use of. To her, it was just an oversized garage, but to Damian, it was obviously much, much more.

"But you don't have any toys right now," Kelly ventured.

"That's because I don't have any place to put them. If I had this space, it would be filled in no time!"

After Damian was done peeking around at things that Kelly didn't understand that had to do with electrical outlets and wiring, they walked back up to the house and stood on the front porch.

"Well, what do you think?" Damian asked expectantly.

Kelly's head was spinning, and she even felt a little light-headed. "Can we talk about this over lunch? I'm starving."

"Of course," he said.

They ended up at their favorite Mexican restaurant, where they dug into the chips and salsa right away. After they placed their orders, Damian leaned across the table and said, "Kell? Are you ok? You haven't said much this entire time. If you don't like the house, just say so."

"No, Damian. It's not that. I actually like the house—a lot. I'm just…this is so sudden. I'm not sure what to make of it all."

"I'm planning for our future, Kell. I love you, and I want to be with you, and I'm trying to make things good for us."

"Things are good for us. You don't have to do this just for me."

Damian sighed and crossed his arms over his chest. "Do you honestly think that I would be content to live in that tiny apartment forever? To creep in an out of your place like a thief in the night? If you know me at all, you would understand how much I would love to have a place of my own, with room to move and a garage to putter around in. A place where I could invite the whole family over for dinner, where Gracie and Ava could run around and play, and eventually my own kids too."

At the start of his soliloquy, Kelly had taken a bite of a tortilla chip loaded with salsa, and now it stuck sideways in her throat. She hurriedly grabbed her glass of water and chugged it down while Damian stared at her with an amused expression.

"What? You don't want kids someday?"

"Well, yes, I do, but…"

The waitress came over and set down their plates, and seeing that Kelly's water glass was empty, she offered to come back with a refill. After she had left the second time, Kelly started over from a different angle.

"About us living together…your lease is up in the spring, but mine isn't up until one year from right now. What do you propose we do in the interim?"

"I would move in and get the house ready. In case you didn't notice, it could use a few updates. The structure is sound, but I don't really care for the cranberry-colored carpet in the bedrooms, do you?"

Kelly giggled. "I noticed that too, but I didn't want to complain."

"Never stopped you before," Damian teased. "What else would you change?"

"The wood floor in the kitchen and foyer needs to be refinished, and the whole place could use a fresh coat of paint. Maybe some new window treatments too."

"Wow. Sounds like a lot of work."

"I don't mind hard work."

Kelly smiled, feeling more relaxed already. "I know that."

"Besides, I'll recruit Zack and my dad to help me. Jim would probably pitch in too."

"So, by the time I moved in…"

"The place would be ready and waiting for you."

The idea was starting to take shape, but there was one small detail niggling at the back of her mind. She decided to shelve her reservation for now and simply enjoy the moment. "So, you think we would do ok, living together?"

Damian swallowed a bite of his enchilada and beamed at her across the table. "I think we'd do just fine. Don't you?"

Kelly tried to drum up some of his annoying habits, but she was having difficulty coming up with one. Truthfully, she probably had more annoying habits than him. Their verbal sparring was mostly over trivial things, and their arguments could usually be resolved with a good, healthy dose of…

"Of course, our sex life will probably go through the roof," Damian said with that wicked gleam in his eyes.

"How so?"

"We won't have to worry about anyone hearing us, kind of like how it was at the cabin."

Kelly glanced around to see if anyone was paying attention to them. Satisfied that no one was listening, she leaned across the table. "And think of all that we could do in front of those windows along the back of the house."

Damian had been eating with his Carhartt on, and now he shoved it off and dabbed his face with a napkin. "Is it me, or did it just get really hot in here?"

Kelly laughed and then turned her attention back to her plate. They had been so busy talking and planning that she hadn't eaten much. Once they were finished and the waitress had cleared the table, Kelly felt much better about everything, but she had to ask, "Have you shared this idea with anyone else yet?"

Damian eyed her suspiciously. "I took Zack to see the house last week. Why?"

"It's just that Emma mentioned something to me on ladies' night, but she didn't know any of the details."

Damian looked at her with a thunderous expression, but she knew it wasn't really meant for her. "I'm going to kill him. I swear it. I should have known that he couldn't keep his big mouth shut."

Kelly tried to suppress her smile. "I'm sure he was just excited for you, Damian, and he tells Emma everything, and then…"

"She tells you. Yes, I know how it works."

"Don't worry. There are lots of things between us that I would never tell."

That seemed to placate him for the time being. "So, what's the verdict? Should I tell Ray that we're interested?"

"There are still some things that we need to talk about, but yes, tell him we're interested."

Damian's smile couldn't get any wider. "I love you, Kell."

She leaned across the table and kissed him. "I love you too."

Chapter 31

Kelly could hardly believe it. She and Damian were seated on the airplane that would take her home for Thanksgiving, and they would get to spend the next four days in the warm Florida sunshine. Damian had graciously offered her the window seat, while he got settled in the aisle seat. Kelly figured that he had wanted the aisle seat so that it would be easier for him to stretch out his long legs, but she was mistaken.

When the plane was speeding down the runway, Kelly glanced over and saw Damian's hands clutching the armrests so tightly that she feared he might leave imprints. "Are you ok?" she asked.

His eyes were closed, and he didn't so much as move a muscle. "Don't talk to me until we're in the air."

Kelly placed her hand over his and didn't speak again, until they had reached a "comfortable cruising altitude." When the flight attendant's voice came over the speaker, announcing that drinks would be served shortly, Damian finally opened his eyes.

"I'm good now," he said and offered her a weak smile.

"Damian, are you afraid to fly?"

"I wouldn't say that I'm *afraid.* I would just say that I don't particularly like it."

The man is chock full of surprises! "I would have guessed that you'd love to fly, since you love cars so much."

He raised his brows at her. "What does one have to do with the other?"

"Duh. They're both machines, they can both go fast, they both have engines, and all that other stuff."

Damian chuckled. "There's one very distinct difference. Cars remain on the ground, and if I'm the driver, I trust myself to be in control. I don't know anything about the guy operating this plane."

Kelly giggled. "I'm sure he's highly qualified."

"That may be, but who knows what his personal life is like. He might have gone to a class reunion last night and had too much to drink. His wife could have left him, and now he's bitter and angry. We just don't know!"

Kelly broke out in full-on hysterics, which she tried to contain when she saw the lady across the aisle glare at her. "Say the pilot did have a rough night. Isn't that what the co-pilot is there for?"

"But we don't know anything about that guy either! He could have an inferiority complex, and feel like he has something to prove. You know the saying, always the bridesmaid and never…"

"The bride. Yes, I know it well." Kelly blanched a little at the implication.

Damian quickly covered up his error. "I wasn't talking about you, Kell."

"Oh, I know," she said, waving her hand in the air like his comment meant nothing. Thankfully, right then, the flight attendant came by with the drink cart, and their conversation was cut short.

After they'd consumed their drinks and snacks, Kelly reached down into her tote bag and pulled out two books. "Here. I have something to distract you from your fear of flying."

"I never said I was *afraid*," Damian growled.

"Well, in any case, you need to start reading this book for our book club meeting. It's only a few weeks away."

Damian accepted the book from her and stared at the cover. "*Wallbanger*?"

The poor lady across the aisle was getting quite the earful! "Shhh…not so loud," Kelly hissed.

"I'm supposed to read this here?"

"Well, you don't have to, but you might want to get started on it. It's a romantic comedy. I think you'll like it."

"But, is there sex?"

"Yes, of course," Kelly replied, trying to ignore the woman across the aisle, who was blatantly staring at them now.

"Ok, then," Damian said, and he cracked open the book.

He got more than a few inquisitive stares from passengers who moved up and down the aisles to stretch their legs or use the restroom, but Damian never noticed. He quickly became engrossed in the story, and since Kelly had already read it, she cracked open a new book.

Occasionally, she'd glance over at Damian, who was either grinning or, at times, chuckling to himself.

My sweet man. Tough on the outside, but a real marshmallow inside!

They got lost in their fictional worlds until the pilot made an announcement for the flight attendants to prepare the cabin for landing. Damian started to bend over the page he was on, but Kelly stopped him. "Oh no you don't," she scolded. "I have a bookmark you can use."

"Seriously? What's wrong with bending the page?"

"Never say that to someone who works at a bookstore! Here you go." She handed him a bookmark with A New Chapter printed on it, along with a picture of the storefront and their hours.

He stuck the bookmark inside and carefully handed the book to her as if he were handing her a rare diamond. "I'll leave it with you for safekeeping."

"Good idea," she said.

Just then, the plane began its descent, and Damian went back to gripping the armrests. This time, Kelly didn't tease. She simply placed her hand over his and gave it a squeeze. His eyes closed, and she leaned over and whispered in his ear. "Before you know it, we'll be at the hotel pool, and I'll be wearing my red bikini."

Damian didn't respond, but his mouth twitched, and his eyelids fluttered. Kelly kissed his cheek and continued to hold his hand until they were safely back on the ground.

A short time later, they were driving down the highway in their rented Chevy Tahoe, en route to the Naples Beach Hotel. Kelly's parents had offered for her and Damian to stay at their condo, but Damian had balked at it. His exact words were "I don't mind spending time with your parents, but I need my privacy too."

When Kelly told her mom that they wanted to stay at a hotel on the beach, Maria accepted the decision with her usual grace. "I remember those days, when your father and I first fell in love. I can understand why you'd want some alone time," her mother had said.

Now they were on the expressway, and Kelly requested that they drive with the windows down so she could feel the warm air against her skin. "Isn't this awesome?" Kelly said as the balmy wind whipped through the windows.

Damian wiped the sweat off his brow and said, "It would be more awesome if I could turn on the air conditioner."

"Are we going to start this already? We just got here."

"Sorry, Kell. While I enjoy the warm weather, it also makes me sweat, and I don't want to stink when I meet your parents."

Kelly glanced over at him and wondered if he was nervous about meeting her parents. He would find out soon enough that Frank and Maria were the most easygoing, fun-loving parents on the planet. At least, that's the way all her friends had described them when she was growing up. Hers was the house that everyone wanted to hang out at, for various reasons. Her mother, Maria, loved to bake, and there was always a variety of cakes and cookies available. Frank, her father, was a prankster who loved to make people laugh, and both excelled at putting people at ease.

"Don't worry. You'll have time to change before they meet us for lunch," she said.

For their first meeting, Maria had suggested that they have lunch right at the hotel restaurant. "It's hard to be nervous when you're looking out at the ocean," she had said, and Kelly agreed.

Damian seemed relieved the minute they stepped into the air-conditioned hotel lobby, and even more so when they entered their hotel room. "How long until they'll be here?"

"Twenty minutes," she said, already rifling through her suitcase.

"Good. I have time for a quick shower. Be right out."

Kelly noticed that he hadn't asked her to join him, but it was probably for the best. They might not be on time for lunch if she did. While Damian was in the shower, she changed into a bright pink tank dress and strappy white sandals. She fluffed up her hair a bit, touched up her blush, and called it good. Then she slipped out onto the balcony to take in the magnificent ocean view. It didn't matter how many times she had been there; she was always drawn in by the sound of the waves crashing on the shore, the squawk of seagulls swirling overhead, and the warm, salty breezes. She was leaning over the balcony rail, watching a group of children build a sandcastle, when Damian came out to join her.

He wrapped his arms around her waist and nuzzled her neck, and now Kelly breathed in his fresh, masculine scent along with the salty air. "You smell good," she said and turned into his arms.

"And you look beautiful," he said, gazing down at her.

"So do you." Damian had changed from his standard jeans and a t-shirt into a pair of khaki cargo shorts and a collared navy blue polo shirt. For him, this was dressing up, and she appreciated the extra effort that he had gone to.

"They're going to love you," she said, smoothing down the collar of his shirt. "Just like I do."

"I hope so," he said and bent down to gently kiss her lips.

Kelly was anxious to see her parents, but with Damian standing before her, looking so gorgeous, she was tempted to delay the visit.

He smirked at her as if he read her mind and said, "We need to get going, princess. There will be plenty of time for other activities later."

Shortly after, they walked into the hotel restaurant hand in hand, and Kelly spotted her parents right away. "There they are," she said, pointing to a table in front of the large plate-glass window where her parents were waiting. As Kelly and Damian approached the table, her parents stood up and held out their arms to their daughter. The three of them embraced for a long moment while Damian waited patiently.

Frank was the first one to disengage from the hug, and he extended his hand to Damian. "I'm the old man. Frank. How do you do?"

"Damian Kostas. Nice to meet you, sir."

"Sir? Wow, I haven't been called that in…geez, I don't think I've ever been called that!" Frank laughed heartily, which broke up the reunion between the women.

"Frank, are you teasing him already? Just ignore him, Damian. I'm Maria, the proud mother. It's so wonderful to meet you." She walked right up to Damian and hugged him, and he visibly relaxed given the warm welcome.

They settled around the table, with Damian seated between Frank and Kelly, and Maria on Kelly's other side.

"So, how was the flight down? Ok?" Frank asked.

Damian shifted in his seat, and Kelly placed a hand on his thigh as reassurance that she wouldn't share his secret. "It was fine, Dad. Smooth as silk."

"Kelly tells us that you're into cars. What is it that you do exactly?" Frank asked, looking genuinely interested.

"Well, sir…I mean, Frank, come January first, I'm going to be the owner of a custom auto shop. I'm taking it over for a buddy of mine who's retiring."

"Custom huh? Are we talking sports cars?'

"All kinds, really. From Cadillacs to Corvettes, and everything in between."

"I'd imagine that's a pretty big business, especially in the Motor City."

"True, but it's big everywhere."

"A few of my golf buddies are into cars. In fact, one guy, Gary, just had a '57 Chevy truck restored. She's a real beauty."

Kelly watched the interaction between her father and her boyfriend and smiled. The more they talked about cars, the more comfortable Damian became, and by the end of the meal, they had planned an outing to check out Gary's restored truck.

After that, Maria smoothly switched topics and asked Damian about his family, another topic near and dear to his heart. Even with the teasing comments that he made about Zack, Kelly was certain that her parents could tell how much his family meant to him.

"We're going to make a trip up to Michigan in the spring," Maria said. "I'm just dying to get my hands on Emma's baby, and meet her new husband too, of course."

"If you come, be prepared to meet the whole family," Damian teased. "Once my mom gets wind of it, you're guaranteed to get a dinner invitation."

Maria smiled warmly. "I would love that."

The four of them enjoyed the food, the drinks (beer for the men, wine for the women), and the gorgeous ocean views while Maria and Frank kept the conversation flowing. Damian participated sporadically, in his usual fashion, but Kelly could tell that he was at ease, and she was happy with that.

"Well, Frank, I think we should let these two enjoy some of the beautiful Florida sunshine while we go home and start preparing for tomorrow's Thanksgiving dinner," Maria said, signaling an end to the luncheon.

"What she really means is that I get to take a nap while she does all the work," Frank teased.

"She still doesn't let you into the kitchen, Dad?"

"Nope. Not that I mind. Your mother is an excellent cook, so I just stay out of her way!"

"I wish I would have inherited Mom's cooking skills," Kelly lamented.

"Yeah, me too," Damian said drily.

Frank patted him on the back and said, "There's always take-out, son."

Everyone laughed, but Kelly was distracted by the term "son." It had slipped out of her dad's mouth so casually that Damian didn't appear to notice, but she did. Kelly took it as a good sign and decided to ignore their teasing about her lack of culinary skills. They walked her parents out to the hotel lobby, where they said their goodbyes. Once again, Maria hugged Damian and said, "We're so glad you're here."

Frank gave Damian another firm handshake and said, "See you tomorrow," and off they went.

After they had driven away, Kelly turned to Damian and said, "Last one in the pool is a rotten egg!"

Chapter 32

After a refreshing swim, they lounged poolside, Kelly in her red bikini and a big floppy sunhat, and Damian in his black board shorts and dark sunglasses. They had brought their books out with them, but neither of them could concentrate. Damian kept trailing his fingertip down Kelly's arm, and she kept giving him sly sideways glances. Every time either of them moved an inch, the other one looked over, and Kelly wondered how much longer this game would last.

"Want to take a walk on the beach?" she suggested, searching for a distraction.

"Maybe later," he replied while pretending to be engrossed in his book.

"Want to go upstairs and get naked?"

He slammed the book shut without marking his place, stood up, and started gathering their things. "Finally!"

"Well, you could have asked me, you know!" Kelly huffed as they hurried into the hotel.

"Sometimes I like it when you initiate sex," Damian said, tapping the elevator button impatiently.

"What are you talking about? I initiate sex all the time."

Thankfully, they were the only two in the elevator on the way up to their floor. "Princess, is arguing your idea of foreplay?"

She couldn't help it. She had to laugh. "You can be so infuriating sometimes!"

"Yet you love me anyway."

"Yes, I do," she conceded.

The second the door closed behind them, Damian backed her up to the bed. He was about to untie her bikini top, but she stopped him. "Damian? Sweetie? Can we please turn off the air conditioner and crack open the patio door? I'm still wet, and it's freezing in here."

Damian glanced down at her nipples as if he needed proof of her complaint. Satisfied, he did as she asked and returned to find that she had already untied the top for him. In fact, she had removed it completely and stood there in just her bottoms, waiting for his next move. When he just stood there, transfixed, she put her hands on the drawstring of his shorts and untied them. She slipped one hand inside and gripped him tightly, causing him to emit a groan.

His hands went to her bare breasts, and he caressed and teased them until she felt the heat between her legs. "Let's get you out of these wet bottoms," he said, his voice ragged and breathy.

"You too," she whispered.

They hurriedly removed their bottoms and tossed them aside before tumbling onto the bed. Kelly was reminded of their time spent at the cabin when they were hidden away from the world in their own private cocoon. She wanted to savor the moment, and Damian seemed to be of the same mind as he lazily trailed his hand up and down the length of her body.

"I love your body, Kell. So soft, so curvy, so sweet."

"Um-hmm. I love your body too, for being the exact opposite." Her hand floated over his muscular pecs and abs before reaching his hard, swollen manhood.

"So, what's the opposite of sweet?" he teased as he watched her stroke him.

"I would have to say…salty. But let me check." With that, Kelly shimmied herself down his body until her head was even with his pelvis. Damian moaned when she took him deep in her mouth and sucked. When she released him, she said, "Yep. Definitely salty."

"My turn," he said and patted the pillow where he wanted her to lay her head. He nudged her legs apart with his hands and bent his head in between them.

Oh boy, she thought, looking around frantically for something to hold onto. She grabbed the empty pillow next to her and held on for dear life as Damian plunged into her with his tongue. He licked, and lapped, and nibbled until she was writhing beneath him and bucking her hips off the bed. *I hope the people next door are out to dinner*, she thought as she was getting close to the edge.

Damian popped his head up and said, "Pillow."

It's amazing how we communicate with so few words, she mused and then pulled the pillow over her mouth to muffle her cries.

Once her tremors had subsided, Damian lifted his head up and smiled proudly. He then licked his lips thoroughly and said, "Yep. Still sweet."

"I'll show you sweet. But first—condom."

Damian scrambled off the bed, rifled through his toiletries bag, and came up with a condom. Once he was sheathed, she patted the space next to her.

"You drivin'?" he asked.

"Oh yeah." She climbed on top of him and made quite a show of inserting him to the hilt. There was no talking after that, unless one-word demands counted.

"Harder…faster…yes," Damian grunted as she rode him like an experienced cowgirl on her favorite steed. At the end, he clutched her hips hard and shouted, "I love you!"

I hope the neighbors are still out to dinner, Kelly thought again while she watched Damian reach his climax, and then she collapsed onto his chest.

A few minutes later, after Damian had cleaned himself up and returned to bed, he pulled her to his side and kissed her gently, almost reverently.

"Whatcha thinkin'?' she said as he pushed the hair back from her face.

"I'm thinking about how good it is between us every single time."

"It is, isn't it? Why do you think that is?"

"I think it's because you're such a generous and loving person, and not just in bed."

Kelly beamed at him and then traced the outline of his handsome face with her fingertips. "Funny. I think the same thing about you."

"Don't tell anyone," he teased.

She giggled. "I promise to let everyone go on thinking that you're big, bad Damian. Even though…the people who really know you believe otherwise."

"You bring out the best in me, Kell."

"And sometimes the worst too," she added.

He chuckled. "Even when we argue, I still love you. I never stop loving you."

Kelly's stomach growled loudly in response. "Do you love me enough to take me out to dinner?"

Damian was already heaving himself off the bed. "I love you enough to take you out for dinner *and* dessert."

"I was thinking we could come back here for dessert," she said and wiggled her eyebrows suggestively.

"That's my girl!"

Thanksgiving dinner was a quiet affair, the opposite of what it had been like the previous year at the Kostas's house.

Kelly introduced Damian to her grandparents and one aunt and uncle (all from her mother's side), along with her parents' closest friends, John and Marsha, who lived a few doors down.

Her Latin American grandmother, Sofia, patted Damian's cheeks and said, "Oh, such a handsome young man." Damian muttered a "thank you" and blushed while Kelly tried to contain her laughter.

Her grandfather, Luis, shook Damian's hand enthusiastically and said, "Greek? Italian?"

"Greek," Damian replied.

"Ahh, it's hard to tell, no?"

"Grandpa!" Kelly scolded, but he was already walking away.

Kelly's Aunt Lucia was her mother's youngest sister, and even though she was approaching fifty, she was still quite flirtatious. She held onto Damian's hand just a little too long and practically batted her eyelashes at him. "Oh, if only I were twenty years younger…"

"Lucia! Behave," scolded Maria.

Lucia's husband, Rich, took it all in stride and shook Damian's hand warmly. "You like football, Damian?"

"Absolutely."

"Game's on in the living room."

Damian looked to Kelly for guidance, and she nodded her head. As soon as he left the kitchen, the women all began chattering at once.

"Marty will be so disappointed when I tell him that you're off the market," Marsha said as she carried some dishes to the table. Marsha had been trying for years to set Kelly up with her son, but Kelly had never been interested. He was a nice enough guy and decent looking, but there had been no chemistry between them whatsoever. Besides, he lived here in Florida, and Kelly lived in Michigan, so she rarely even saw him.

"Your babies will be so beautiful," Lucia said while she stirred the gravy on the stove.

"When are you getting married?" Sofia said.

All heads popped up at once when Damian reentered the room.

"Um…excuse me, ladies. I just came in to grab a beer."

Kelly hurriedly stuck her face in the refrigerator to avoid eye contact with him and came up with a beer. When she handed it to him, he smiled broadly. "Thank you, princess," he said and sauntered out of the room.

Maria crossed her hands over her heart and said, "Oh, how sweet. He calls you princess."

Kelly rolled her eyes and said, "Ok. That's enough, everyone. Time to talk about something else."

Damian was relaxed and attentive toward her throughout the rest of the afternoon. If he had overhead the conversation in the kitchen, he never let on. While Kelly helped her mom clean up after dinner, she heard him yelling at the football game along with the rest of the men. At one point, he came in the kitchen to grab another beer, and this time, he kissed her on the cheek. "Come and join us when you're done," he said sweetly.

Maria and Kelly were the only two left in the kitchen, since Maria had shooed the other women out. She hugged her daughter tightly and said, "I can see how much that man loves you."

"I love him too, Mom."

"I know, and I'm so happy for you."

Kelly peered through the doorway to make sure that no one was coming, and then she said, "Damian's going to buy a house in the spring, and he wants me to move in with him."

Her mother didn't flinch. "Oh. Well, that's a good thing, right?"

"Yes, it is, but…"

"But what, sweetie? What are you worried about?"

Kelly peeked out again, and satisfied that they were alone, she continued. "There's a part of me that wishes he would have asked me to marry him first." There. Finally, she had shared what had been bothering her ever since Damian had shown her the house. She hadn't realized that she was a traditionalist until he had asked her to move in with him. While she wanted to be with him always, she wanted them to commit to each other first—to truly commit to each other, in front of their families and before God. Kelly had been struggling with her revelation and was trying to decide how and when to tell Damian, but now she felt better just having shared it with her mom.

"Oh, sweetie," her mom said and gathered her in for another hug. "Maybe he wants to take things slow."

"But that's just it. Damian and I don't do *slow*. Our relationship has been full speed ahead since the beginning."

"Well, then I think you need to tell him how you feel."

"But I don't want to pressure him into it."

"Pressure me into what?" Damian asked, strolling back into the room.

Think quick, think quick! "Um…Dad wants to take you to see Gary's truck tomorrow morning, but I didn't want you to feel pressured into going."

"Ha! That's no pressure, Kell. Your dad and I have already talked about it. He's picking me up at ten tomorrow morning."

"Oh. Ok, then," Kelly replied, breathing a sigh of relief.

"Terrific! While you two are gone, I'll get to spend some more time with my daughter," Maria said smoothly.

Shortly after that, Kelly and Maria served dessert in the living room and enjoyed it with the rest of the guests. When the football game ended, Kelly announced that she and Damian were leaving. "He promised me a walk on the beach," she said to the room, and there was a collective "Ahh." Everyone understood that the lovebirds wanted to be alone.

After a hearty round of goodbyes, some more pats on Damian's cheeks from Sofia, and a wink from Lucia, they were out the door.

On the way back to their hotel, Kelly asked, "So, what did you think?"

"I think your Aunt Lucia's a trip!"

Kelly giggled. "But did you have a good time?"

"Yes. Compared to my family gatherings, that was easy! I enjoyed myself."

"Good," Kelly said, turning her attention out the window.

"I am curious about one thing though."

"What's that?"

"All the whispering going on in the kitchen. What was all that about?"

Kelly kept her eyes trained out the window. "Oh, that. That was nothing," she said dismissively, and she hoped like crazy that he believed her.

Chapter 33

While Damian was off with Frank the next day, Kelly and her mom went shopping in downtown Naples. It was Black Friday, but it was difficult for Kelly to get into the Christmas mood when it was eighty-five degrees out! She snapped a picture of herself and Maria in their shorts and sandals and sent it to Emma. A few minutes later, she received Emma's response in the form of a picture of Gracie playing outside in the snow!

Kelly enjoyed the one-on-one time she got to spend with her mom as they meandered in and out of boutiques, behaving more like friends than mother and daughter. Kelly even bought a few racy pieces of lingerie that she knew Damian would love while Maria pretended to look the other way.

When it was nearing lunch time, Damian sent Kelly a text letting her know that he would be eating lunch with Frank and his friend Gary and that he'd meet up with her later at the hotel. Kelly tried not to feel disappointed (he was with her father after all!), but she couldn't help it. Today was their last full day in Florida, and she wanted to enjoy the time with Damian as much as possible.

Maria suggested a popular gourmet hamburger restaurant for lunch, and they sat outside at a table with an umbrella so they could enjoy the breeze. Kelly giggled after the waiter had set down their heaping plates of hamburgers and fries.

"What's so funny?" Maria asked.

"Oh, it's just that before Damian, I dated someone who didn't eat red meat," Kelly replied.

"Well, that never would have worked," said her mother.

Kelly laughed again. "I know! Damian and I are much better suited."

Kelly and Maria had been operating under an unspoken agreement that they wouldn't talk about Damian today, but since she'd brought him up…

"So, when are you going to tell Damian how you feel about moving in with him?" Maria said.

"I don't know for sure. Maybe tonight. Although it is our last night here, and I don't want to ruin it."

"Being honest with him shouldn't ruin things, Kelly. Honesty is the cornerstone of a good relationship. Well, that and a few other things…"

"Mom! Are you talking about sex?"

"Shh…I might know some people around here," she scolded, although she was fighting back a smile.

"Anyway, I'm just not sure how to bring up the topic of marriage without scaring him off. Damian was engaged once before, a long time ago, but he still bears the scar from it."

If Maria was surprised, she didn't show it. "You'll figure it out, sweetie. Don't worry. You might even discover that Damian is on the same page with you."

"Hmm…we'll see."

Maria dropped Kelly off at the hotel in the middle of the afternoon, but Damian wasn't there. He sent her another text stating that he and Frank were at a coffee shop talking and not to worry. Coffee shop? Damian? In the middle of a hot Florida afternoon? None of it made any sense, but Kelly figured that he was probably too polite to tell her dad that he wanted to get back to the hotel.

Since she had some time on her hands, Kelly decided that she might as well go for a swim. She donned her red bikini and a mesh cover-up, grabbed a towel, her book, and some sunglasses, and headed down to the pool. Kelly received more than a few admiring stares from some of the men lounging outside, but she barely noticed. She was too busy thinking about Damian and wondering what she might say to him later.

She settled into a lounge chair furthest away from the majority of the sunbathers and cracked open her latest romance novel. She immersed herself in the world of fiction for a while until she felt overheated, due in part to the sexy scenes she had just read, so she set down her book and then dived into the pool. Some of the same men who had taken notice of her before perked up and watched the dark-haired beauty in the red bikini swim laps across the pool.

Kelly was practicing her backstroke when a large splash interrupted her musings. *Probably some kid doing a cannonball*, she thought and continued her backstroke until she reached the edge of the pool. When she stood up and flicked her hair back off her face, there was Damian standing right next to her with a bemused smile on his face.

"Showing off your swimming skills, I see," he teased.

But she was in no mood for teasing. "It's about time," she huffed. "I was beginning to think I'd be spending our last night in Florida alone."

"Well, you wouldn't be alone for long. Not with all these men ogling you." With that, he pulled her into his chest and covered her protests with his lips.

She thought about resisting but melted into him instead. She had missed him, the big lug! Once they broke apart, she said, "You did that on purpose."

"Damn right I did. Can't have these dudes thinking that you're a single lady."

This could be the opening that I need. "But, technically, I am single," she ventured.

Damian scowled at her and muttered something under his breath.

Ok, maybe this wasn't the best time to bring it up. "So, what took you so long with my dad?"

"Well, first we went to Gary's house and talked cars for a long time. Then we went to lunch at a nearby deli, and after we dropped Gary back off, I asked your dad if we he wanted to go for a coffee."

"But you don't even drink coffee!"

"I know, but I thought it was a nice thing to do. Don't tell me you're mad at me for spending time with your dad."

He was right, damn it! "No. It's just that this is our last day here, and I wanted us to spend it together."

Damian wrapped his arms around her again, oblivious to the attention that they were attracting. "We're together now, and we'll be together all night long," he said, his voice becoming deeper, huskier.

"That's true," Kelly admitted, softening against his rock-hard chest.

"There's something that I want to do tonight."

"Me too," she said, giving him that look.

"Besides that, I mean."

"Oh. What else?"

"I want us to be on the beach at sunset."

Kelly had a hard time hiding her surprise. Damian wasn't one for overly romantic gestures, preferring to show his love for her in simple ways. "Ok…"

"Frank mentioned that the sunsets on the beach are spectacular, and I'd like to see one before we leave."

Wow, Damian and my dad must have really bonded! "I'd love to watch the sunset with you tonight," she said.

"Good. Let's go get something to eat so we're back in time," he suggested.

The men around the pool got one last glimpse of the long-haired beauty with the sensuous curves as she was escorted into the hotel by the equally attractive Greek man. Or maybe he was Italian, who knew?!

Kelly was mostly unaware of the attention, although she thought she heard someone mutter, "Lucky bastard," as they walked by.

They decided to eat dinner at the hotel restaurant so as not to miss the sunset. Kelly almost ordered a salad, since she had downed a hamburger earlier, but changed her mind when she saw a plate of fried shrimp being delivered to a nearby table.

"Oh, what the hell! I'm on vacation," she said aloud.

While she and Damian tucked into their meals, they talked about various "safe" topics, such as the auto shop, the bookstore, and their families. Ever since Kelly had sent Emma a picture of sunny downtown Naples earlier, she had been barraged with photos of the snow scenes awaiting them in Michigan. Apparently, Zack had been doing the same thing to Damian, and they shared a good laugh over it.

Talk turned to Emma and Zack's wedding, which was just two weeks away. Since they were on the topic of weddings, Kelly considered making some joke about her and Damian getting married someday, but she couldn't bring herself to do it. They were having such a wonderful time, and it was their last night there, and…

"Something on your mind, Kell?" Damian asked after the waiter had cleared their plates.

"No, not really. Just enjoying our last night together."

Damian reached his hands across the table and entwined their fingers together. "You keep saying that as if we're not going to have any other nights together except this one."

"Sorry. I didn't realize that I was doing that."

"C'mon. Let's get out of here. I want to find a nice, private spot on the beach."

What is his fascination with the sunset tonight?

When they got down to the beach, Kelly slipped off her sandals and tucked them into her tote bag. Damian took her hand, and as they walked, he glanced over at her every few minutes and smiled.

It was a beautiful evening. The ocean breeze tossed Kelly's hair around, and the sound of the waves lapping at the shore soothed her. They passed several other couples, who, like them, were scoping out a private patch of sand on which to watch the sun go down. Of course, there were plenty of families too, their children playing hide and seek with the sea as the cool water tickled their toes before receding.

They walked for a long time while the sun set itself up for its final bow of the evening. Finally, they left the packed sand along the water's edge and trudged into the soft, white, powdery sand that sunbathers had been laying out on earlier that day.

"Here looks good," Damian said, and then he helped Kelly spread out their oversized beach towel that was big enough for two.

Damian sat down first and then patted the space between his legs for Kelly to sit between. He wrapped his arms around her waist from behind and tucked her in close. People were still walking by, but they were far enough away to afford Kelly and Damian some privacy.

Kelly was so enraptured by the colors of the setting sun—the reds, oranges, and yellows—as it descended over the vast expanse of ocean that the sound of Damian's voice almost startled her.

"So, I told your dad about the house," Damian began.

"Oh yeah? What did he have to say?"

"He said he'd like to help me work on it in the spring if your mom lets him."

Kelly laughed. "Ever since Dad had that health scare last fall, she's been worried about him. What else did you two talk about?"

"You. Us."

Kelly twisted her head around to study his expression and asked, "What about us?"

Damian pointed at the sun and said, "Turn back around, or you'll miss it."

She reluctantly did as he directed, and they both watched as the sun slipped into the ocean, leaving them in the purplish dusk. She then turned back around to face him. "Why did you talk to my dad about us?"

Damian inhaled deeply and gazed at her intently, and Kelly sensed that he was on the cusp of revealing something big. "What is it, Damian? Tell me."

"I asked your dad for permission to marry you."

Kelly's hands flew to her mouth. *Did he just say what I think he said?* "Could you repeat that please?"

Damian threw his head back and chuckled. "I told your dad that I loved you and that I wanted to ask you to marry me, but I wanted his permission first."

Kelly's head felt like it was going to explode. Shock, joy, elation, and a thousand other emotions flooded her body, and for a moment, she was tongue-tied.

"The thing is…I don't have a ring. I didn't even know until we got here that I was going to propose. I was going to wait until after Zack's wedding."

Kelly was still trying to find her voice, but Damian, for once, was doing all the talking.

"And then I figured that you might want a say in what your ring looks like. You'll have to wear it for the rest of your life after all." He reached out and pried her hands away from her mouth to hold them firmly in his.

"I'm doing this all wrong. I didn't have it all planned out, but Kelly, will you do me the honor of becoming my wife?"

The tears came then, and she shook her head back and forth because she still couldn't believe it.

Unfortunately, Damian misread the gesture and said, "No? Is it too soon? Should I have had the ring first?"

Kelly shook her head even harder, and then she finally spat out the words. "No, it's not too soon! It's perfect timing!"

"So, no really meant yes?"

Kelly flung her arms around him then and tackled him to the ground. "Yes, yes, a thousand times yes!"

And then he kissed her.

Later that night, after they had made love, Kelly and Damian made a plan.

"I don't want to upstage Zack's wedding," Damian said. "I'll never hear the end of it."

"I agree. We'll tell everybody at Christmastime."

Damian pulled her close and ran his fingers down her naked back. "We can set the wedding date for whenever you want, but I have one request."

"Anything," she said, idly tracing his tattoo.

"Remember when I agreed to wear the Batman costume and you said you'd owe me a big favor?"

Kelly halted her movements and swallowed nervously. "Yes…"

"Well, I'm going to call in my favor. For our honeymoon, I want to go somewhere where we can go hiking."

"Like Alaska?"

"No. We'll work up to that. I was thinking about renting a cabin in the Smoky Mountains."

"Hmm…I like the sound of that. You and me, alone in the mountains. I can handle that."

"So, it's a plan, then?"

"It's the best plan ever," Kelly said.

Epilogue

Emma and Zack's wedding took place on a sunny yet cold December Saturday at the church that the Kostas family had attended for years. The bride and groom looked gorgeous and content as they said their vows in front of their closest family and friends. Kelly and Damian were the only two members of the wedding party, other than Gracie, who served as the very proud flower girl.

As Emma and Zack recited their vows, Kelly kept sneaking peeks at the best man, who cut quite an impressive figure in his well-fitted black and white tuxedo. Damian looked less than comfortable though as he periodically tugged on the tight collar. She smiled softly with the knowledge that he would much rather be wearing his faded jeans and a t-shirt, along with his rugged work boots. Still, every time she glanced at him, he took her breath away.

The reception took place at Buhl Estate, a historic manor home set in a nearby county park. Zack teasingly referred to the venue as the "scene of the crime." He and Emma had attended a wedding there when they were first dating, and Emma had ended up quite drunk. They had both loved the setting so much though that they had decided to have their own reception there. The estate was decorated for Christmas, and the sparkling white lights, Christmas wreaths, and poinsettias added to the festive ambiance.

Kelly and Damian were in a celebratory mood along with the rest of the guests, and the secret that they shared only heightened that mood. When they sat next to each other at dinner, Kelly relished the press of his thigh next to hers and the possessive way he rested his hand on her leg beneath the table.

She couldn't wait until the music started up so they could dance together; however, Damian didn't share her enthusiasm. "I'm not a good dancer," he had warned her ahead of time. "I don't have the moves."

"Oh, yes you do," Kelly had argued.

Damian had given her that sexy grin and said, "Ok, I've got moves, but none that are appropriate in public."

When the bride and groom took to the dance floor, Kelly thought that she had never seen Emma look so radiant. *That's what love does to you*, she mused as she watched Zack spin his bride around the floor. When the DJ called Kelly and Damian to the floor, she eagerly jumped up and took Damian's hand. His expression told of his reluctance, and the few people who were sitting nearby laughed, including his parents.

"C'mon," Kelly whispered. "It'll be good practice."

The minute that she was in his arms, the rest of the world melted away. It was only her and him, their bodies pressed tightly together like two pieces of a puzzle that fit perfectly. When Damian gazed into her eyes, she saw all the tenderness, affection, and desire that she needed to know that she was well and truly loved.

Zack and Emma sidled up next to them on the dance floor, and Zack said, "So, when do Emma and I get to stand up for you two?"

"We'll let you know," Damian replied with a wink, and then he purposely danced Kelly into the crowd that now occupied the dance floor.

Kelly glanced over his shoulder and saw that Zack and Emma were still watching them with a mixture of curiosity and joy on their faces.

Kelly just smiled, her focus on the best man, who had pulled her in even closer and had leaned down to nuzzle her neck. "I can't wait to make you mine," he whispered.

His words were like an aphrodisiac, and she shivered against him. "I already am yours, Damian. I've been yours since the moment we met, even though it's been a bit of a rollercoaster ride to get here."

"I'm sorry about that."

"Don't be. I've decided that I like rollercoasters."

Damian chuckled. "I love you, princess."

"And I love you."

THE END

Also by Susan Coventry

"As Coventry describes the complex issues of age and love that Jason and Sam must navigate, she also touches on other weighty topics, such as grief, friendship, and emotional renewal. She tells the story at a fast clip, building the suspense in a way that will keep even the most experienced romance fans engaged. The story artfully explores the difficulties inherent in unconventional relationships without skimping on steamy sex scenes." - *Kirkus Reviews*

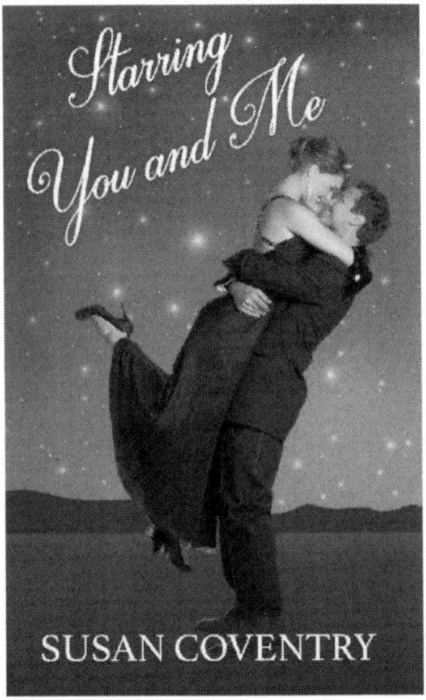

Nikki Branson swore off men a long time ago. She runs a successful real estate business and has a cuddly cocker spaniel to keep her company. What more could she possibly need? When a Hollywood agent contracts Nikki to find a rental home for his superstar client, she hadn't even heard of Nate Collins. Her first mistake, looking him up on Google...

Nate Collins is Hollywood's latest sensation and most eligible bachelor. All he wants is a quiet place to stay while he's in Michigan filming a movie, and who better to find it for him, than the most sought after real estate agent in town. When Nate and Nikki meet, sparks fly, but their lifestyles are worlds apart. Logic tells Nikki it will never work, now if she could only convince her heart of that...

Emma Murphy first laid eyes on the tall, dark and sinfully handsome Zack Kostas when they stood up in a wedding together. Five years later, they meet again, both newly divorced, and in the process of rebuilding their lives. Emma finds comfort in the bookstore that she owns, while Zack is busy caring for his four-year-old daughter Gracie. Despite their attraction, Emma and Zack decide to be "just friends," but soon discover that staying in the friend zone is easier said than done! Sometimes love comes along when you least expect it, but when will Emma be ready to trust her heart again? How will she know when the time is right to begin...*A New Chapter?*

62403530R00181

Made in the USA
Lexington, KY
06 April 2017